"Since things seem [...] **you, maybe you ca** [...] **Springs."**

"Mr. Murphy, I don't understand..."

"You're a nanny and I need someone to keep Louie out of trouble. So maybe you could be his nanny. Now, I can't pay you a lot, but I can pay some. But if you would agree to stay through the winter to give folk here time to simmer down about Louie, then I'll buy your ticket back to Boston in the spring."

Hazel thought about the child. He would certainly be a handful, but she'd always loved a challenge.

She focused her gaze on Mr. Murphy. "I accept your proposal."

This wasn't going to be like caring for a child she'd known his or her entire life. However good Mr. Murphy's intentions, he had not disciplined the boy.

Perhaps this was God's plan in the first place. For her to help bring order into the boy's mind and heart. And perhaps she could help Mr. Murphy, too...

Tracey Bateman has published over forty novels for the Christian market. Now an empty nester alongside her husband of thirty-two years, she is enjoying writing romance, watching her kids be adults and introducing her grandbabies to the wonderful world of books.

Books by Tracey Bateman

Love Inspired Historical

The Nanny Proposal

The Nanny Proposal

TRACEY BATEMAN

LOVE INSPIRED
INSPIRATIONAL ROMANCE

LOVE INSPIRED®
INSPIRATIONAL ROMANCE

PLEASE RECYCLE · THIS PRODUCT IS RECYCLABLE

Recycling programs
for this product may
not exist in your area.

ISBN-13: 978-1-335-90966-4

The Nanny Proposal

Copyright © 2021 by Tracey Bateman

This edition published by arrangement with Harlequin Books S.A.

For questions and comments about the quality of this book, please contact us
at CustomerService@Harlequin.com.

Love Inspired
22 Adelaide St. West, 41st Floor
Toronto, Ontario M5H 4E3, Canada
www.LoveInspired.com

Printed in U.S.A.

A man's heart deviseth his way:
but the Lord directeth his steps.
—*Proverbs* 16:9

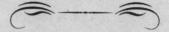

For my fellow romantics.
You, who love love. You, who still light candles
and spread rose petals.
For you, who cry and sigh at a happy ending.
For you, who could be cynical but choose to
be hopeful. This is for you.

Chapter One

Tucker Springs, Iowa; October 1870

It seemed only fitting that a sky-shattering crash of thunder accompanied Chester Rubles as he stormed into Murphy's General Store, clouds of anger darkening the contours of his face. "Murphy!" The word exploded from Chester's throat, a startling contrast to the otherwise silent room.

Ezra Murphy swallowed down annoyance as the burly blacksmith yanked off his battered brown hat and slapped it against his thigh, flinging rain onto a display table of dime books.

Years of experience behind the counter had taught Ezra that a smile and a pleasant tone of voice could do wonders to soothe an angry customer. Even if that customer were Chester Rubles. So he planted a smile on his face and forced a cheerful tone, despite the fact that at least some of those books were likely going to have to be reduced to five-cent novels. "Hey, Chester," he said. "How's the weather out there?"

"How do you think?" Chester snapped, clearly not in the mood to have his anger soothed by Ezra's attempt at humor. "We need to talk about that boy of yours…again."

If Ezra had a nickel for each and every time he'd heard those words spoken in outrage, bewilderment or just plain anger, he would be able to purchase every novel on the table—at full price.

Ignoring the rug by the door, Chester stomped up the aisle, leaving muddy boot prints in his wake.

Mud. The bane of Ezra's existence lately. He'd taken to keeping the scrub bucket filled and handy—for all the good it did. The entire main street had become one big slough over the past week due to the cold October rains. Tempers flared in the misery, and even folks who were generally good-tempered were getting their feathers ruffled over the smallest things.

Holding up his hand, Ezra halted the complaint before the red-faced fellow could give voice to it. "Now, Chester, I know Louie dumped your water pot yesterday and almost broke Mr. Taylor's new wagon wheel, but whatever's got you all riled up today, Louie couldn't have done." He jerked his thumb toward the outer wall, the direction of the town café. "He's over at Avery's having a late lunch with Jennie." The Avery family had practically adopted Ezra and his brother into their family years ago—and they treated Ezra's nephew, Louie, like he was one of their own. Jennie and her brother, Wyatt, were Ezra's closest friends. He trusted them implicitly. "Louie's been there for the last hour. It's fried chicken day."

"Is that a fact?" Chester's cheeks puffed out with indignation. "Then how come I saw the boy running through my place with that wet, stinking dog just when I was hammering new shoes on Johnny Gable's old plow horse? Scared the nag so bad, she went to kicking and bucking and liked to have killed me."

Ezra frowned. Chester might be a bitter old man, but he wasn't the sort to tell an out-and-out lie just from spite. "And you're certain it was Louie?"

"Of course I'm sure! I'm telling you, it was him. And his dog! You think I'm blind? And let me tell you, I heard him laughing."

"Laughing? At the dog?" Ezra frowned.

Chester shook his head in disgust. "He was laughing at the bucking nag. Then he just took off." He stopped to catch his breath. "This has got to stop. And I mean it has to stop now."

The bell above the door jangled to announce the entrance of a trio of men—half the town council. They stood just over the threshold, shaking rain from their coats and swiping their muddy shoes across the rug that Chester had completely ignored.

Chester leveled a distinctly satisfied gaze at Ezra. "I told you last time that boy made trouble, it was bound to come to this."

Mr. Lowe, the town banker and head of the council, led the entourage, reaching the counter first. "Good afternoon, Ezra." The other men murmured half-hearted pleasantries as Ezra braced himself for what was to come. "As you've probably guessed," Mr. Lowe said. "We've come on official town business."

Chester slapped his hand down on the counter again. "All right, men, let's get on with this so's I can get back to the smithy." He leveled a pointed gaze at Ezra. "I got a lot to clean up when I get back."

"No one's stopping you from going. We can take it from here." Mr. Lowe tossed him an exasperated glance. "Besides, I thought you were going to let us handle it."

"That was before the boy acted up again. Don't I got a right? He just about broke a wheel yesterday and would've if I hadn't moved it lickety-split. And then today he tore up the place. And look here." Chester bent over the counter and showed off an angry knot the size of a mountain smack dab in the middle of his balding head. "He spooked a horse that shoved me so hard, she knocked me into an anvil. I'll be seein' stars for a week."

Ezra winced just looking at the injury and was about to offer to pay for a doctor visit when Mr. Lowe cleared his throat to speak. The other two council members stood behind him—like Aaron and Hur holding up Moses's arms.

Ezra felt very small under the weight of their judgmental stares. Worst of all, he had no defense to offer. There was no excuse. Not for him. Not for Louie.

"We've always thought highly of you, you know that." Mr. Lowe hesitated before continuing. "But it seems as though things with Louie have come to something of a crossroads. People have been complaining about the mayhem Louie causes."

"Well," Reverend Harper said in the soft way he had of speaking, "I'd call it more mischief than mayhem."

Ezra met his kindly gaze. "Thank you, sir." He offered a grateful smile. "Mischief" was how he tended to view it, too. Louie wasn't sly or vicious, just high-spirited—curious and playful, with an abundance of energy and a knack for getting himself into trouble. He never meant any harm.

Of course, that didn't actually stop him from *doing* harm, whether he meant to or not.

"Mischief!" Chester bent toward the preacher, pointing to the knot on his noggin. "Does this look like a child's mischief? I'd say menace is more like it."

Ezra gave a helpless shrug. "I've made restitution where necessary. And if I've missed anyone, all they have to do is speak up." His nephew—his son, in every way that mattered—was his responsibility, and that meant shouldering all the costs that Louie's particular brand of mischief seemed to accumulate.

"I'm afraid paying for the damage isn't enough. Folks around here want to see the damage stopped—and as the boy's pa, they expect you to discipline him to make that happen. If you don't…" Samuel Lowe reached into his coat pocket and retrieved a piece of paper. His face spoke his hesitance as he handed it over. "Those folks are threatening to do their trading elsewhere."

Ezra studied the list, trying without success to shove down the rising disappointment. The names were more than just faceless people. He had known these folks most of his life. He couldn't believe they'd truly turn their backs on him and his business just because his boy had made a little trouble. "So, they're threatening to go all the way to Jamesburg to do their trading?"

"For the most part, I'm afraid. But you'll be given a chance to change their minds. You're invited to come to the town meeting tomorrow night and state your case. It's your chance to explain what you're going to do to change things around here."

"Humph," Chester snorted, shaking his head with a vehemence that waved the loose skin around his jowls like a hound shaking off after a splash in the creek. "It sure as shootin' had better *be* an explanation and not just more excuses. I'm sick and tired of empty words, mister. And I ain't the only one. You best come with a plan of action to back up your words. Something to show that you're finally going to take that boy in hand after all this time of lettin' him run wild."

Robert Bohannon stepped forward and looked Ezra square in the eye, firmly but not without sympathy. "We know it's not an easy thing to ask…taking a firm stance with the boy, considering his ma left and all…"

"I don't see what that jezebel has to do with anything." The words nearly exploded from Chester's throat. "And we ain't askin'. We're saying plain as day—"

"Chester," Mr. Lowe snapped. "You've said your piece. No one has to guess how you feel about any of this. Now you stay quiet and let us conduct our business with Ezra without your interference."

The blacksmith slapped his hat onto his head, then winced as it pressed against his injury. "I got to be going, anyways. It's fried chicken day at the café." He narrowed his gaze and pointed a meaty finger at Ezra. "You'll be there tomorrow night, Murphy, if you know what's good for you."

He stomped back up the aisle, knocking into a barrel of apples from Tillman's orchard. Ezra's eyes widened and he sucked in a breath as the fruit began to roll across the floor and the barrel tipped more. Chester turned at the door and narrowed his gaze. "I'll just let you pick those up," he said. "I got messes enough to clean up, thanks to you Murphys. This one's on you."

Ezra waited until the door slammed behind Chester, then he turned to the three members of the council. "Am I the only item on the meeting agenda?"

Reverend Harper shook his head. "We have to talk about fixing the church roof, too, and Robert's hogs smelling up the town."

Mr. Bohannon scowled. "I don't know what anyone expects me to do about the smell. Wash 'em down with sweet-smelling soap from Paris?" He snickered. "You have any of that for sale, Murphy?"

Ezra's lips stretched into a wry grin. "'Fraid not."

Reverend Harper reached down and picked up an apple that had traveled to the counter. "We can wait until you get those picked up before we discuss any more. Let us help."

Ezra felt a surge of affection for the aging minister. He'd known the man for most of his life, had been baptized by him and then had grown up as childhood friends with the reverend's daughter. The man was as decent and kind as they came—but he also wasn't a young man, by any stretch. The idea of making him stoop and fetch things off the floor didn't sit right with Ezra. "I'll pick them up as soon as we are finished here."

"Well, we just wanted to let you know that you'd likely better show up tomorrow night." Reverend Harper drew in a deep breath and rubbed the apple on his shoulder before taking a bite.

He smiled and patted Ezra's shoulder. "I'll be there to speak up for you—and to push for a solution that eases everyone's concerns while avoiding either scapegoating Louie or damaging your business," he said around the bite. "And I'm not the only one hoping for a peaceful resolution, without anyone shunning your store." He looked up at the shelves behind the counter and rubbed his palms together. "In the meantime, I could use a pound of sugar. My girl plans to bake a cake for that new husband of hers. And how much do I owe you for the apple?"

Grabbing a bag of sugar from the display behind the counter, Ezra shook his head. "Take as many as you like—I'm giving them away. Tillman brought in that barrel after that storm two nights ago. It shook his trees so hard that the apples are all over the ground. Matter of fact, he said anyone can take a basket and pick up as many as possible before they rot."

The reverend smiled. "I'll pass that along."

The door opened a little and Ezra's best friend, Wyatt Avery, stuck his head inside. "Stagecoach is rolling in!" he announced as though he were a self-appointed town crier, then he left as quickly as he'd come.

"I best be running along." Mr. Lowe turned up his coat collar. The other two men nodded.

"Don't be anxious," the reverend said at the door. "The Lord's will be done."

Swallowing past a sudden lump in his throat, Ezra nodded. What was there to say to that? He wanted to trust that the Lord had some extra mercy set aside for him and Louie…but based on Mr. Lowe's list, it hardly seemed likely. Maybe the best thing he could do was find his son and keep him close for the next twenty-four hours. No need to stir anyone up with new mischief right before the big meeting.

"Jeremiah!"

His young stock clerk stuck his head out of the storeroom. "Yes, sir?"

"Mind the store for me. I have to go find my son."

As the door closed behind him, Ezra thought he heard the sixteen-year-old mutter, "Again?" But he ignored it and walked quickly along the boardwalk. He would check the café first, but if Louie had escaped Jennie as Chester claimed, he wasn't sure where the boy would have gone. One thing he was pretty certain about—if he headed in the direction of the nearest ruckus, he was bound to find Louie smack dab in the middle of it.

"Rollin' into Tucker Springs!"

The wheels that carried Hazel O'Brien through the muddy streets of her new hometown slid one way and slogged another as she fought valiantly to keep from tumbling onto the stagecoach's floor. Her traveling companion, she noted, wasn't having as much success. She wasn't quite on the floor yet, but she was certainly on the verge of it, sliding all over the seat. When the stagecoach steadied temporarily on a straight patch of road, Hazel slid to the other seat.

"What on earth are you doing?" the elderly lady huffed.

"Keeping you in the seat, ma'am."

They had shared the stagecoach since they boarded this morning in Iowa City. Miss Tucker, she knew from Benjamin's letters, was a very wealthy spinster and part of the founding family of Tucker Springs. It seemed Benjamin was rather besotted with the woman, as he devoted at least a paragraph here and there to her with each letter he had written. Despite that, Miss Tucker didn't seem to know who he was—hadn't recognized the name when Hazel had explained why she was moving to town. A circumstance, Hazel had already decided, she would not reveal to her fiancé.

After a day of shared travel, Hazel had learned that the woman ran both bitter and sweet, and Hazel never knew which would flavor their conversation. Still, the risk of being rebuffed seemed outweighed by the threat of an old woman falling and breaking a bone.

"Well, I suppose I'm grateful." She sighed. "Aging isn't pleasant, I must say."

"Yes, ma'am."

"Oh, what do you know about it? You're all of twenty-five years old."

Hazel smiled at her. "And a spinster. We have that much in common."

She scoffed. "Not for much longer. Have you spied your young man yet?"

"No, ma'am." Hazel peeked out through a tear in the canvas flap covering the window. She watched in bewildered silence as the tired, bedraggled little settlement passed by, one shabby storefront at a time. She pressed her lemon verbena–scented handkerchief to her nose, trying with little success to escape a fetid stench that squeezed into the coach, despite the canvas, and seemed to bounce from wall to wall.

At least the canvas was doing a tolerable job of protecting them from the mud churned up by the coach's wheels. The rain had been a constant and most unwelcome companion since Hazel and Miss Tucker had boarded the stagecoach seven hours earlier, just after dawn. She had scarcely dared to roll up the canvas at any point for fear of ruining her blue velvet gown. Of all the hand-me-downs she'd received from her employer, it was her favorite. Mrs. Wells had risked her husband's ire by slipping it out of her own closet into Hazel's as a parting gift. At least she had known Hazel was innocent, even if Mr. Wells would not listen to any of her protests. If things went as she hoped, the gown would also serve as her wedding attire before the day ended.

Hazel held her breath and pushed against the wall with one hand and the ceiling with the other to steady herself as the driver yelled to the horses. She exhaled and sent up a prayer of thanks when the horses finally settled down and the swaying stopped.

"Well, here we are." Miss Tucker adjusted herself upright, suddenly the regal figure she had been before the jostling of the wagon. "Return to your own seat, please."

"Yes, ma'am." Nerves overwhelmed her stomach as

she peeked behind the canvas and scanned the board-walk for Benjamin. Would he take one look at her and be disappointed? Or would he think her beautiful? At twenty-five years old, Hazel had not minded being considered a spinster. In truth, she had thought herself superior to all the twittering, silly women who could think of nothing but ensnaring some man and making a home for him. To her way of thinking, independence had been preferable…but only for so long as she could earn her way. Marriage, in the end, was better than begging on the street to survive. Or worse. And Benjamin Gordon had presented himself well in the letters he'd written over the past three months—well enough, in fact, that Hazel felt a real and true affection for the farmer.

He loved his hometown, and she was moved by his eagerness to share it with her. To build a home and family together. The thought warmed her and almost took away the sting of being sent away from the three Wells children without so much as a farewell. Of course, she hadn't said a word to Benjamin about her dismissal. And truthfully, they had begun their correspondence afterward. By the time he had proposed, Hazel had spent almost every penny she had saved of her meager salary on the smallest attic room in the dingiest, but proper boarding house she could find.

In the interests of presenting herself in the best light, and securing Benjamin's affections, she had omitted other minor details about herself that might mean a lot more to her intended, but she would naturally reveal the harshest truths before she allowed Benjamin to become bound to her in holy matrimony. Her husband-to-be would have the right to know about her pa and his tendency to steal anything not nailed to a strong, sturdy surface. She would probably even tell him about her sister, who wasn't a thief at heart but could not seem to break her childhood ties with their pa's dishonest life.

"Well?" Miss Tucker said. "Is the town everything that romantic heart of yours had hoped?"

"It's not quite what I envisioned. But perhaps that's only because I didn't think to envision rain and mud."

Miss Tucker chuckled. "One rarely does in dreams."

Hazel stared out at the dismal, grimy, gray town and sighed. It appeared that she wasn't the only one who had been less than forthcoming in order to cast circumstances in a rosy hue. Neither Benjamin's advertisement in the Boston newspaper three months ago nor any of his subsequent letters had said a word about ramshackle buildings or revolting, pervasive smells that, frankly, caused a sickening burn at the back of Hazel's throat. As a matter of fact, the advertisement had clearly stated: "Twenty-five-year-old bachelor seeking a bride to share a life in the charming town of Tucker Springs, Iowa."

Surely Benjamin had not purposely deceived her— but charming? She glanced down at the tintype she'd been clutching for the past hour. Her fiancé's handsome face stared back at her. A strong jaw, neat, well-kept hair and eyes that—despite his slightly exaggerated description of this town—appeared honest and kind. Hazel had shown the tintype to Miss Tucker, hoping for some stories of his youth or accounts of his generosity or heroism as a man that he had been too humble to share. But

Miss Tucker only said that while he did look familiar, she wasn't one to keep up with everyone's names.

At the very least, she hadn't known anything negative about him, which had given Hazel hope that he was just as he'd presented himself—even if the town didn't quite live up to his promises. Shaking her head, she carefully tucked the image into her reticule and slid the ribbons over her wrist. Not that it mattered in the long run, she supposed. A home of her own—even in this town composed of mud and stench—was still better than living in alleyways or burned-out buildings. She shuddered as images of her childhood flashed across her mind. She forced back the memories as the driver walked by the window and gave her a nod.

"I reckon you best wait until I unload your trunk."

"Thank you." She leaned as far out of the window as she dared in the drizzling rain. "Are you quite certain *this* is Tucker Springs?"

Miss Tucker chuckled at the question.

"Yes, ma'am," the driver answered. He frowned in a way that indicated he might have been wondering if she was quite sane.

"Tucker Springs…Iowa?"

"Only one I know of." He spat a revolting stream of tobacco juice into the mud. "Now you just sit tight. I'll be there to help you down in two shakes."

Hazel scanned the crudely built boardwalk, carefully examining the faces of the few men standing outside the stores along the walkway. There were three very old men huddled together next to a leather shop. They were definitely not Benjamin. Sitting on a bench outside the café were a couple of men closer to her age, but they also were not her fiancé.

There was a knock on the stagecoach door, and Hazel drew in a sharp breath. She glanced at Miss Tucker. "Do I look…presentable?" She wanted to ask if she looked beautiful. Would Benjamin find her attractive?

The wise old woman seemed to see through her hesitation and uncertainty. "You are a lovely young woman, Hazel O'Brien. I am sure the young man will find you pleasing in every respect. In five years, I'll see a passel of redheaded children darting along the walk as I drive through town, and I'll remember you. Now, open the door, please."

Hazel did as bidden. Her eyebrows went up at the sight of a slim, tall man of about sixty years of age who most definitely wasn't Benjamin.

"Ah, Smith," Miss Tucker said. "Meet Miss O'Brien. Soon to be missus something or other."

"Delighted, Miss O'Brien." He nodded his head respectfully but barely smiled. His proper manners and speech indicated he was a servant trained in a wealthy household. He reminded her of the Wellses' butler. He turned to Miss Tucker. "I shall have to carry you, madam. The mud is deep."

Miss Tucker allowed herself to be swept up into the man's arms. She turned to Hazel. "It has been a pleasant enough journey. You may come see me, if you like. Just ask for directions from anyone."

"I will, Miss Tucker. It has been a pleasure traveling with you."

As Hazel watched them walk away through the

ankle-deep mud toward the fine carriage that seemed to be waiting for them, worry edged its way through her. That heavy sense that something was not right had been a lifelong companion, a result of her precarious childhood. Only during the last seven years had she been able to quiet the voice of foreboding, thanks to the stabilizing influence of her work for the Wells family—a position secured for her by her teacher Miss Hastings. Two years later, Hazel had procured a maid position for her sister, Rose, hoping that honest work would be the boon to her sister's comfort and peace of mind that it had been to her.

The eldest of the Wells children had been no more than a year old on Hazel's first day of employment, and two more children had followed during her time as their nanny. Her arms ached for the children. Her heart ached for them, as well. But Mr. Wells had been resolute in his dismissal. A woman whose sister was a thief was not a suitable nanny for his children. Oh, if only she hadn't recommended Rose for the post.

Hazel watched as one of the men from the boardwalk stepped down to help the driver carry her trunk, and the two men who had been sitting on the bench laid boards down between the stagecoach and the boardwalk to provide her a path somewhat less hampered by mud. The driver returned, breathing heavily from his exertion. He offered her his hand. She nodded her thanks and stepped onto the crude wooden plank, looking at the few people walking back and forth in front of the storefront buildings. Could one of the men be her Benjamin? For the life of her, she couldn't imagine why he hadn't stepped forward to claim her. She'd telegrammed him to let him know when to expect her. He was supposed to be here to meet her.

Soft mud sucked at her new shoes as the board sank into a good two inches of the stuff. If only she'd worn sensible boots. Dainty shoes were not meant for a day like this—as was proven when the mud sucked one of her shoes right off her foot.

Irritation rose in Hazel as she looked back at it. Wrestling it out of the muck seemed likely to tip her over. And even if she retrieved it, what then? It was already quite ruined. There was no choice but to consider the mud a burial ground for shoes.

"Pardon me. Miss O'Brien?"

Hazel forced a pleasant expression and glanced up at the soft sound of a female voice coming from the boardwalk a couple of feet away. The young woman standing there was tall and willowy with blond hair piled atop her bare head.

A frown touched Hazel's brow. "Yes. Do I know you?" Obviously not. But the woman seemed to know Hazel.

"I'm Ivy—" She hesitated for a beat. "Gordon. Ben got your telegram and he—well, he's been delayed, but I offered to come meet your stage until he could get here."

That explained it. Benjamin would certainly have spoken about her to members of his family. "Then you must be Ben's…" She frowned. This woman could be a sister, sister-in-law, cousin, niece. Well, gracious, why guess? "I'm sorry, but what relation are you to Ben?"

The woman's face reddened suddenly, and she

reached a trembling hand to the cameo pinned at her throat.

"Did I say something to upset you?" Hazel asked.

Miss Gordon glanced over Hazel's shoulder. "Please, Ben will be here any second. Come out of the street, and when he arrives, we will discuss the situation further."

"Further?" Hazel said, beginning to be annoyed at the woman's evasiveness. "We haven't discussed anything..."

She took one soggy step toward Miss Gordon, but the sound of a high-pitched bark behind her, followed by a child's equally high-pitched yell, stopped her in her tracks.

"Ar-r-r-chiiee!"

Instinctively, she spun toward the commotion.

"Louie, no!" the other woman screeched.

With a gasp, Hazel caught a glimpse of a blond blur dashing toward her just as her feet became entangled with something small and energetic that was too twisted up in her skirts for her to identify. Nothing on earth had the power to stop the inevitable as the ground rose up to meet her. She had just enough presence of mind to put her hands out, catching herself in time to avoid a mouthful of mud.

"Oh no!" The sound of a man's voice broke through the commotion. *Please, dear Lord, let that be Benjamin.*

"Miss O'Brien!" the other woman called out. "Are you all right? Oh, dear! Someone help her. Ezra!"

Sputtering, indignant, completely unaware of what had happened, Hazel sat up, shaking her arms, flinging mud from her hands. She glanced about, trying to gather her wits.

Something wiggly and furry moved beneath Hazel's legs. She gave a yelp and yanked on her skirts, finally revealing a truly pathetic, mud-matted little dog as a series of terrified yips and whimpers filled the air. The entire ordeal was just so…ridiculous. "Oh, for mercy's sake. Come here, little one." She reached forward to reassure herself the wretched animal wasn't injured.

From the corner of her eye, Hazel could see someone walking toward her. She turned, hoping to see her Benjamin, but instead a man in the shopkeeper's apron closed the distance. "Louie," he said. "Apologize to the lady."

"But you saw how she almost killed Archie, Pa." A towheaded boy, no more than five or six years of age, swooped down and snatched up the tiny dog. He glared at Hazel. "You leave him be!"

The man quickened his steps. "Louie!"

"Little boy," Hazel said sternly as the man stopped beside the child. "I will gladly leave your animal be. It is unfortunate the dog didn't give me the same consideration. If it had, I wouldn't be sprawled in the mud like the prodigal son, regretting his waywardness, now, would I?"

Clearly unswayed by the truth of the matter, the little boy continued to glare at her, his wide brown eyes flashing in anger. "You almost squished him!"

"Louie," the man said, a distinct warning in his tone that the boy seemed intent on ignoring.

"But Pa, she's a minnow to society," he protested.

"And you know what Miss Stewart said about minnows to society. They shouldn't be walking around all alone getting in trouble."

"Is that so?" Working hard to suppress a smile, Hazel glanced at the boy's father before she turned back to the little boy's stormy gaze. As a nanny, she'd learned the importance of staying stern in the face of misbehavior—even when the misbehaving child in question said or did something that made it almost impossible to keep from laughing. "I'm sure you mean menace. However, if there is a menace in the general vicinity, I'd wager it is that animal and possibly his young owner." The father reached out to help her. She accepted the man's assistance and soon found herself back on her feet, her two hands wrapped in his. "Thank you."

"I hope you will accept my apologies." His eyes grazed over her mud-soaked gown. "I'm truly sorry for the trouble. I promise you, I'll deal with my son."

She gave a short, unsteady laugh. "Well, it wasn't so much the boy as it was the dog." Assured that she was steady, she pulled her hands from his.

He slid his hands over the shopkeeper's apron he was wearing, wiping mud from his hands. He smiled, a sad kind of smile that caused crinkled lines at the corners of his eyes. "The dog was supposed to keep him from getting lonely and make up for him not having a mother, but it was probably not my best idea."

Hazel's stomach dipped deeper than it had during the two days of swaying and bouncing in the stagecoach. Was it compassion for this man's obvious loss or something else? Guilt seized her at the very thought that she could get absolutely lost in those deep dark eyes. *Stop it!* she commanded herself and forced herself to avert her gaze away from his perfectly squared jaw and full, smiling lips.

"It looks like you lost a shoe."

"I beg your pardon?" Bewildered at the direction of her own traitorous thoughts, Hazel had forgotten all about the shoe in the mud. He bent down and retrieved it.

"Thank you," she said. "I thought it was gone forever."

He chuckled, deep and pleasant. "It probably should be."

She lifted her muddy foot, stumbled and caught herself by grabbing on to his shoulder.

"Let me help." He wiped the mud from the top of her shoe and slipped it deftly onto her foot. "There," he said. As he unbent, her hand slid from his shoulder to his forearm. "All set."

"Now I just have to keep it in place until I reach the boardwalk," she said wryly. "A few minutes ago, I would have thought that an easy enough task. At the moment, though, I'm not so sure."

"Perhaps all you need is an escort." Taking hold of her hand, he moved it from his forearm to curve around his elbow. "May I?"

"Thank you. I am sorry for the trouble." For some reason, his kindness eased some of the apprehension she'd felt since she'd seen Ivy Gordon's flustered expression.

He leaned in closer as though sharing a secret. "This

drizzle and all this mud, now that's trouble. Helping a pretty lady get where she's going is a pleasure. By the way, welcome to Tucker Springs."

Hazel's cheeks warmed, and her heart lifted a little. She wasn't sure how to respond, and thankfully she was spared as he continued, "I'm Ezra Murphy. I own the general store…for now, anyway."

For now? What a curious thing to say. But he didn't elaborate, and she didn't feel as though she had the right to ask. "Hazel O'Brien. From Boston." She wasn't sure why, perhaps because his boy was so unruly, but she added, "I was a nanny before I…well, came here." If he wanted advice on how to deal with his son's misbehavior, she'd be happy to offer it—but she wouldn't say anything unless she was invited to. He might consider it rude or intrusive, and she didn't wish to cause trouble with the man who would supply her and Benjamin with so many of their daily needs. She highly doubted that this town had more than one general store. Besides, for all she knew, this man might be one of Benjamin's friends. No, she'd keep her thoughts to herself until and unless her opinion was solicited.

"Nice to meet you," he said as they reached the boardwalk. He dropped Hazel's elbow and tipped his hat to the tall woman waiting there. "Ivy." He smiled. "You didn't happen to see which way Louie and the dog went, did you?"

"I'm sorry, he must've slipped away."

He expelled a heavy sigh. "I'd best go look for him. This is Miss O'Brien, from Boston. She's a nanny.

This is Ivy. Her pa is the reverend and her husband is a farmer."

"Yes, Ezra!" Miss Gordon—Mrs. that was, apparently—said with an edge to her voice. "We have met. Louie is probably in the café with Jennie."

"I'll look." He tipped his hat and sauntered into the café that was just behind them.

Mrs. Gordon offered a piece of crumpled paper to Hazel. "We only received this a few hours ago. We had no time to prepare."

Hazel glanced down at the telegram, recognizing the message she had sent Benjamin.

I am coming to you, my love STOP
Will arrive by stage this afternoon in Tucker
Springs STOP
Yours, Hazel STOP

"Prepare?" Hazel repeated. "We? I don't understand."

The other woman's gaze shifted to focus behind Hazel, and relief flooded her face. "Ben, sweetheart. Here is Miss O'Brien."

Hazel spun around and stared into the eyes of the man she recognized as her fiancé. "Benjamin." What an odd thing to finally meet in person the man she had come to know so well through letters. Her heart pounded. The stranger she was about to marry.

"Miss O'Brien?"

"Of course." She had sent along her own picture— he should have had no difficulty in recognizing her.

Though she supposed she was rather cleaner in the photograph.

"You're all…" His gaze slid over her.

"I took a tumble in the mud."

"Louie and Archie waylaid her." Mrs. Gordon's pitch seemed unnaturally high.

"I see. Well, there's no easy way to say this." Ben's voice cracked, his tone curiously stilted. "I'm so sorry you've come all this way. Ivy and I…we…she left town and I thought we would never see each other again. But when she came back, I knew…we knew…" His face flushed and he frowned. "I sent you a telegram telling you not to come."

"Not to come?" Though she usually prided herself on her keen understanding, Hazel was still reeling from the fall in the mud coupled with the exhaustion from the trip. She could hear what Benjamin was saying, but she couldn't make the words into any kind of sense. She felt like she was looking through a fog and could not grasp the full picture. "Why?"

"Ivy and I were married three days ago." He stepped around her and took his place beside the willowy woman.

Hazel stared dumbly, unable to speak. This couldn't be right.

"Miss O'Brien?" Concern creased a frown between Ivy's eyes. She reached out to Hazel.

Hazel stepped back, her breath catching as if the shock had made her lungs forget how to contract and expand properly. Black spots formed in front of her eyes, slowly growing and covering the faces of the two people in front of her. Even though she wanted to stomp away and not look back, she felt herself falling. Just as suddenly, she was caught in a pair of warm, strong arms. Before she could wonder who rescued her, everything went black.

Chapter Two

Ezra burst into the general store with Hazel lying limply in his arms. Louie followed him more closely than he ever had. "Is she dead, Pa?"

Instinctively, Ezra looked down at the woman's long eyelashes sweeping gracefully across her mud-spattered pink cheeks. If she were dead, those cheeks wouldn't have still been pink...would they? As if to settle the matter, she chose that moment to take in a deep breath. Ezra felt himself sigh a bit in relief. Not that he'd truly believed she was dead. But he had never seen anyone living be so still.

"She just fainted." He saw the worry flee from his son's eyes and be replaced by something else. Excitement? "Run ahead into the storeroom and straighten up the bed." They sometimes slept there on the rare occasion when they had to stay the night. Louie didn't hesitate. By the time Ezra reached the doorway, the boy had smoothed the covers and fluffed the feather pillow. Sometimes in the storm of life with Louie, Ezra forgot how capable he could be for a five-year-old—and kind, too, though he couldn't always find a constructive way to show it.

Before Ezra could lay her down on the bed, Hazel's eyes opened and she wiggled out of his arms, planting her feet on the floor. "What happened?"

"You fainted."

Her large green eyes widened. "Fainted?" As soon as the word left her mouth, the blood drained from her face again, and Ezra could tell she was replaying the humiliating discovery that Ben Gordon had married someone else after leading her on. Which—in Ezra's opinion—made him an idiot.

She swayed a little, and Ezra took hold of her arm. "Sit down, over here." The bed no longer seemed appropriate now that she was awake, so he led her to the tattered armchair in the corner.

Hesitating, she looked down at her mud-covered gown and flinched. "I'm filthy."

Ezra chuckled. "A little mud won't hurt that old chair."

Her lips trembled a little, and she swallowed hard. "Thank you. You're very kind." She sank into the chair. Her gentle sigh shot straight into Ezra's heart.

"We'll get you some warm water for washing up." He nodded to the key in the storeroom door. "You can lock the door from the inside. Do you have clean clothes to change into?"

Her face flushed, but she nodded. "If you can bring in my trunk."

"Consider it done." He nodded and excused himself.

What was it about this jilted woman from Boston that so moved his heart? He couldn't be sure. Maybe it was the way she'd treated Louie and Archie after their unfortunate encounter. She'd been firm without being harsh, not ignoring the misbehavior but not turning her temper on the child or the animal, either. It was a balance that few in town had mastered when it came to Ezra's son, and he admired her for it. He also admired the good humor with which she'd handled her dousing in mud…and the way her green eyes looked—verdant and lovely—when they met his. He found himself wanting to right the world for her. To make all her troubles blow away like a prairie wind.

Of course, that was a foolish notion. Hadn't Marie taught him not to trust a woman with fancy clothes and city ways? Even though she'd been dead for the past four years, he still had a tendency to tread lightly when it came to women who had no place in his world. No matter how pretty their eyes might be.

When he stepped out of the storeroom, the store was bustling. It hadn't taken long for word of what happened on the boardwalk to spread, and apparently everyone who was already in town, including other shopkeepers, had made a beeline to his door to see what would happen next. To their credit, most of the people were making selections among the goods, willing to spend a little money to satisfy their curiosity. Many of the customers, Ezra noted with more than a little satisfaction, were names on the list the councilmen had shown him earlier. He nodded to his clerk, Jeremiah, who was busy behind the cash register. Since Jeremiah seemed to have things well in hand, Ezra could continue to focus on helping Miss O'Brien.

He hurried to fill a big pan of water and place it on the top of the potbellied stove, then headed out to the boardwalk to retrieve the lady's trunk.

Fifteen minutes later, after hoisting the trunk, dodging questions, and maneuvering through displays and shoppers, he reached the storeroom door and tapped with his free hand. When there was no answer, he pushed the door open. Miss O'Brien was still in the chair, sitting up but sound asleep. Louie sat in front of her on an old wood chair, with that muddy ball of fur in his lap. They both were intently watching the sleeping woman.

"She was telling me about a dog she used to play with when she was a young'un," Louie said. He shrugged and shook his head. "She fell clean asleep, right in the middle of the whole story." He patted the dog's head, and Ezra thought that might be the calmest he'd ever seen the two of them. "Archie and I figured we'd best look out for her while she sleeps."

Apparently, Louie felt a sense of responsibility for the stranger. It was a striking change from Louie's accusations earlier that she was a "minnow" to society. Apparently, her story had made a good impression. Or maybe he was won over by a woman who didn't yell at him when he misbehaved. Regardless, it looked as if she had quite a way with children after all.

But while Ezra was glad to see the boy care, Louie knew better than to bring Archie inside in that condition. "You go tie that pup up outside and you can come back and keep watch over Miss O'Brien until the water is ready."

Louie looked like he would protest, but he stood and took Archie to the door. He stopped and looked back at the sleeping woman. "You think she might be dead, now, Pa?"

Ezra pretended to seriously consider the matter. "I don't think so."

The crowd had thinned somewhat when he reentered the store. He stepped to the counter to relieve Jeremiah. Finally, the last three ladies stood in line with their purchases. He suspected these three were last in line due to their determination to wait until they could see the jilted bride emerge.

He handed Mrs. Lowe her bag of peppermints and took the five cents in exchange. "It was unfortunate that your Louie caused such a public ruckus today of all days, Ezra." She sounded as if she had seen the whole thing.

"Yes, ma'am," he admitted. "I couldn't agree more. I suppose it'll come up tomorrow night at the meeting."

Mrs. Green, who was next in line, scoffed. "That goes without saying."

"Well, you have many friends in Tucker Springs." Mrs. Lowe clicked her tongue in sympathy. "We are all here to help in any way we can, aren't we, ladies?"

Mrs. Green, who worked alongside her husband running the *Tucker Springs Chronicle*, gave a shrug of her meaty shoulders. "I will speak with my husband, but what he decides is entirely his business." Her gray eyebrows rose high on her forehead. "Although if I were to, say, have access to an interview with a certain poor young lady, there might be one more vote in your column." She turned an exaggerated gaze in the direction of the storeroom.

"Rebecca Green!" Her sister, Miss Joy Reagan, shook her head and gave a scolding frown. "You leave that poor woman alone." Of course, being a spinster herself, Miss Joy probably sympathized more than anyone else with Miss O'Brien's uncomfortable situation.

With a scowl, Mrs. Green shrugged again. "Well, better to get the story straight from the horse's mouth than to print secondhand information. You know folks will expect to read something about it in next week's edition of the *Chronicle*. I will not disappoint my readers."

Ezra had known Mrs. Green all his life. He knew the best way to get her focus off one story was to redirect it to another. Leaning across the counter, Ezra met her eye to eye. "Will you have enough print space, what with covering the meeting tomorrow night? Mr. Lowe mentioned the agenda includes a discussion about the leaks in the church's roof. Not to mention people have been complaining about Robert Bohannon's pigs."

Miss Joy wrinkled her nose. "Oh, those hogs of his!"

Mrs. Green frowned. "It's going to be a long meeting, isn't it?" She took in a breath, then gave an abrupt nod. "I'll make it work. I can always leave out the poetry section."

Miss Joy gasped. "But that's my section."

"Yes, sister, and I'm sorry if it comes to that. We may have no choice but to make the sacrifice. It depends on how heated the meeting becomes. And I'm thinking…" she added, eyeing Ezra closely, "…it might become very heated indeed."

Miss Joy sniffed. "It's not right, what they're trying to do to Mr. Murphy. After he took that boy to raise all alone." Turning to Ezra, she added, "I'm on your side, and I don't care a bit if sister cuts my little contribution to the newspaper. If there's anything I can do, you just let me know."

Hope rose in Ezra's heart. "If you truly mean that, I could use someone to look after Louie tomorrow night."

"Y-you mean during the town meeting?"

Was he mistaken, or had Miss Joy's face gone pale?

Mrs. Green shook her head at Ezra. "You know well and good my sister wouldn't stand a chance going up against that boy of yours. Like a tumbleweed in a twister."

Ashamed that he'd even put the sensitive Miss Joy in that position, Ezra gave her an apologetic smile. "I understand, Miss Joy. I should never have asked. Louie's a handful to take care of even for me."

Miss Joy stammered. "Well, i-it's just that…"

"I know. Let's go back and pretend I didn't ask."

"You're very kind. You know I would watch him if…"

"I know." He dropped an extra stick of licorice in her bag and handed it to her.

Ezra's best friend, Wyatt, came in from outside as the three ladies were leaving. He stepped back to let them pass. Mrs. Green lagged behind, glancing back toward the storeroom as she left.

Wyatt chuckled as he crossed the room toward Ezra. "I take it Miz Green was hoping for an interview with the lady from Boston."

Ezra nodded. "Tried to barter with her husband's vote in my favor at the meeting tomorrow if I could set up an interview."

Wyatt snickered. "That doesn't surprise me. The woman is like a hound when she smells a story. But what are *you* going to do about Miss O'Brien?"

Ezra frowned. "Let her rest for now, I reckon. She's bound to be exhausted—first from her journey and then from the emotional toll of finding out her intended…"

Wyatt grinned. "Never intended to marry her in the first place?"

Ezra frowned. "In all fairness, I think Ben did plan to marry her until Ivy came back, but I feel bad for Miss O'Brien. I'm pretty sure she gave up a position as a nanny to come here."

"Ben tell you that?"

Ezra shook his head. "She did. Well, she mentioned being a nanny. So, I'm assuming she gave it up to come and marry Ben."

"It occurs to me that there's an easy solution to your problem and hers."

Ezra stared at his friend. "What solution?"

"Well, she came here to marry a stranger—and she has experience with children. Meanwhile, Louie needs to be looked after before you get starved out of town." He shrugged as though he were suggesting the most obvious thing in the world. "Why not just marry her?"

Ezra laughed at the absurdity. "You think I ought to

marry a woman I don't know just to have someone to look after Louie?"

Wyatt lifted his shoulders in a shrug. "Why not? Louie could use a mother. And if you were planning to go courting, you'd have gotten around to it before now. It's not like anyone in Tucker Springs has caught your fancy since Marie hightailed it out of here."

The words stung, and Ezra felt an inward wince. "Who are you to talk about courting? You haven't looked at a woman since Sarah over in Jamesburg married David Grey."

"We ain't talking about me." He kept his tone pleasant, but Ezra could see the mention of the only girl Wyatt ever had eyes for had hit a nerve. Good. Maybe that would help him remember that some topics were off-limits, even for friends who were as close as brothers. "Besides, you're the one who needs someone to look after your son."

"But not a wife," Ezra said firmly. "I'll figure out... something for Louie."

"Like what?"

"I don't know. But *something*." There must be another way forward. Something that would appease the town and protect his son. Something other than marriage to a woman he didn't know and wasn't sure he could trust.

Something. There just had to be something.

Hazel jerked awake and found herself staring into a pair of startled brown eyes.

"I reckon you ain't dead, then."

"No, I'm most certainly not dead." She peered closer

at the boy. Someone had made him clean off the mud he'd been covered in earlier. He now wore trousers and a dark shirt with a pair of red suspenders. The tow-headed little boy was actually a pretty handsome fellow when he was scrubbed clean and tidy. Of course, she had a feeling that pleasing appearance wouldn't last long. "Where's your dog?"

"Aw." He kicked at the floor. "Pa don't let him in the store."

She gave him a wry grin. "Because he's a minnow to society?"

He scowled. "Menace."

"Exactly." She couldn't help but smile. Hazel could forgive almost anything from a child who was willing to learn a thing or two. "So, if your pa doesn't allow Archie inside, where is he?"

"Tied up outside." He sighed and tipped his chair back on two legs. "You figure he'll be mad at me?"

Hazel was pretty sure the boy wasn't referring to his pa. "The dog? Even if he is, he'll forgive you." She smiled. "Discipline is hard, but profitable. And dogs are predisposed to love owners who love them."

The response seemed to help ease his mind, though he did nothing more than nod.

He narrowed his gaze and studied her. "You been sleeping practically all day. I figured if you didn't wake up soon, Pa would be calling for the undertaker. But you did. So, no need for that. Buryin's are fun, though."

"I'm sorry I couldn't oblige you." It was a good thing for her there'd been no need for a buryin'. Who would have mourned her? Certainly not Benjamin! Or his wife!

Hazel shoved back the tears that threatened. She absolutely wouldn't allow self-pity to get the better of her—especially not in front of the little boy. "Tell me, why do you like *buryings*, as you call them? Most people don't, you know. Especially children."

"They don't?" He scrunched his nose and frowned. "How come?"

"In my experience, children are frightened of funerals. The black carriage and viewing the body of the deceased…"

He waved her off with a chubby hand. "Well, I ain't ever seen a black carriage, and the only time I saw someone dead was when Henry Avery and me snuck a look at old man Carter through the window."

"Then I'm sure I can't imagine what you find so appealing about the whole ordeal."

"The food is what I like."

"Food?"

"Sure. After someone gets buried, folks eat together." He gave her a bewildered frown. "Don't they do that where you come from?"

"I don't really know." She had never attended a funeral. Her dear mother had passed away quietly one wintry evening in the freezing, burned-out tenement building where they'd been squatting for months. Mama and the baby had been taken away and she'd never known where they were laid to rest. Her guess was a pauper's field. After that, Pa hadn't allowed them to mention her again. There'd certainly been no funeral—much less a funeral feast. Shoving aside the maudlin memory, she focused back in on Louie. "What sorts of foods do you eat after a funeral?"

"There's always potato salad and fried chicken and cakes and such. Sometimes Mr. Bohannon roasts a pig. But mostly he just does that for festivals. And Mrs. Bauer over at the post office always makes potato dumplings."

"Potato dumplings? I've never heard of them."

He nodded. "Mrs. Bauer's pa and ma brought her over from the old country when she was no bigger'n me, and that's how she learned to make the potato dumplings. She talks a little funny. Mr. Bauer came over from the old country when he was a lad, he said. He talks real funny."

Hazel's lips stretched into a smile. "Which old country?"

He frowned again, then shrugged, clearly deciding not to be bothered with such a small detail. "I don't rightly know. How many are there?"

"A lot. As a matter of fact, just about every country in the world is an old country compared to America. We are just shy of one hundred years old." Which, it occurred to her, the child should already know. "Do you attend school yet, Mr. Murphy?"

"I did, but not anymore." He rocked back onto two legs of the chair. "Miss Stewart says I ain't allowed. She said I got to learn to behave myself and use my manners before I can come back. And she doubts that'll be any time soon."

Worry gnawed at Hazel's stomach, as the boy's feet barely reached the floor. "I think you'd best not lean back like that. You could fall."

A frown scrunched his nose. "Aw, I do it all the time."

"Fine. So no school?"

He shrugged. "I went for a couple days, and it wasn't that great anyway. I think I'm better off just stayin' away from that place."

"What didn't you like?"

"Staying put, for one thing. And Archie couldn't go." He scrunched his nose. "And Miss Stewart kept trying to teach me my letters."

"You don't want to learn to read?" Feeling a bit more like herself, Hazel inched herself up. "You have to learn your letters to read."

He scowled. "I already learned. Miss Jennie showed me all the letters and told me how they sound. It's easy."

"Well, I wouldn't give up on school altogether. I'm sure there are still things for you to learn. And you seem like a very bright boy."

His face lit up at the praise, but before he could respond, the chair legs slid out from under him, and he and the wooden chair made prompt contact with the ground.

"Gracious, are you hurt?" She stood to help him, but before she could reach him, the elder Mr. Murphy stepped in the room, a steaming pot of water in his hands.

"What was that crash?" His eyes widened at the sight of the boy on the ground. "Are you hurt?"

"No, sir." Louie stood up, clearly a bit dazed but seeming otherwise intact.

"Is he bothering you?" For a second, Hazel was too intent on looking over the boy, making sure he wasn't hiding or ignoring an injury, to realize that Mr. Murphy was speaking to her.

She shook her head. "I appreciate the company. It kept me from thinking too much about…other things."

He nodded before he carefully poured the water into a washbasin that sat on a table next to the wall. Once that was taken care of, he squatted down and put his arm around his son. "You sure you're not hurt, son?"

The tenderness in his voice as he spoke to Louie broke down the emotional wall that Hazel had been hiding behind ever since the scene on the boardwalk.

She'd thought she was going to have that for herself. Not a loving father, no—life had long since disabused her of ever achieving that dream. But someone to love and cherish her, someone to care for her comfort and work for her happiness. All through the journey to reach this miserable town, she'd reminded herself that every stomach-turning, bone-jarring mile of the journey was taking her that much closer to her husband, who had promised to love her, to protect her, to build a life with her. She'd been just on the verge of having all that, of knowing that she'd never have to be alone again.

And now, it was all gone. Her hopes, her dreams, her plans. They'd all come to nothing in the end. Tears filled her eyes, and she swallowed against a sob. She had been jilted in front of an entire town by a man who would never deliver on all the plans they'd made. The wedding, the husband, the home. The children that they would cherish together as this man in front of her did his son. None of it would ever happen now.

She closed her eyes against this awful reality.

"She's falling asleep again, Pa. What's wrong with her?"

Even through her overwhelming sadness and disappointment, Hazel felt a tiny twinge of amusement at this boy and his innocent question. She opened her eyes. "I'm not asleep." She allowed a small smile through her tears. "And I'm still not dead." She would have liked to assure him that nothing was wrong with her, but she refused to lie.

She glanced around and realized her trunk was on the floor next to her. She looked up at Mr. Murphy, who was regarding her with an unreadable expression. "Thank you so much for your kindness."

He shrugged. "It's the least I could do after the day you've had."

He turned to the boy. "Louie, let's give Miss O'Brien some privacy." The boy bounded out of the room, and at the door, Mr. Murphy glanced back at her. "Like I said, you can lock the door. I'll check on you in an hour or so, if that's all right?"

She nodded. "Thank you again."

He closed the door behind him, and she stepped over and turned the key in the lock.

As she opened her trunk and chose clean clothes, she thought about her situation. She had been through too much in her life to waste any more time dwelling on the devastating blow Benjamin Gordon had dealt her. She was as much at fault as he, she supposed, for having foolishly fallen for his sweet words and promises. The first sixteen years of her life, she'd been surrounded by half-truths and confidence games. She'd thought herself too wise and too cautious to be taken in, so the thought that she had allowed herself to be a victim of that kind of ruse sickened her as much as anything. There was certainly no way to salvage the life that she had hoped for in Tucker Springs—a new start as a respectable wife and member of the community where no one knew that her pa was a thief and that her sister was following in his footsteps. But for better or for worse, she was here now and would have to figure out her next steps. There was nothing to do but force her muddled brain to clear and her tired legs to move, gather as much dignity as she could muster, and face the people who were undoubtedly mocking her mistake.

Her mood had improved some by the time she was presentable once again. She was grateful for the dry warmth of a clean dress and equally grateful that she had some sensible boots she could wear that were more suited to the weather and the condition of the roads.

A knock resounded through the room. She twisted the key and opened the door. A middle-aged woman stood there, holding out a covered plate. Whatever was under that towel smelled delicious. Hazel was suddenly reminded of just how long it had been since she had eaten anything.

"Hello, dear," the rather round woman said. "I'm Caroline Avery." She bustled in and set the plate on the small table by the basin. "We own the café next door. You must be starving. I brought you something to tide you over until supper. While you're in town, we expect you to eat lunch at the café. Breakfast, too, if you're so inclined."

"Thank you. I'm not sure…" How could she afford

the luxury of eating meals at a restaurant? She'd need every penny she still had—and then some—just to get back to Boston. How could she afford the luxury of eating at all?

"Obviously, we want you to eat there as our guest," Mrs. Avery insisted. "It's rare that we get a new woman in town. It'll be lovely to hear all about living in Boston. Must be exciting to be a nanny to fine folks."

"H-how did you know about that?" Had Benjamin bragged about his trickery to the townspeople?

"You told Ezra you came from Boston and that you were a nanny."

"I did. I'd forgotten telling anyone."

"And not only that, but I cornered Ben the second Ezra carried you off and made him tell me the whole story." Mrs. Avery offered a bit of a sheepish smile. "I'm not proud that I waylaid him to get the information, but his ma was one of my dearest friends for thirty years, and I felt it my obligation to do what she can't—rest her soul."

"Well…" Hazel had no idea what to say to that.

Mrs. Avery waved her hand. "You don't have to say anything. I know Ben and Ivy didn't mean for you to be caught in the middle of their mix-up, but that does not excuse how poorly he handled things. I wouldn't have blamed you if you'd slapped him."

Hazel's cheeks warmed. "I've never cared much for violence."

"Of course you haven't. I can tell you're a fine Christian woman."

Fine Christian? Hazel believed in God, but she was

not at all certain that she walked in the Lord's grace. Surely the Lord didn't approve of her choice to withhold the entire truth from Benjamin—that she'd been dismissed from her position before she ever answered his advertisement for a wife. Perhaps she was reaping what she'd sown. Deceit for deceit.

Mrs. Avery planted her work-worn hands on her generous hips. "Now, I've been told your name is Hazel O'Brien, but what do I call you?"

Hazel offered the best smile she could muster. "Hazel, please."

Mrs. Avery nodded and smiled in return. "Then you must call me Caroline, or at least, Miz Caroline. I insist. You'll find that while we try to be proper, we are not very formal in Tucker Springs."

"Mrs. Avery—"

She shook her head. "Caroline."

"Miz Caroline—" Hazel couldn't help but feel warmed all the way through by this woman's kindly demeanor and friendliness. "Thank you so much for bringing me food."

She nodded. "I'll go get you a glass of water to go with it."

"Thank you."

Grabbing her reticule, Hazel quickly counted her money while Miz Caroline was out of the room. She had enough to book her stagecoach ride back to Iowa City. To fund the rest of her journey, she would need to sell some of the finer things Mrs. Wells had generously given her over the years.

Now that her thoughts were beginning to get organized, she took in a deep cleansing breath, then exhaled. After she ate, she would send a telegram to Mrs. Wells and beg her for help securing a new position. Mr. Wells would not allow her return to that household, but surely Mrs. Wells had friends who would be willing to give her a chance.

As she stuffed the bills back into the reticule, her fingers brushed against the tintype of Benjamin. She pulled it out. Staring at his face brought back all the feelings of hope that had carried her to this town. The dreams of building a life with a husband and finally becoming a part of something—a family, a community. Tears sprang quickly to her eyes and rolled down her cheeks.

"Here we go." Miz Caroline returned carrying a glass of water. She stopped short at the sight of Hazel wiping away the tears. "Oh, honey. You're going to be just fine. God always has a plan."

"I know. I truly do. It's just so hard to see hope during these awful times." Hazel swiped fruitlessly at the tears that continued to fall. "I'm so ashamed about all of it."

"Hogwash. You've done nothing wrong. Ben Gordon is the one who should be ashamed." Miz Caroline snatched a small towel from a shelf. She poured a little of the cool water onto the cloth, then handed it to Hazel.

As anger at Benjamin replaced despair, Hazel's tears ended. "You'll get no argument from me on that point." She wiped her face with the cool cloth. "But I still feel foolish for never even considering what I would do if our arranged marriage did not take place." She checked her appearance and twisted her hair back into place. "Do you know where I might stay tonight? I'll take the stagecoach tomorrow and return to Iowa City."

"I hate to tell you this, but the stage only stops in Tucker Springs twice a week. The driver won't be back until Monday."

Hazel's stomach clenched, and her thoughts went to the few scant bills rolled inside her reticule. "Then I suppose I'll need several nights' lodging. Can you recommend someplace to rent a room?"

"'Fraid not, hon." Miz Caroline shook her head. "The hotel has been closed since a twister came through town a couple of months ago. Several buildings were damaged—I'm sure you noticed that when driving through town—but the building with the saloon and hotel was practically split in two."

"And that was the only place to rent a room? There are no boardinghouses?"

Again, she shook her head. "There used to be one, but the widow who owned it found a fellow over in Missouri and up and moved. They sold the place to the Bullocks, who have eight children and no spare rooms to let."

"Eight! Mercy."

"Honey, I have ten. All ages—from my oldest, Wyatt, who's close to thirty, all the way down to little Henry, who's just eight." She laughed. "Most of the folks around here are packed into their houses tighter than a drum, but don't you worry. We won't leave you out in the cold, even if I have to stuff you into a corner with my girls. And for tonight that's just what I'll do, if you're amicable to it. The Lord has a remedy for every problem that arises. All we have to do is ask for guidance."

"Yes, ma'am." While she didn't doubt God's ability to turn all things for good, in Hazel's experience, God was in no hurry to reveal His plan.

"Good. That's settled, then." Miz Caroline planted her hands on her generous hips. "Well, then. My son Wyatt is over at the livery hitching up the wagon, and just as soon as my daughter Jennie closes the café and gets herself on over here, we'll go out to the house."

Hazel nodded. "I thank you for the kindness."

Miz Caroline chuckled. "Honey, just wait to thank me until after you spend the night with a roomful of girls. Trust me, you'll have to put up with a lot of talking, a bit of arguing, some giggling and lots of girlish emotions."

It sounded like a lot of love to Hazel. "I have a sister, too." Rose and she had lived a life with few occasions to giggle. But while they were growing up, they had taken advantage of the opportunities that came. When she had gotten Rose the job with the Wells family, she'd hoped that they could resume their closeness—but it was Rose's closeness to their father that she should have noticed, before it ruined everything. She still recalled seeing her sister for the last time two weeks after their dismissal from the Wellses'. Hazel had begged her to return the pin, but their pa had already sold it and spent the money, and Rose had only had tired excuses to offer.

"I'm glad you think so." The creases by Miz Caroline's eyes deepened as she smiled. "Let's see how nice you think it is tomorrow after a night of it."

Hazel felt a surge of envy and tried to repress it. Miz Caroline—and Mr. Murphy as well, for that matter— had been nothing but kind and generous. She was grateful to them. But she couldn't help feeling saddened at the comparison of her life to theirs. They had so much more than they knew. And she had almost joined them in living a life with family and friends in a community where everyone looked out for the other.

Instead, she was homeless again, with no prospects. Rather than seeing the last of Boston or New York, where she'd spent her uncertain childhood, she was going to be forced to return in disgrace.

This life that she'd dreamed of—stable and safe with a home and family that couldn't be taken away—all that simply wasn't meant for her. She'd been foolish to believe otherwise. She was intended to live poor and isolated. The sooner she resigned herself to that, the better.

Chapter Three

At Mr. Murphy's generous insistence, Hazel left her trunk in the storeroom so that there was no need to haul it to the Averys' home. She had stuffed the smaller, more portable carpetbag as full as she could with items to last her the next four days. Even though the Averys had only extended their invitation for tonight, it was clear that wherever she ended up, her burdensome trunk would be an inconvenience. Best to leave it at the general store, where it would be convenient for the stage-coach driver to fetch it when he came on Monday.

Jennie Avery, a cheerful young woman with kind blue eyes and her mother's welcoming manner, had come over from the café in short order, and the women had departed for the Averys' home. When they reached the two-story farmhouse seven miles outside of town, they were greeted by a tousled boy that Hazel assumed must be Henry—the youngest Avery child and the boy with whom Louie Murphy had sneaked a peek at the unfortunate Mr. Carter in his deceased state. She smiled at the child. "Hello."

"Hello." He held out his hand for her satchel.

"Oh, it's very…" She was going to say "heavy," but his eyes narrowed in annoyance before she could even get the word out of her mouth. She was too familiar with the pride of boys that age to think that her warning would be taken as anything other than an insult. Instead, she nodded. "Well, you look pretty strong. I'll leave it to you to decide what you can handle."

He beamed with pride as she handed the bag over… but then his arm jerked downward as he took it, and his face grew red.

"Oh, Henry!" Jennie snatched the bag from the lad. "What are you trying to prove?"

"I can do it."

"Ma! Would you do something before he hurts himself?"

Miz Caroline heaved a heavy sigh as she closed the distance between them, a scowl on her face for her daughter. But her expression softened as she touched the boy's shoulder. "I believe you could do it. But I could use help taking boxes to the kitchen. Would you mind? It'll take strong arms."

Henry's chest puffed out, and he gave Jennie a satisfied smirk.

Miz Caroline had brought food from the café that wouldn't keep. Hazel suspected supper would consist of leftovers. Not that she minded, if it was anything like the food the kind woman had generously brought her earlier.

As the boy grabbed a box more in keeping with his size and followed his ma inside, Jennie rolled her eyes.

"I don't know why Ma encourages him that way." Jennie gave a huff. "Well, let's get you settled." She motioned for Hazel to follow her into the house.

"I wish you'd let me carry my satchel," Hazel tried to argue. "I know it's dreadfully heavy." Once inside, she glanced around in wonder at the beautiful carvings and handmade wooden furniture. Miz Caroline had been right when she said they weren't fancy, but there was no denying the beauty of this home.

Jennie shook her head. "It's nothing!" But her breathing was just a little too heavy as they climbed the steps for that to be completely true. Shaking her head, Hazel followed silently. At the top of the wooden steps, Jennie turned right. She glanced over her shoulder with a grin. "So, tell me, Hazel O'Brien, do you enjoy no privacy, a lot of company and children crawling all over you at night?" Her blue eyes crinkled. "If so, I have just the room for you."

A laugh shot through Hazel. "I'm sure I'll be just fine. Trust me, it'll be better than sleeping in an alley." Realizing what she'd said, Hazel cringed as Jennie frowned with confusion.

Trying to explain away the comment would only lead to revealing information she'd rather keep to herself, so Hazel averted her gaze and tried to will away the traitorous blush she could feel creeping up her cheeks.

To Jennie's credit, she let the subject drop as they stopped in front of a room. "Welcome to our humble abode, cramped though it may be." Hazel stood in the hallway as Jennie stepped inside. "One set of twins, Josie and Julie, share this bed," she explained, pointing to indicate. "They're fourteen next week. Bethany and Bess—short for Elizabeth—share this one. They recently turned seventeen, and they're both madly in love with a couple of boys who are more interested in riding and roping than courting. Hopefully whispering and giggling won't keep you awake." She turned to smile again at Hazel. "The bed by the window is mine. It's one of the few benefits of being the oldest sister in the room," she said wryly. "And Ma sent Wyatt out to set up that cot just in case you agreed to squeeze in with us."

Hazel grinned back as she stepped into the room. It was exactly what Miz Caroline had said it would be: crowded and cozy. Nearly all the space was occupied by three beds, side by side. The cot—which Hazel assumed was for her—sat against the wall. With the wardrobe and a table holding a chamber pot and a washbasin and pitcher, there was barely room to walk without running into something. "I feel terrible putting you all out."

Jennie chuckled. "Oh, Hazel. You're probably going to feel a lot more put out than we will. One more person in the room won't change much for us. But you're about to sleep in a room with five other people—and there's a very good chance you'll wake up to one or two of the little children jumping in your bed."

"I thought the children were older except for Henry."

"Henry is the youngest. But my older sister, Sally, moved back in with her two children while her husband stakes a claim out West. She's with child again, so they didn't want her to travel all that way until her husband has the household built and the land settled."

"So, the two children…"

Nodding, Jennie grinned. "Sally and her children are in my old room. Wyatt moved in with Ezra and Louie, and the other two older boys are married and out West. Henry sleeps in an old lean-to for now. Fair warning, my nieces inevitably make their way to our room at least four or five times a week. We never know whose bed they'll turn up in."

Hazel smiled as she followed Jennie inside. "It wouldn't be the first time a child woke me up with a knee to my ribs or an arm thrown across my face."

The other woman dropped her satchel on one of the beds. "That's right, someone mentioned that you used to be a nanny. Did you enjoy that?"

An ache drifted through Hazel's heart as she thought about the three children she'd practically raised. She nodded. "Very much."

"How old was the child you looked after?"

"Children—there were three. I came to the Wellses' home when the oldest was only a year old. He just turned eight."

"It must have been so difficult to leave them. I can't imagine how I'll feel when Sally and her girls finally do head West."

Gathering a shaky breath, Hazel sank onto the cot and nodded. "Yes. But they weren't my children. And I came here to build a life and family of my own."

"I'm sorry it turned out the way it did."

Unable to respond without bursting into tears, Hazel nodded.

"Listen," Jennie said, sitting on the bed across from Hazel. "I know you're probably sizzling mad about Ben and Ivy right now—and, trust me, there's not a person in town who would blame you if you are—but before you leave on the stage Monday, Ivy would like to speak with you. I told her there were no guarantees that you'd agree, but she begged me to try. She truly is a kind and gentle soul. She knew nothing about you until Ben showed her the telegram this morning."

Averting her gaze, Hazel breathed in and out. "I am not sure there is any reason for us to meet. As you say, I'll be leaving on Monday. It's not as if I intend to stay and make any trouble for them."

"She isn't afraid of that. It's just that she feels awful about the way Ben behaved—about the entire situation. I think she just wants to look you in the eyes and tell you that she is sorry."

The sound of Ben's name so casually connected to another woman—his wife—formed a vise of pain around Hazel's heart. Didn't these people realize that she had fancied herself already halfway in love with the man she had agreed to marry? She was struggling with all her might not to hold any bitterness toward the woman who had taken her place—but meeting her and being forced to listen to her excuses seemed rather too much to ask.

On the other hand, the Averys were being phenomenally kind, and Hazel didn't want to refuse Jennie's request outright. "I—I'll think about it."

Jennie nodded, then further demonstrated her kindness by changing the subject. "Will you go back to the children in Boston, now that…"

She let her question trail off, but Hazel knew what she meant: now that she had no reason to stay.

Hazel shook her head. "Mr. Wells hired a new nanny just a few days after my…" She would have said "dismissal" but caught herself just in time. "Departure."

"How unfortunate." Jennie nodded toward the bed by the window—the one where she'd set Hazel's satchel. "That's where you'll sleep. One of the Js will use the cot, and I'll sleep with the other one."

"Oh, please don't. I can't push you out of your own bed. The cot will serve me just fine."

But Jennie had begun shaking her head before Hazel finished speaking. "Ma gave me strict instructions to give you a real bed. And Ma gets what she wants. Always. So don't even try to argue." She laughed. "Trust me, you'll just be wasting your breath."

"Well, I can't deny a clean, comfortable bed will certainly be a blessing after so many days traveling. First on the train, then the stagecoach." She'd spent most nights on the train sleeping while sitting up. Once she boarded the stagecoach, she'd spent one night at an overnight station, and she'd slept on a thin pallet on the floor.

Hazel pushed herself up from the cot and walked to the bed. Opening the satchel, she pulled out the dress that she'd packed for tomorrow. She could only fit one dress, a nightgown, her Bible and another set of undergarments. Best to start getting used to making do with only two dresses from now on. Mrs. Wells had kept her well supplied in expensive hand-me-downs, so her trunk was filled with dresses that would, hopefully, fetch a decent sum. They were hardly worn, even if they were secondhand. Hazel was reasonably sure that if she sold all but two, she could finance her trip home.

"Where may I hang my things?"

Jennie gestured toward the wall above Hazel's bed. "There are two pegs we emptied for you. We weren't sure how many dresses you'd be bringing."

"I just brought one besides the one I'm wearing." She held up the dress in her hands—blue with little white flowers. "My others are in my trunk."

"It's darling. And how fashionable, that it has a bustle." She smiled broadly. "Ivy made me a gown with a bustle a few months ago, but I haven't had the courage to wear it yet."

Hazel narrowed her gaze. "I don't understand. Everyone is wearing bustles." At least, everyone in Boston was. It suddenly occurred to Hazel that she hadn't seen any in town. Were they considered unsuitable out here?

Jennie gave an offhanded wave. "Oh, no one thinks it's inappropriate, if that's what you're worried about." She took the dress from Hazel and held it up by the shoulders. "It's just not a fashion the women around here have caught on to yet. But now that you are here, it won't seem so strange to everyone. We'll both be the front-page story in the *Tucker Springs Chronicle* the second Mrs. Green gets a look at us come Sunday."

Hazel couldn't help but imagine such a thing. What would it be like to be such a part of community that your choice to wear a new dress would be considered headline news?

It sounded wonderful.

The sound of scrambling footsteps coming up the steps stopped the conversation, and they both looked toward the door. Henry stood there, gulping for breath. "Ma says hurry, the sheriff's here with Mr. Murphy and Louie."

Louie jumped out of the wagon before it had even come to a full stop. Ezra sighed but didn't bother calling after him. If he tried to scold and say it wasn't safe, Louie would just nod along and then do the exact same thing the next time he had a chance. There was nothing for Ezra to do but shake his head and follow after Micah Lane—the local sheriff—as they headed toward the house.

Micah had waved him down just as he and Louie were leaving the store to head out to the Averys' for dinner. It was common knowledge that Micah was sweet on Jennie, but that wasn't the reason for his trip to the farm. He clearly had a more unpleasant task at hand. While he hadn't shared the details—given that he planned to tell Ezra and the Averys at the same time—he had let Ezra know that there was some trouble in town and that he was going around to talk to all the business owners.

Will Avery, Miz Caroline's husband, was waiting to greet them at the door.

Mr. Will nodded toward the sheriff. "Good to see you, Micah. Everything okay?"

"There's some trouble, I'm afraid."

"Well," Miz Caroline said, "why don't you come on in and have supper with us? The girls have everything almost ready. We'll go into the sitting room, and you can tell us what trouble has come to Tucker Springs."

Micah managed a smile at that. "Thank you, ma'am. I sure would appreciate it."

Jennie had just come down the stairs when they walked inside. "Hey, Micah. What brings you out this way?"

"Come into the sitting room, Jennie," her father said. "The sheriff is here on official business."

Jennie's gaze shifted to Ezra's and she frowned, her eyes asking a question.

He shrugged, hanging back as the others went ahead into the other room. He glanced past Jennie.

"If you're looking for Hazel, she's putting her things away."

Ezra's ears warmed at being so easily caught out. "Is she getting settled in okay?"

"I think so. Ask again in the morning after she spends the night in that crowded room."

"By the way, your ma invited Micah to stay for dinner."

Jennie blushed. "She's determined to get me married off."

"You couldn't do much better."

She looked unconvinced. Ezra knew that it wasn't because she didn't like Micah. Rather, it was because she hadn't ever gotten over Ezra's brother, John. Even though John had fallen in love with someone else before he had died in the war. He wanted to tell her that there was no need to stay loyal to the memory of a man who'd left her behind twice over. But he knew his words would fall on deaf ears. Only Jennie could say when she'd be ready to let John go from her heart. For Micah's sake, though, Ezra hoped it would be soon.

There was no more time for talk. They each took a seat and looked at the sheriff, who stood in front of the fireplace.

"Don't keep us in suspense," Jennie said.

He turned his gaze to her and nodded. "I'm telling all the business owners. There's been some robberies in town. One last night and one this morning."

"Robberies?" Miz Caroline frowned. "What do you mean? Who exactly has been robbed?"

"Blake Stone at the leather shop had near fifty dollars stolen from his cash box."

"Gracious!" Miz Caroline said.

"And Chester left the blacksmith shop unattended for a while this morning, and when he came back he said some of his tools were missing."

Miz Caroline scoffed. "He better not try to blame Louie for that one."

Ezra appreciated the support of his second family. The blacksmith was always quick to name Louie as the source of all his troubles—but hopefully even Chester would have to admit that Louie was no thief.

"Well, I haven't noticed anything missing from the café," Jennie said. "But I can't claim to keep too close of an eye out for that. If someone steals food, they likely need it worse than we do."

Micah's eyes softened as he looked at her. "And it's kind and generous to think that way. But anyone who would steal cash or tools isn't someone who is just hungry and in need of a meal. So be careful when you're at the café alone after dark."

Ezra turned to Micah again. "Do you have any idea who might be stealing? I can't imagine it would be anyone we know."

"I don't have a suspect in mind yet. I can't imagine that anyone in Tucker Springs would do such a thing. But no one seems to have spotted any strangers in town except for the woman who came in on the stage."

Miz Caroline chuckled. "Well, I can assure you that Hazel has been accounted for every minute since she rolled into Tucker Springs. And the only criminal behavior around here is what Ben Gordon did to her!"

A gasp drew their attention, and Ezra saw Hazel standing midway down the steps, her face drained of color.

"Miss O'Brien," he said.

"I—I'm sorry to intrude. I heard voices."

Miz Caroline beckoned her with a wave of her hand. "Come on down, hon. The sheriff was just telling us that Tucker Springs has a thief running around. And apparently," she said wryly, "you're the only stranger in town."

Rather than coming down, Miss O'Brien backed up one step, shaking her head. Somehow, her face turned even paler until Ezra was seriously concerned that she might faint again. "I didn't. I…I wouldn't."

Micah held up a hand to stay her retreat. "I wasn't suggesting you are the thief, Miss O'Brien. Both robberies happened before the stage got here."

"Oh, I see." Miss O'Brien descended the remaining

steps, and Ezra noted the color beginning to return to her cheeks. Bewilderment drifted across his mind. Why on earth had she gotten so frightened?

"Ezra," Micah said, pulling Ezra's thoughts back to the conversation. "Please take extra precautions. You, too, Miz Caroline." He turned to Jennie, and his voice got a bit gentler and a bit warmer. "And you. Especially when you're there alone after dark."

"Won't you be there to protect me?" She grinned teasingly, but there was a definite blush staining her cheeks. Ezra smiled, hoping her feelings might finally be shifting. The sheriff would be good to her. Everyone knew how much he loved her.

Apparently oblivious to the undertones of romance between his daughter and the sheriff, Mr. Will frowned at the man mooning over Jennie. "We should've been told earlier, before we closed up the café. We might have taken extra precautions."

"Pa!" Jennie said. "It's not Micah's fault."

Micah shook his head. "No, Jennie, your pa's right." He turned to Will. "When it was just Chester reporting the theft, I hoped—assumed, actually—that it was just unruly youngsters and the stolen items would show up when they were done with their pranks. Then Blake stopped by the jail. He was robbed first, but it took him longer to realize because he thought his wife took the money to make some purchases. It was only when he went home to her that he learned the truth and came to report the theft to me." He shrugged. "I should have taken Chester more seriously."

"Well, he's always stirring things up, so it was a

natural reaction for anyone. Don't blame yourself," Mr. Will replied, his stern look giving way to understanding. One of the older twins showed up at the door and announced that supper was on the table. "Let's go eat. We can talk about this later."

While they ate, Ezra couldn't help but notice that Miss O'Brien barely spoke and barely touched her food. Before he was half-finished, she stood and excused herself. Ezra frowned and caught Jennie's gaze. She followed their guest, only to return a moment later. "She has a headache."

Miz Caroline clicked her tongue, shaking her head. "Well, of course she does. She is likely beyond exhausted. Poor thing." She narrowed her gaze and looked around the table, focusing on her children and grandchildren. "Miss O'Brien has had a very trying journey here and an even more trying day. I expect all of you to be on your best behavior as long as she's our guest. And girls, you keep quiet when you go to bed. Am I clear?"

After the young folks assured her that they understood, conversation resumed, though it was not as hearty as it had been before Miss O'Brien's departure.

As they drove back to town, Micah brought up the woman's unfortunate situation. "Can't blame her for feeling rattled after a shock like she's had," he said.

"True enough," Ezra agreed.

"You're the one who's spent the most time with her," Micah said. "Was she shaken like this the whole time she was at the store?"

"Actually, no," Ezra said after thinking about it for a minute. "I walked in while she was talking with Louie, and she seemed pretty at ease. Though I guess that makes sense, seeing as she was a nanny back in Boston. She's likely used to being around children."

"A nanny, eh? Say, that could work out real well for you, couldn't it?"

"For me?" Ezra rolled his eyes. "Like I told Wyatt, I'm not marrying someone just to get a ma for Louie."

Micah chuckled. "I wasn't suggesting you do. I'm just saying that it sure seems like a nanny would solve your problem."

Ezra heard a squawk behind them from where Louie was sitting, but the boy didn't say anything as Ezra and Micah continued making casual conversation for the rest of the way back to town. After they dropped Micah off at the sheriff's office, Louie climbed up to the front seat and sat next to Ezra, sulking.

"And what's that pout for?" Ezra asked.

The boy shrugged and snuggled closer against Ezra as a brisk wind blew across them.

"I think I might know." Ezra needed both hands to drive the horses or he would have slipped his arm around the boy for added warmth and comfort. "I think you heard what the sheriff said about Miss O'Brien becoming your nanny, and maybe you don't want to be reined in. If you have someone keeping an eye on you, it means you and Archie can't run off hither and yon all day. Is that it?"

When there was no response, Ezra glanced down. Even in the dark, he could see Louie's eyes were closed, his long lashes brushing the tops of his plump cheeks. His shoulders moved up and down rhythmically. Ezra smiled. He'd always marveled at the way a child could sleep anywhere. Falling asleep against someone else meant complete trust. Peace that nothing would happen, that you could close your eyes and fade away without worry. He hadn't felt that in a long time. Not since his pa had passed away.

He only had fragments of memories of a man with twinkling eyes, a kind smile and a ready laugh. He remembered being thrown in the air and hugged so close he could barely breathe. And then he remembered emptiness and grief when that warm, loving presence was lost forever.

A month after his father died from pneumonia, Ezra and his ma were on a wagon train headed to Iowa. She had answered an advertisement to become a bride for Mr. Murphy, who was a shopkeeper in a prairie town called Tucker Springs. While his ma hadn't had the same experience as Miss O'Brien, in that her fiancé had married her as promised, that didn't mean her experience had been entirely good. Certainly, Mr. Murphy had been nothing like Ezra's pa. Ezra supposed his sympathies for Miss O'Brien went beyond common decency. Perhaps he wondered what would have become of his ma and him had his stepfather not been, at least, a man of his word. Not to mention, his brother, John, would never have been born.

Ezra started as Louie stirred. "I just don't want her," Louie said. "I want my ma." The words were more mumbled than truly said as the boy nodded off again, but they twisted Ezra's heart all the same.

"You know that's not possible, Louie," he whispered, as much to himself as to the boy.

He thought about Marie. The child couldn't possibly remember her, any more than he could remember his real pa, John, who had died at the end of the war. Ezra's brother was the sort of man anyone would have wanted—as a father, brother, husband, friend. Ezra knew he could never hold a candle to him, but he had been determined to be the best father to Louie that he could. Even though Louie wasn't his own son, from the moment the boy had come into his care, he'd been committed to treating him with nothing but love and kindness. Louie would not be raised with the harshness Ezra had experienced in his own childhood.

Perhaps he had gone too far in the other direction. Been too lenient. Well, that would have to stop. If he had a chance of appeasing the town and keeping his business, which would one day be Louie's inheritance, he had to start getting better at disciplining the boy.

The sound of Miz Caroline's voice echoed in his memory. "God always has a remedy. Even when it doesn't look like He's paying attention."

"Well, Lord." His voice sounded odd and intrusive as he spoke into the night. "I suppose You know what You're doing. Just let me know, and I'll follow Your lead."

Chapter Four

Bleary-eyed after a night of tossing in his bed, Ezra arrived at the store with a bright and bounding Louie by his side and Archie trotting alongside the wagon. "Can I go on over to the café, Pa? I'm hungry."

Ezra flushed, feeling guilty. For the first time in longer than he could remember, he had overslept. Wyatt had even awakened first and left by the time Ezra woke up. He'd had to rush through the chores and had been forced to leave home without feeding Louie breakfast. The smell of bacon and bread and whatever else they were cooking next door made his mouth water and his stomach growl. He didn't blame the boy for wanting to head right over. He wished he could join him—but checking on the store had to come first. "Sure. Tell Miss Jennie I'll be over in a bit. And ask Wyatt if you can sit at his table."

Louie hopped down, and Archie jumped up and turned around on his hind legs. "Wait! Louie." Ezra grabbed the rope from the back of the wagon and tossed it to the boy. "Tie Archie to the railing in front before you go inside."

"Aw, Pa! He don't want to get tied up."

"It's either that or you wait for me, and Archie runs off while we're eating. Your choice."

With a huff, Louie bent and looped the rope around Archie's neck. Ezra could hear him speaking to the animal but couldn't make out the words.

As he unlocked the door, the hairs on his arms stood on end as an unnamed instinct warned him that something was wrong. His mind traveled back to the sheriff's warnings about thieves in the area. His gut tightened with dread. It was only logical that if other shops were going to be robbed, he would be next on the list. He glanced around the store. With a glance, he could see that shelves and displays had been disturbed. But he couldn't tell if things were missing in the dimness of the room.

He took the cash out of the money box each night, so he knew if a thief did break in, they wouldn't get any money. But as he checked, he saw that the box had been opened and tossed onto the floor. Thwarted from stealing cash, had the thief decided to go for something else? There were plenty of goods and wares that would bring a price. Ezra stopped short, his blood going cold, as he heard the back door creak open. Was the thief still in the store?

"Who's there?" he yelled, then inwardly kicked himself. He wasn't armed, and most likely a thief would be. The door slammed, he heard the sound of glass shattering and before he could even reach the storeroom, he heard a horse's hooves speeding away. He ran to the door, but the intruder was gone, likely vanished through one of the trails in the woods.

Ezra glanced around, and his heart sank. Miss O'Brien's trunk had been flung open and looked practically empty. He could see books and odds and ends of various items flung around the room.

How on earth was he going to tell the poor woman that she'd lost not only her intended groom but also most of her belongings?

"Oh, oh, oh. Oh no!"

Ezra turned sharply at the sounds of dismay and found himself looking straight at the victim of the latest crime. Miss O'Brien stared at the trunk, then at him. "I—can't. Mr. Murphy, what happened?"

He shrugged helplessly. "I'm sorry. It must've been the thief the sheriff warned us about last night."

"Then…" She glanced over her shoulder. "But nothing is missing from the store, is it?"

"I'm not certain, but I don't think so. Just some messiness." He didn't know what to say to soothe the poor woman. "I think I interrupted the thief in the process of rummaging through things." His eyes traveled back to the flung-open trunk. "I suppose your belongings seemed more valuable—or more easily transportable— than my stock of canned goods and plows. I'm so sorry."

She stumbled into the room, shaking her head in disbelief. "It's just…" With a heavy sigh, she sank into the old corner chair. "All of the gowns…they were gifts. Hand-me-downs from my former employer. Expensive dresses, in good condition. I was going to sell them once I got to Iowa City to pay for my return to Boston."

"You don't have passage back home?"

She shook her head, barely focused on him. "I wasn't expecting to need passage, since *this* was supposed to be my new home." She stood and began picking up the books and other items the thief had deemed unworthy of taking. She placed them carefully in the trunk. He wanted to help but sensed she would rather do it herself so as to assess what was left.

Suddenly she gasped and crossed to the back door. She got down on her knees near some broken pieces of green glass. She covered her face with her hands, and he could see her shoulders rising and falling in silent sobs. He stood in respectful silence. Whatever the thief had dropped at the door was obviously more important to her than the dresses or the money they would bring.

She stood, and he could see her wiping tears away. When she turned, her expression was resolute. She lifted her chin. "If you will fetch the broom, I will sweep up the broken glass."

He shook his head and crossed the room. "I can get it." He glanced down at the floor. "This meant a lot to you?"

She nodded. "Yes. It is—was—a trinket box. It belonged to my mother and…" Her eyes filled again and she averted her gaze.

Ezra touched her shoulder. "It's all right. I'll get this cleaned up." The trinket box had broken into six pieces that were all big enough to pick up in his hands. He quickly scooped them up.

She turned away and retrieved an apron from the floor. "Well, at least they left this. It's what I was coming for. I finally convinced Miz Caroline and Jennie to let me help in the kitchen of the café today to show my gratitude for their hospitality." She slipped the apron over her head and tied the strings behind her back. "There's nothing I can do about this theft, but I can keep my word. The café is getting busy."

"I'll walk you over, if you don't mind."

"I'm sure no one is going to try to rob me in broad daylight between here and the café, but I appreciate it." He could tell she was making a concentrated effort to shrug off the pain the thief had caused.

Ezra smiled. "I don't open the store this early, anyway. I usually eat breakfast at the café. After you finish helping the Averys, I can accompany you to the sheriff's office."

She gasped. "The sheriff?"

"So that we can both report the theft."

"O-oh, of course." She shuddered. "That won't be necessary. The sheriff is having breakfast with Wyatt Avery."

Wyatt, seated with Micah, spotted them as they walked inside and waved Ezra over. Ezra took Miss O'Brien by her elbow and escorted her, surprised to feel her tense as they drew closer to the table.

"I really should go back to the kitchen and help Miz Caroline," she protested. "I'm sure you can tell the sheriff about my trunk."

For the second time in two days, Ezra had the feeling that Miss O'Brien wanted to avoid Micah. "The sheriff will want a description of what's missing so he can tell the other small towns around here to be on the lookout. A thief is likely going to sell those stolen items."

She nodded. "I suppose that's true." He could see the hesitation in her eyes, but she complied, allowing him to escort her to the table. With halting words, she explained what had been taken, and the two of them answered the sheriff's questions as best they could before Miss O'Brien excused herself and went to help in the kitchen.

He couldn't help but admire how quickly she adapted to the hustle and bustle of the café. By the time he and the others had finished their food, the breakfast rush had tapered off. He watched Miss O'Brien take her apron off and say something to the other women. He excused himself, then made his way over to Miss O'Brien. "Are you going somewhere?"

She spun around. "I must send a telegram back East."

Ezra's heart jumped into his throat. Sending a telegram likely meant she would be contacting her old employer to ask for her job back. Or perhaps she'd ask that employer or some other friend to lend her the money to pay for her passage, since she no longer had the dresses she'd intended to sell. Either way, a telegram back East signaled that she was moving forward with her plans to return—and Ezra didn't want that to happen. The more he'd thought about Micah's words the previous night, the more they'd made sense to him. Hiring Miss O'Brien to be Louie's nanny could be the answer to his troubles…if he could convince her to accept.

"I'd be pleased to escort you, if you have no objection," he blurted out. He didn't want to make his offer in front of everyone in the café. Bringing it up during the walk would feel more natural. Besides, she didn't know her way around and would probably appreciate the escort.

"Oh, but what about the store?"

Across the café, he caught his friend's eye and gestured toward the store. Wyatt nodded, and Ezra knew the message had been received. "Wyatt is going to open for me. He's done it before." No one would mind if Wyatt's carpentry shop opened a little late. Everyone in town would know to look for him at the general store or the café if he wasn't in his shop, anyway.

She smiled and nodded. "Then if it wouldn't be an inconvenience, I'd appreciate having a guide." There was no doubting the relief washing over her face. "Not to mention, I would prefer not to walk alone."

Ezra turned to Louie, unsure if he should make the boy walk with them so he could keep an eye on him or instruct him to stay put. Louie hadn't seemed pleased with the idea of Miss O'Brien as his nanny, and Ezra didn't want him saying anything to put her off the idea while he made his offer. On the other hand, if he left the boy behind and Louie got into mischief again, that might make Miss O'Brien withdraw her agreement.

With a wry grin, Miz Caroline waved both of her hands toward Ezra and Miss O'Brien. "You two go on. Louie will be here with me when you're done at the telegraph office." She pinned the boy with a motherly gaze. "Won't you, Louie?"

Louie shrugged. "I reckon I don't got a choice."

With everything arranged, Ezra escorted Miss O'Brien out of the café and onto the boardwalk. "What will you do now that there is not a reason for you to stay on in Tucker Springs?" Ezra felt his palms growing damp as he shored up his courage.

She took in her bottom lip between her teeth, then let go and shrugged. "I've been asking myself the same thing. I hope my former employer will be able to recommend me for another position, perhaps with one of her friends."

They had reached the end of the boardwalk and stepped down. The post office and telegraph shared a building just across the street. Several boards were stretched out in the street to aid in walking, of course, but mainly so wagons didn't get bogged down. Ezra took Miss O'Brien's elbow to help steady her. "Miss O'Brien, may I ask another question that might seem intrusive?"

"You may ask, Mr. Murphy." Her eyes glinted with amusement as she allowed him to support her across the wobbly, uneven boards. "But as to whether or not I will answer your question, well, that remains to be seen."

"Fair enough."

Together, they ascended the two shallow steps to the boardwalk in front of the post office and stepped into the building, the closed door providing some respite from the bustle of the street. No one was behind the counter—Frank must have stepped away.

Ezra's heart picked up a little as he tried to formulate the words in his mind. The question would have to be asked before she sent her telegram back to Boston. Which meant he could delay no longer.

He turned to face her and looked down into her large, wide green eyes.

"I know you came here to marry Ben. And I'm sorry that it didn't work out for you." He raked his fingers through his thick hair and rested his hand against the back of his neck.

Her cheeks grew pink, and though Ezra hated to embarrass her, he found it difficult to look away. She was a very fetching woman.

"Mr. Murphy," she said, looking him square in the eye, "to be honest, I've decided to put all of that behind me. When the stagecoach returns, I'll head back to Boston and get on with my life. The events of the past few days will just be a chapter that is closed."

"I can't say I blame you. But I'm hoping you'll change your mind about returning when you hear what I have to ask you."

Her brow creased into a frown, and something like horror filled those pretty eyes of hers. Ezra realized, too late, what she thought he was going to ask her. He shook his head. "Oh, I——"

Frank Bauer came bustling through the curtain hanging from the doorway into the back. "I am sorry to haf keep you waiting. That bell is not working again."

"It's fine."

The postmaster's gaze rested curiously on Miss O'Brien. "You, I have only heard about. I am sorry for your troubles in our town."

Miss O'Brien's cheeks bloomed with a fiery blush.

"I assure you, there is no need to be sorry. I would like to send a telegram, please."

"Of course."

Ezra's heart hammered against his chest, and he held up his hand to Frank. "Wait." He knew it was now or never. He turned to Miss O'Brien. "I know I'm not the man you came to Tucker Springs for. But I think we might need each other. Will you hear me out before you send that telegram?"

Hazel sucked in a sharp breath, horror filling her as Mr. Murphy's eyes beseeched her.

Mr. Bauer stood on the other side of the counter and smiled as though he were part of the conversation. "Oh, yes, yes," he said, nodding. "Is a very good plan, I am thinking."

Mr. Murphy turned to him with a little frown. "Hey, Frank. Give me a minute to speak with Miss O'Brien, will you?"

"Oh, sure, sure." His round head of thinning blond hair bobbed as his smile widened. But he stood planted, his gaze darting between them.

"Frank?"

"Huh?" Then, understanding seemed to spread over his face at last. "Oh, my. Of course." He shook his head. "I will go and fetch my Gilly. She will wish to say hello to Miss O'Brien." He grinned again. "Is a good match, you two, I think. I will ask Gilly. She knows about such things."

Hazel stared, mouth agape at the retreating form of the little man. She gathered in a steadying breath and stepped away from Mr. Murphy. He was a kind man. And she had to admit, he seemed likable enough. And he was certainly handsome. More handsome than Benjamin, though she felt catty for thinking it. Still, she couldn't marry for convenience alone. She had come to wed Benjamin on the basis of several months of correspondence and a certainty that they wanted the same things for their future. She barely knew Mr. Murphy at all. "Sir, you honor me…"

But he was shaking his head, his eyes wide and filled with…something other than what one might expect of a man about to propose marriage. He held up his hands and took a step back as though he felt he needed protection. "Miss O'Brien. I fear there's been a misunderstanding. I'm sure not looking for a wife."

Hazel felt the humiliation—and perhaps a little disappointment that she'd never admit to in a million years—all the way to her toes. "That's good," she began slowly, hoping her tone held an edge of dignity and not the tremble of tears she was fighting hard not to give in to. "I may have come here with the intention of becoming a bride, but I am certainly not willing to marry just any man who asks me, even if I did get robbed. So I'm relieved to hear that we're in agreement on that point."

His tense expression instantly softened to relief. "All right, then. I didn't mean to get you all riled up. It's just a simple misunderstanding."

"Just so we are clear, Mr. Murphy. I am not *riled up* over the misunderstanding." Now that she had set the record perfectly straight, she lifted her chin and looked him square in his lovely brown eyes. "But since you implied you have some offer for me, what is it that you wanted to ask?"

"You've met Louie."

"Obviously."

"Well, here's the situation. The town is threatening to stop patronizing my store because Louie tends to get himself into trouble while I work."

Hazel frowned. To be sure, Louie was high-spirited. And given how he and his dog had landed her in the mud just the previous day, she knew that he was not exactly a model of deportment. But was he truly so ill behaved as to justify withholding their business from his father's store? It seemed extreme—perhaps even cruel. Mr. Murphy was raising his child alone. Did that not warrant him some compassion and understanding? "I'm sincerely sorry that you find yourself in such a situation, but I don't know how I can help. I'll be leaving as soon as the stagecoach returns."

"Here's what I was thinking. Since things seem to be unsettled for you, maybe you can stay on a bit longer in Tucker Springs."

"Mr. Murphy. I don't understand…"

"I'm doing this so poorly. And I'm sorry for all the confusion. But you're a nanny, and I need someone to keep Louie out of trouble. So, maybe you could be his nanny."

Hazel tried to make sense of what he had just said. Mr. Murphy's need for childcare was clear, but how would the arrangement work? Typically, quarters were provided for the nanny in the same house with her charges. But she certainly couldn't live in the home of an unmarried man with only a child for a chaperone.

As though he read her mind, Mr. Murphy spoke up before she could decline. "My pa and ma lived in a log cabin a little ways behind the store when they were first married. Louie and I live on the homestead in the larger house my pa built a couple of years later. The cabin has been empty since my late brother's wife left Tucker Springs a few years ago—you'd have it to yourself and could keep Louie there during the day. I'm open from eight in the morning until six in the evening and half days on Saturdays. But Louie goes to the Averys' with Wyatt on Saturdays so you'd have the weekends to yourself. You'd be responsible for giving him breakfast and lunch through the week—but food and necessities are included as part of your compensation. Anything you need to set up housekeeping you can get from the store. Now, I can't pay you a lot, but I can pay some—and as I mentioned, you'll have no expenses as far as food, housing and home goods are concerned. And if you agree to stay through the winter to give folk here time to simmer down about Louie, then I'll buy your ticket back to Boston in the spring."

Hazel's heart sped up at the possibilities his words whispered to her heart. A cozy little cabin? The very thought seemed too wonderful for it to be real. She wanted to jump into this pool of hope with both feet but stopped short of giving him a resounding "yes." Hadn't that sort of blinding hope gotten her into this bind in the first place? She squared her gaze at Mr. Murphy. "What happens when Louie returns to school, as I assume he will be doing soon? You won't need a nanny in that case. If he was suspended…"

Mr. Murphy shook his head. "The teacher isn't willing for him to attend ever again. She said she has her doubts whether he's even bright enough to learn."

She frowned. "Is that so? From what I observed, he seems quite bright."

His eyes lit up with pride. "I agree, but I reckon every parent thinks their child is exceptional."

"And usually they are correct. May I ask, how old is Louie?"

"He's five, six next month."

Hazel thought about the child. He would certainly be a handful, but she'd always loved a challenge. And she couldn't abide the thought of a child not getting an education because the teacher refused to try.

She focused her gaze on Mr. Murphy. "I have no need to send a telegram, after all. I accept your proposal."

As Hazel and her new employer walked back to the general store, they discussed the terms and expectations of her duties. Hazel realized that even though her salary would be meager compared to the amount she received from the Wellses, she would have her own home, and her duties would be lighter since she would only have Louie when Mr. Murphy was at the store.

"Occasionally, I might ask you to keep him during other times when I have errands to complete. But you are free to refuse."

Hazel nodded, still mulling over the new circumstances in which she found herself. "When may I see the cabin? It would be lovely to move my things from the Averys' home soon." Noting a slight hesitation, Hazel frowned. "Is something wrong?"

"Well, the cabin has been sitting there collecting dirt and critters for a few years. Wyatt said if you agreed to stay in town that he'd start cleaning it up while I mind the store today." His expression turned sheepish. "It isn't that I'm unwilling to handle it myself, but with the meeting tonight, it's not a good idea to keep the store closed all day. People might think I'm calling their bluff about taking their business elsewhere. But I'd rather you wait to see the cabin until it's clean and ready."

"That's very thoughtful of you," she murmured, feeling a bit overwhelmed at the quick turn of events.

"The most important thing we'll need to get if you agree is a new mattress for your bed." His brow furrowed. "If you've never slept on a straw tick, you might want to plan to spread a quilt or two for padding. The straw tends to poke through."

Hazel blushed. "I'm sure it'll be just fine." True, straw mattresses weren't what she'd been used to at the Wellses' home, but if he only knew that, as a child, she would have welcomed a pile of straw to sleep in and never complained if pieces poked through her clothes.

When they reached the store, Wyatt Avery was just walking out. He grinned in his easygoing way. "Jeremiah just got to work in there, so I reckoned I could get along to my shop."

"Thank you for opening for me," Ezra said.

"Think nothing of it." Mr. Avery turned to Hazel. "You get your telegram sent?"

Hazel wasn't sure how to answer, so she hung back and was grateful when Mr. Murphy spoke up instead. "She decided she didn't need to send it."

Mr. Avery's eyebrows rose beneath his hat. "Is that right?"

"She agreed to stay on till spring and help out with Louie."

"That's right good news." Wyatt's grin spread across his face as his eyes twinkled.

"Why, Pa? What did you go and do that for? We don't need her. I can help out in the store. That'll keep me out of folks' hair, won't it?"

Hazel and Mr. Murphy swung around to find Louie kneeling in front of Archie as he untied the knot that secured the animal to the railing. He'd clearly been listening to the whole conversation. Hazel looked into the boy's stormy gaze.

"I'm sure there are many chores to be done at the cabin from day to day."

"I don't need you telling me what to do," Louie said. He scowled and ran off with Archie.

Hazel watched him run away. This wasn't going to be like caring for a child she'd known his entire life. The Wells children hadn't been perfectly behaved, but they'd trusted her completely and had never questioned her authority. Louie was proving to be quite another matter.

However good Mr. Murphy's intentions, it was clear he had not disciplined the boy, and Louie seemed very angry at the idea that he wouldn't be getting his own way. Hazel was starting to understand why the town felt he was such a behavior problem. There was a good boy underneath the bluster—she was sure of it. But if he didn't learn to mind his manners, no one would take the trouble to find that hidden goodness.

Perhaps this was God's plan in the first place. For her to help bring order into the boy's mind and heart. She could only pray that she would succeed.

Chapter Five

After Mr. Murphy brought Louie back to the store, Hazel spent the morning with the sulking child. She'd decided there was no reason that she shouldn't begin her position right then and there. Despite his surly attitude, she discovered he quite enjoyed writing his letters and even making small words. She set him to the task of writing a series of letters and words and began to make a list of items she believed one would need for housekeeping.

It was a surprisingly challenging prospect. She had never kept a house herself. There'd been nothing resembling a proper home in her childhood, and once she was old enough to work, she'd been with the Wellses, who had a full staff of servants to handle housekeeping. She was simply at a loss as to what a small, simple home might require.

A deep sigh drew her attention to Louie. He sat with his elbow on the table, chin resting on his palm as he squirmed and grumbled and did everything possible to exaggerate his boredom, as he had for the past two hours.

"Louie, for your next assignment, I'd like for you to try to write down ten things from your kitchen at home."

He scowled. "What if I can't spell it?"

She smiled. "That's what I'm here for."

When he was finished, he seemed pleased. She took the slate tablet he was writing on and read the list out loud.

"Stove, bucket, wood, plate, coffeepot, spoon, pot, towel, sugar, cup."

She was about to ask if he could think of anything else when Mr. Murphy came to the back room. Proudly, the boy snatched the slate tablet from her hand and shoved it at his pa. Mr. Murphy took a look at the list and frowned.

"Is this your list or Louie's?"

"Well, I thought we could combine my list with his lesson and have him help me come up with ideas for what I might need." She lifted her chin. "Why, is something wrong? I though he did a lovely job, despite the few misspellings." It was perfectly reasonable to think *bucket* was spelled without a *C*, and it wasn't as if she couldn't tell what he'd meant.

Mr. Murphy winked at Louie. "You did a wonderful job, son. Go get yourself a peppermint stick while I speak with Miss Hazel."

When the boy was gone, he looked back down at the list.

"Please, Mr. Murphy, if there's something wrong

with the list—not as an exercise but as an actual list—tell me and I will modify it."

"Not wrong exactly. But..."

"Oh, I'm so sorry. It's too much, isn't it?" Hazel could kick herself. "I'm so sorry. Just omit anything you feel is extravagant."

"Stove?" His eyebrows narrowed.

"Oh. You prefer I cook over a fireplace? Of course. How silly of me. There's no need to go to the expense of a stove for a nanny." She shook her head and held up her hands. "Ignore that item. I don't need it at all."

"You don't need a cookstove?"

Confused, Hazel frowned, then met his gaze and noticed a smirk.

Mr. Murphy laughed. "There's already a stove. And actually, most of these items are already there. Well, not the coffeepot and coffee."

She was so relieved she didn't even mind the teasing. "Well, good. Then I guess I'm all set."

"Not exactly. You'll need all the staples. Flour, sugar, salt, meal. You'll need bedding and a washtub—which I believe Wyatt said is still there and fine."

Hazel's eyebrows rose at the news. It had not occurred to her that there would be anything usable left inside an abandoned old cabin.

Apparently reading her expression, Mr. Murphy inclined his head slightly. "Most of the household items are long donated to folks in need or just plain worn from age. You'll just need to look around and decide what you'll be needing, I suppose."

Feeling frustrated and uncertain, Hazel raised her

hands and let them drop. "Mr. Murphy, I am a nanny. I'm not a housekeeper. I do not know which items I will need." She couldn't even cook. But she would never admit that to him.

"Don't worry. You'll have everything you need to set up housekeeping. And if you think of anything else you might need, we'll see to it." He cleared his throat and set the tablet on the table. "It's lunchtime, and we usually have our lunch at the café. Please join us."

Heartily relieved to be done with the conversation, at least for now, Hazel was more than happy to accept.

Hazel clasped her hands together to contain the inexplicable joy rising inside her as she stepped across the threshold of the dusty cabin that was to be her home for at least the next few months. Her own home. The first she had ever had.

At the Wells home, the only space she'd had to call her own had been a small room connected to the nursery that held little more than a narrow cot. And she'd been ever so grateful for what had seemed then like an incredible luxury. The night after she'd moved into the Wellses' home, she had slept securely for the first time in her entire life. But this was different. It was an entire house—all to herself. She could choose when to sleep and when to eat. She could arrange things however she pleased. On her days off, she wouldn't be awakened by children pouncing on her, demanding her undivided attention. They were dear children—she loved them, and they loved her. But they could never seem to understand that she wasn't theirs to command. Especially on her day off! But that would not be a problem here, in this veritable palace of her own.

Well…perhaps not quite a palace.

The ragged door sagged on its hinges, previewing the worn, bedraggled state of everything inside. Despite the effort Mr. Murphy's friend had made, dust layered the floor and furniture. And some rodent or other—likely several of them—had clearly made use of the place. The log walls would need to be sealed up, as several open spaces between logs were definitely letting in cold air. It was warm enough, though. A fire already crackled in the fireplace, and a box on the hearth was practically overflowing with firewood.

"I'm sorry." Ezra scowled and shook his head. "You can't stay here. Not until I get it fixed up properly. Wyatt only had a few hours today to do the essentials. I should've known better than to think that would be enough."

Alarm seized Hazel's stomach, as he seemed on the cusp of escorting her right back outside. If he sent her away, where would she go? There was simply no other option. "Mr. Murphy," she said quietly as she removed her hat. "There is nothing wrong with this house that a good cleaning and airing out won't fix. And perhaps some minor repairs. It doesn't have to be fancy to be livable."

She wanted to say it was nicer than any so-called home she remembered from childhood and that she'd certainly made do with worse before. But that would invite questions that she didn't want to answer. She badly needed this position. She would tell him about her past and about Rose's thievery, but not yet. Not until she'd proven to Mr. Murphy that he could trust her—and he'd proven that she could trust *him* not to cast her aside because of the actions of others, the way Mr. Wells had done.

Louie had already settled himself in one of the two rickety chairs by the equally rickety kitchen table. Mr. Murphy handed the boy a bag that seemed to contain a few books. "If you're sure you don't mind staying," Mr. Murphy said, "I reckon a good sweeping and dusting would make it livable for tonight, and we can fix up the rest tomorrow. I'd stay and help with it myself, but I'm afraid I have to be going so I can be there for the town council meeting. You're sure you don't mind watching Louie while I'm there?"

Relief threatened to weaken her knees. She nodded. "Of course, it's fine. I can sweep and dust while you're gone. I'm sure Louie won't mind reading his book while I clean a little. Right, Louie?"

The boy shrugged. "I don't care."

The door creaked open, and they turned as Wyatt Avery stepped into the cabin carrying a load of firewood. "Hey, you three are here." He grinned and nodded at her, then looked straight at Mr. Murphy. "By the way, I about tripped over that dog. Why do you got him tied up?"

"So he won't run off," Louie offered glumly. "He don't like it a bit."

Hazel's heart went out to him, but not enough to allow a filthy dog inside to undo any cleaning she was about to do.

"Thank you for the firewood—and for the cleaning you've already done," she said to Mr. Avery.

"Wyatt's already offered to make you a new table and chairs, and I took him up on his offer," Mr. Murphy added.

"I see." Hazel smiled at the man as he strode across the floor and dropped the wood into a large box on the hearth. "Then thank you yet again, Mr. Avery. I truly do appreciate it."

"Please, call me Wyatt," he said with a warm, friendly smile. "Everyone does. We're proper hereabouts, but we ain't formal."

The exact words his mother had said. Hazel couldn't help but grin. Apparently proper names weren't the norm in Tucker Springs. Society ladies in Boston would've swooned at the informality. She'd never even heard Mrs. Wells refer to her husband as anything but Mr. Wells, unless she was speaking to the children, and then she always said, "your father."

Wyatt turned to Mr. Murphy. "I got the cold cellar cleaned out and ready to store food." Turning to Hazel, he added, "Ma sent over some smoked venison and some canned beans and carrots and a few potatoes to get you started. She also donated a straw tick mattress and some quilts. I brought those from home. The old mattress was pretty much done for."

"I—don't know what to say. Please thank her for me."

He pointed toward the door that Hazel assumed went to the bedroom. "I set your satchel in there. And your trunk." He looked up apologetically. "I sure am sorry that it is mostly empty now."

Hazel shrugged off his sympathy. She was overwhelmed at everything Ezra had asked this man to do for her—and everything his family had given up so willingly. "I don't know what to say. You've both been so kind." Mrs. Wells had been generous in a casual way, giving Hazel unwanted or already used items that would otherwise have gone in the trash, but she'd never given up anything she actually valued, and she'd certainly never put in the time to make or build anything for Hazel. No one had ever gone out of their way like this for her before. No one but Miss Hastings, that was.

Wyatt's eyes sparkled when he smiled, and Hazel couldn't help but like him. They'd met in passing at dinner last night and then at the café this morning, and she'd thought even then that he was very like his mother. That impression was only reinforced now. The same kindness, the same twinkle in the eye. "It was no problem at all for the lady willing to help out Ezra and his ornery boy. And don't be too ready with the thanks. I didn't do much cleaning except for sweeping up in the bedroom and fixing you a place to sleep. You still have a big cleaning job to do. The new kitchen table and chairs still have to be built, and I was thinking I can provide some more chairs for the sitting area and a little table for next to the bed. The one in there got chewed up by something. Probably the same squatters that chewed up the old mattress."

Hazel forced her legs to move forward, praying diligently that whatever had chewed the table and mattress had vacated the premises and would not scamper out underfoot at any moment.

Mr. Murphy must have seen her gaze darting back and forth to every knothole along the floorboards. He chuckled. "Don't worry. Whatever critters have been squatting in the cabin will vacate as soon as they realize you're the one who belongs here."

She knew he was jesting, but hearing him say that Hazel belonged filled her with a sense of well-being. Wasn't that what she had hoped for when she accepted Benjamin in the first place? To belong somewhere. To stop being the outcast.

She turned to Wyatt. "You make furniture?"

"Yes, ma'am," he said. "I can make any kind of furniture there is." There was no arrogance about it, as though it was the most natural thing in the world for a man to create furniture from logs. "I can make you more than one table. Or a bigger one if you think you will need it."

"I—I don't…" Entertain? She had never had a friend, let alone a place to invite one to. Was all that about to change? The wonder of the very idea filled her with a sense of hope.

"Wyatt really can build anything out of wood." Mr. Murphy looked around. "Wyatt, maybe you could add a couple of chairs for the sitting area and four for the table, just in case someone comes for dinner." He turned his gaze on Hazel just as she was about to protest the generosity. "You never know. You might want to host a ladies' knitting or canning day or something."

Wyatt nodded. "Glad to do it. I will have them done soon."

Hazel did not know what to say. "Thank you both again."

"Well," Mr. Murphy said. "I hate to leave you to this mess, but I really do have to get to that meeting."

She glanced at Louie. "We'll get along just fine, won't we?"

Wyatt ruffled Louie's hair. "I'll be headed out, too. Be nice to Miss O'Brien," he said. He turned to Hazel. "I'll be by tomorrow with more supplies. I'll be doing some patching on the roof, and I want to re-place those shutters on both windows. A cold front is coming through, and it feels like there might be some rain or even ice or snow with it." With those ominous words, he left.

Mr. Murphy frowned. "I've already asked Jeremiah to work at the store tomorrow so I can be here to help get the place ready, too. You can officially start on Mon-day, if that suits you." At her nod, he turned to his son. "Do whatever Miss O'Brien tells you. I'll be back as soon as the meeting is over."

Louie exhaled heavily, but he nodded. "Yes, sir."

Hazel shut the door behind Mr. Murphy and pasted a smile on her face. "Well, I tell you what. Get your book from the bag and you can read while I do some clean-ing in here, like I told your pa. How does that sound?"

"I don't care."

Hazel desperately wished she had lemonade or some sort of goodie for the child. She wasn't keen on spoil-ing children with sweets, but she needed something to break through to him and get him to see her as something other than the enemy. They'd never get anywhere if he was so closed off to her. She added a log to the fire, searching through her memory of the day's events, trying to land on anything that might help.

Then an idea came to her, as though God Himself had placed it in her mind. She looked around the kitchen area. Sure enough, there was a washtub hanging on the wall, and a bucket sat on the counter next to the cookstove.

"Louie," she said. "I'll be right back."

The little boy watched with interest as she grabbed the bucket and walked out to the pump in front of the cabin. Archie was such a small dog, one bucket of water in the washtub with one more for rinsing should work just fine. Next, she walked into the bedroom. She was acutely aware that Louie had risen and stood in the doorway watching. "What are you doing, lady?"

"You'll see. And you may call me 'Miss Hazel' or 'Miss O'Brien.' You may not, however, call me *lady* again. Am I clear?" Clear rules were crucial. If Louie chose to be disobedient, then that would be a problem she'd have to deal with—but she got the sense that a large part of his misbehavior came from truly not knowing what he shouldn't do or say. She could help with that.

He gave a loud huff but surrendered without argument. "Yes, Miss Hazel."

"Miss Hazel it is, then."

"What kind of name is Hazel, anyway?"

The question wasn't exactly polite, but there was no

meanness to his tone. "It's the name my mother gave me when I was born. I was named for her grandmother."

"What was her name?"

"Hazel." Hazel waited for the obvious to sink in.

A sheepish grin spread across his face, and Hazel noticed his bottom front tooth was so loose it was barely hanging on.

She opened the wardrobe and found a couple of old sheets folded on the top shelf. The one on top was covered in dust, but the one beneath wasn't too bad, so she took it down and grabbed one of the quilts Miz Caroline had graciously sent. Guilt hit her at what she had in mind. But she would only do it once, and it was for a good cause.

"Now," she continued. "The name Hazel comes from the word *hazelnut*."

Louie snickered.

"Don't be rude, please."

"I wasn't."

"You laughed at my name. That's rude."

A solemn expression washed over his face, and his eyes grew serious. "But I didn't laugh at Hazel. Just *hazelnut*." He shrugged. "It's kind of a funny word."

"Well," she conceded. "I suppose it could sound funny in the odd sense of the word if you haven't heard it before. Is that what you meant?" She opened her trunk and began to rummage about until she found an apron to cover the entire front of her gown, along with a bar of soap Mrs. Wells had ordered through a catalog from Paris. The wealthy woman hadn't fancied the scent and had passed it along to Hazel. She turned to

Louie. "Well? Is that what you meant? That *hazelnut* is an odd-sounding word?"

"I reckon so." He frowned. "Miss Hazel, what are you doing?"

She handed him the sheet and the soap. "Go and sit next to the washtub."

His face blanched. "I ain't taking no bath. And I especially ain't taking one in front of a lady. And I can say lady in that odd sort of way."

Hazel laughed. "Oh, Louie. I'm not suggesting you have a bath." She slipped on the apron, then walked across the room and opened the front door. Poor Archie shivered and whined. She untied him, gathered him up and brought him inside.

"What are you doing?" Louie gave her a deep frown. "He don't like getting a bath, if that's what you're thinking. You best just put him down and forget that idea."

"Now, listen." She leveled her gaze at the boy. "I think Archie could be a very nice inside dog."

"He's the nicest dog alive, that's all."

"I'm sure he is. And I don't mind allowing him inside while you are here. But Archie absolutely cannot stay inside unless he has a bath. Now, he's your dog. So, you decide. Bath or back to the rope outside?"

He turned his soulful gaze onto an unsuspecting Archie. "I reckon a bath is for the best."

"You've made a very wise decision. Now roll up your sleeves, because I'll need your help."

Once Archie looked and smelled presentable, Hazel wrapped the dog in the sheet from the wardrobe and handed him to Louie. Archie had put up a valiant struggle, and Hazel's arms were tired from the effort of holding him still. Not to mention the fact that she and Louie were as wet as the dog. But as she looked at the pure joy on Louie's face as he snuggled Archie close to his chest, Hazel felt it a small price to pay.

The meeting was just being called to order when Ezra stepped inside and found a seat close to the back.

The members of the town council sat in the front. Mr. Green, who owned the local newspaper, Frank Bauer from the post office, Mr. Will, the reverend, Mr. Lowe and Mr. Bohannon. Ezra figured he could for sure count on Mr. Will and Reverend Harper to vote in favor of giving him another chance. But he couldn't be sure.

For the first twenty minutes, they discussed the funding and labor for the church roof, which had to be replaced before winter set in. Already, the reverend was using every single pot he owned to collect water during every rainstorm.

Once the roof issue was agreed upon and Robert Bohannon grudgingly agreed to move his pigs farther from town, an awkward silence filled the room.

"Well, for mercy's sake," Miz Caroline finally said. "Let's get this nonsense over with so we can all go home."

As head of the council, Mr. Lowe stood. "We have a complaint against one of our town members." He cleared his throat, and Ezra could see the hesitation in his eyes as he lifted the paper from the table. "We've spoken to Ezra already, so he's not blindsided by any of the names on the petition."

"Hey!" Rufus Jenson burst out. "I was told that thing was anonymous."

"Well, it wasn't," Mr. Lowe snapped back.

Mr. Will pointed an arthritic finger toward Rufus. "A fellow ought to know who's against him."

Rufus turned to Ezra. "I wouldn't say I'm so much against him," Rufus tried to argue, but he quailed under Mr. Will's stern stare. "I...I reckon I'll withdraw my name," he said at last. "The boy ain't bothered me all that much."

"Then why'd you sign it in the first place?" Miz Caroline's exasperated voice cut through the room.

Rufus shrugged and waved a hand toward the front. "You go on and cross my name out." He stood and motioned for his wife, Betsy, and their three children to leave with him. Ezra knew the man was ashamed. He'd fallen on hard times last year after he'd been laid up from an accident in the field. Ezra had extended credit since. He couldn't just see a family do without. He nodded toward Rufus as the family left.

Chester stood, and the buzzing room grew instantly quiet. "Now listen, I like Murphy just as much as everyone else. But the fact is my smithy was torn up yesterday when Louie Murphy and his dog scared Johnny Gable's horse while I was shoeing it. And I won't even mention the damage to my head."

"You just did." Miz Caroline glared at him. It was no secret that there was no love lost between those two. Not since Wyatt apprenticed for him five years ago and Chester let him go, citing a distinct lack of ability on Wyatt's part. Everyone knew he was right, but no one would say it to Miz Caroline. So she still carried the wound in her soul, despite Wyatt assuring her he'd much rather do carpentry than work with iron.

"What is it that you would have Ezra do, Chester?" Mr. Bauer spoke up in his calm tone.

"As I've said repeatedly, Ezra has to take charge of the boy—find a way to keep him occupied. Otherwise, what's to keep the boy from terrorizing the citizens of this town and destroying property?"

"It gives me no joy to agree with Chester," Mr. Bohannon said. "But the boy has set my pigs loose twice in the past two months."

"But not on purpose." Ezra spoke up, hoping to explain. "He was trying to get Archie out of the pen." He winced as he realized his statement probably did little or nothing to help his cause. As a matter of fact, it was further proof of Louie's lack of supervision. If Louie and Archie hadn't been wandering around town alone, Archie wouldn't have gotten near the pen—and if he had, there would have been an adult to take care of the situation rather than Louie opening the gate to go after him. Ezra himself had helped round up the hogs both times, so he did feel for Mr. Bohannon.

"I hate to say it," Mr. Bohannon said. "But unless we can come up with a solution, I'll be joining Chester and Miss Stewart and getting my goods at Jamesburg."

"As will we," Mr. Green, the newspaper editor spoke up.

With a sinking heart, Ezra watched as one by one, the townsfolk "regretfully" joined Chester's boycott.

Miz Caroline stood at the front of the room. She

looked at Ezra, then lifted both hands, palms forward. "Stop this right now. All of you. Now, think about what you're saying. If everyone takes their business to Jamesburg, and Ezra can't make ends meet, that means he and Louie will have to pack up and leave town. Is that really what you all want? To drive away Ezra, when he grew up in this town? When he's been a part of this community since he was no bigger than Louie is now?" She took in the rest of the room. "We don't push each other out in this town. We're like family." When no one spoke up in agreement, she scowled. "It so happens that this is no more than a tempest in a teapot anyway. Ezra, it's time to tell everyone what you've done to help Louie stay out of trouble."

"Well, Ezra?" Chester said, "What's happened since yesterday that will have any bearing on the outcome of the meeting?"

Ezra knew that hiring Miss O'Brien was simply the first step in winning back everyone's trust. But it was a start. Thankfully, Ben and Ivy Gordon hadn't attended the meeting, so bringing up Miss O'Brien wouldn't be quite as awkward as it could've been.

"I know many of you have heard about the lady who came in on the stage yesterday."

A smattering of chuckles pecked at the room until Mr. Lowe rapped the table with his knuckles. "Let him speak, please, and try to hold your responses until he's finished."

"Thank you, sir." Ezra swallowed hard and glanced around at the stoic faces of his friends and neighbors. "Miss O'Brien, the lady in question, was a nanny for several years in Boston. Since she found herself in need of a new situation after she arrived, I hired her."

Reverend Harper stood, his eyes sparkling with humor. "Well, I call that providential." He gave a laugh and glanced around. "And I should know."

Mrs. Green stood up. "You mean the woman that Ben Gordon jilted is going to stay here in Tucker Springs?"

Ezra held back a groan at Mrs. Green's question. She held her ever-handy paper and pencil, ready to add town gossip to tomorrow's edition. But now that she had brought it up, everyone seemed to be leaning in to hear the answer. "Yes, that's right. She was planning to take the stagecoach back East on Monday, but I asked her to stay on until spring and take care of Louie."

Mrs. Green gasped. "Do you mean to tell me you hired a stranger to look after your son? Why, you don't know what might happen to him. He could be kidnapped."

"I'm reasonably sure that won't happen," he said. Then he couldn't resist a grin. "But if it does, think about the front-page story."

"Aw," Frank Bauer said, scowling as much as the perpetually smiling postmaster could manage. "You folks. First you tell Ezra, you must control the boy. Then he finds someone to do that and you tell him, this is not good enough. Well, the woman is here through no fault of hers. I haf met her, and I liked her a lot."

"Where will she live?" Mrs. Green looked down her nose at Ezra. "Surely not with you and the boy?"

"No, ma'am. She's going to live in Ma and Pa's old cabin back behind the store."

"Humph. I hate to think of the work it will take to get that place livable."

"I'm organizing a workday there tomorrow. Maybe you should bring your oldest apron and some cleaning supplies and come help," Miz Caroline said.

"Well! I never…"

Miz Caroline nodded. "That's what I thought."

"It's settled, then," Mr. Will said, not quite concealing a smile at his wife's handling of Mrs. Green. "Ezra's hired himself a nanny."

Chester scoffed. "It's not settled until we get some proof this is going to settle things down."

"Well," Mr. Lowe said. "I vote that we give this nanny a chance. As long as Louie is no longer allowed to run wild, I see no reason to take further action."

Relief washed over Ezra as one by one the council members voted against a boycott. When it was Robert's turn to speak, Ezra's stomach grew tight.

"I'll be moving my hogs out of town anyway, so it's unlikely the dog will get into the pen anymore, nanny or no nanny. As far as how things will be in town…as long as the woman settles him down, I can't see a good reason to drive all the way to Jamesburg for our goods. I say we give it a chance."

Ezra slipped away before the meeting was dismissed so that he wouldn't be forced to answer questions about Miss O'Brien, particularly questions from Mrs. Green. Gratitude filled him as he drove the wagon to the cabin. As he replayed the day in his mind, he became swept up in a sense of well-being he hadn't felt in quite some time.

Smoke came from the chimney, and he could see

the lamplight flickering through the spaces he needed to patch in the walls. He'd tend to that tomorrow along with the roof and several other small fixes. He wasn't as skilled as Wyatt, but he knew how to patch or plaster a hole well enough. He was a little ashamed of himself that he'd let the place go to such an extent. It was his property, and it was a man's job to take care of what was his. By the end of another day, Miss O'Brien would be all set, snug and cozy in the cabin. He smiled and nodded, satisfied with himself. It felt good to know things were beginning to head in the right direction.

He set the brake and hopped down, excited to share the good news.

He tapped on the door, but there was no answer. With a frown, he pushed it open and peeked inside. A lump formed in his throat at the sight of Miss O'Brien seated on a chair in front of the fire, and Louie and a very clean Archie curled up together on the floor by her feet.

His mind went back to the last woman who had occupied this cabin. How different that had been from now. Marie had shown up just after the war with a tiny newborn Louie in her arms. It had been a shock to learn that she was John's wife. She was lovely, to be sure, beautiful, even. But there was a coldness to her beauty that couldn't be more different from Jennie Avery, who had been John's sweetheart before the war. If not for the letter of introduction that had accompanied her, Ezra might not have believed her at all.

There had been no mistaking John's handwriting, nor had there been any question that Ezra would honor his brother's request.

Dear Brother Ezra,
If you are reading this, I didn't make it home.
Please take care of my wife and the child she is
carrying.
John

Ezra shook off the memory as Miss O'Brien stirred and slowly lifted her head. She opened her eyes, then gasped. "Oh! Mr. Murphy!" She stood suddenly, startling Louie and Archie awake. Archie shot up, barking. Then he darted toward the door, which Ezra had failed to shut behind him.

"Get him, Pa!" Louie scrambled to his feet. "*Archie!*"

Ezra took swipe at the fleeing animal and missed. Archie shimmied through his legs and took a flying leap…straight into the mud, and then scurried into the night.

"Archie!"

"Whoa, there, fella." Ezra caught Louie just before the boy could slide past him and go after the dog. Ezra heard a soft feminine sigh. He turned slowly and looked helplessly into Miss O'Brien's bewildered face.

Her hands rested on her hips as she stared at the opened door, shaking her head. "But we just gave him a bath," she murmured, more to herself than to him.

Ezra felt the need to apologize anyway. "I'm sorry. I should've closed the door." In the second it took him to get lost in Miss O'Brien's eyes, Louie broke free. In a beat, the boy had followed the dog, right into the mud.

As he thanked Miss O'Brien for keeping Louie and told her of the council's decision, his stomach sank a little as reality sank in. Having a nanny didn't necessarily mean that Louie's rambunctious behavior would end. He was still a boy who wanted to chase his dog in and out of mud puddles and all over town. Could Ezra really expect that to change, nanny or no nanny? Nothing he'd said had ever curbed his son's behavior, even after nearly six years of trying. Was it plausible that this woman would have more success—and that the success would happen fast enough to appease the town?

If she wasn't able to get him in hand soon, the council just might change their minds and suggest the town shun his business. And then where would they be?

Chapter Six

Hazel rose early Saturday morning to get ready for Mr. Murphy, Wyatt and Louie's arrival. She was dressed and ready to start her day by the time the sun peeked up over the horizon. The trees, already beautiful in their autumn colors, seemed to glow a mixture of red, orange and yellow with the first golden rays of the sun providing a spotlight. She lingered on the porch for a minute, and just thanked God. She could not believe that the turmoil of the past few days, past few months, even, had brought her to this moment.

Movement caught her eye, and she waved as Mr. Murphy's wagon came down the small lane. Before she could turn to go back in the house, she noticed another wagon behind it and another. She recognized the Averys and the Bauers, and there were other families she didn't know. They all pulled up onto the grass and disembarked from their wagons with cheerful shouted greetings and plenty of bustling around. She watched the men carrying roofing and carpentry tools make a beeline for Mr. Murphy who gestured toward the barn and chicken coop, then turned toward the house. He lifted his arm in greeting as she caught his eye. Overwhelmed, she waved back and turned as Miz Caroline and several other women descended on the cabin with buckets and rags and lye soap.

Speechless, Hazel stepped back and allowed them to enter.

She knew that this outpouring of love and support was for the Murphys more than for her, but she could not help but be touched by it.

Miz Caroline directed each woman to a different area, then turned to Hazel. "Ezra mentioned that you haven't kept a home before. Correct?"

Hazel nodded. "I've been in service since I was old enough to work, but only as a nanny. I know how to care for children. And I can take care of myself and my quarters. But I've never had more than a room to myself. I've certainly never had my own kitchen."

"Your ma didn't show you anything while you were growing up?"

"She died when I was younger than Louie is now."

"You work with me then," Miz Caroline said kindly. She lowered her voice. "Watch what I do and ask me if there is anything you don't understand about the way I do something."

Hazel nodded and made sure she was ready for every job Miz Caroline gave her. At lunchtime, Gilly Bauer and Jennie showed up with baskets of food for the hungry workers.

Amid the loudly talking men, the chattering women,

and the shouts and laughter of several children who had played outside all day, Hazel felt herself fade back until she leaned against a wall, observing the love and friendship between the townspeople. She had to wonder, if they knew her past, would they be welcoming her into their lives this way?

As she watched the scene all around her, her gaze repeatedly rested on Mr. Murphy. Even as disheveled and dirty as he was from the morning's work, he was so handsome. His lips curved into a smile, and Hazel felt her heart start to beat faster. No man had ever made her feel whatever this was. He stood, and for an instant, she thought he would cross the room and come to her.

"Ezra!"

Like a splash of icy water, Jennie's voice broke into the moment, and Hazel woke from whatever stupor she'd been in. She pushed away from the wall, made her way to the door and slipped outside for a minute of fresh air. *Now you listen*, she admonished herself. *What you're feeling is nothing more than gratitude. You did not stay in the town after being humiliated and jilted just to fall in love with the man who was kind enough to hire you.*

She felt marginally better after closing her eyes and reminding herself to stick to her plan. She would use this time in Tucker Springs to gain some independence. She'd be able to save some money, gain new housekeeping skills and write letters back to Boston to see if she could scout out job prospects for the spring. She'd smooth the way for her future—which wasn't here, and certainly wasn't with Mr. Murphy.

She turned to go back inside just as a pair of men exited. Wyatt grinned as he passed her. "By tonight, you'll have a palace fit for a queen."

Mr. Murphy scoffed and clapped his friend on the shoulder. "Miss O'Brien, you'll learn that Wyatt here tends to exaggerate. You won't have a palace, but at least the walls won't let in a draft and the roof won't leak."

Wyatt feigned confusion. "Isn't that what I said?"

Hazel couldn't help but chuckle at their silliness as she stepped past them back into the house. The ladies were cleaning up from lunch.

"Oh, Hazel." Jennie smiled as she called from the kitchen. "I'm leaving the leftover ham and beans for your supper. Also a few of these corn muffins I hid under a napkin for you—if I'd left them in plain sight, that brother of mine would have wolfed them all down." Hazel stepped in to help, and the next several hours passed in a whirlwind of scrubbing and chatting and laughter.

By the end of the day, her muscles ached, but her heart felt lighter than it ever had.

She stepped out on the porch with Miz Caroline and almost bumped into Mr. Murphy. "Whoa there," he said, catching hold of her arms to steady her.

"Well," Miz Caroline said with a wry grin on her lips, "I'd say today was a success. I'll see you two at church in the morning." She shook her head as she stepped stiffly toward her wagon. "These old bones are going to feel this for a couple of days. Henry Avery! It's time to go."

Louie came running up to the porch as Henry followed his mother. Louie took his place between Hazel and Mr. Murphy on the porch, and they waved until the wagons disappeared down the road.

"Well, it's been a long day," Mr. Murphy said. Dirt smudged his forehead where she suspected he'd wiped the sweat from his brow. He seemed exhausted but satisfied. Hazel's stomach twisted with something that felt like a revelation. She'd never seen her pa work this way. And Mr. Wells didn't do the sort of work that roughened a man's hands. A new respect formed within her not just for Mr. Murphy, but for all these men and women who worked the land and survived from the fruit of it. This wasn't the kind of life she'd been born to, but for the next few months, this was her world.

Hazel understood Mr. Murphy's satisfaction as he looked across the yard, the barn, the chicken coop. Despite the aching arms and back, there was a satisfaction—more than satisfaction, there was *joy*—in doing a hard day's work in her own spot in the world. Her own kitchen, sitting room, bedroom.

Mr. Murphy glanced at her over Louie's head. "Would you like for us to pick you up for church service in the morning?"

Hazel's heart lifted at the thought of fellowshipping with other believers. "Yes, I would."

"All right, then. We'll see you in the morning."

"Mr. Murphy," she called after him as he led Louie toward the wagon.

He stopped and turned. "Yes?"

There was so much she wanted to say to this man who had given her a home. A real home. But the right words to express the depths of her gratitude eluded her. All she could manage to say was "Thank you for this."

He seemed to scrutinize her, then simply nodded. "This is part of your pay. And even with this included, I still feel like I should thank you. It's not every day a fancy nanny from Boston agrees to look after the son of a simple shopkeeper. I know this cabin is not everything you're accustomed to, but I hope it'll do."

Disappointed, somehow, by his response, Hazel simply nodded. "It's just fine."

"Good, then. We'll see you in the morning. Tell your nanny good-night, Louie."

The boy turned. "'Night, Miss Hazel."

As she watched them leave, a little joy went out of Hazel's day. It was idiotic for her to be disappointed. But with his response to her gratitude, Mr. Murphy had made the lines between them very clear. He had not come and worked on her home out of friendship, but simply as a duty from an employer to an employee.

She was too exhausted to pull out the dinner Jennie had left for her, so after cleaning herself up, she crawled into her bed in the scrubbed room that looked and smelled fresh. She stared at the ceiling, reliving the day. The week was ending much differently than she had expected. Instead of starting her life as a wife, once again, she was a nanny. At least she knew how to take care of children. Even precocious children like Louie. The rest, she wasn't so sure. If those women had taught her anything today, it was that there were many things a woman needed to know in order to run a household.

And she barely knew how to build a fire in the cook-stove, let alone how to cook on it.

But she had always done whatever had to be done. She'd do it again. She'd been gifted a few recipes by the women who had come, and she would learn how to cook from them even if she had to cook a hundred meals that were barely edible while she learned. She'd learn to build a fire, even if the first hundred tries failed. And if she had no prospects arranged yet for employment when Mr. Murphy sent her away in the spring after his troubles with the town were over, well, somehow she would find a way to live. After all, God had provided this remedy for Mr. Murphy and for her. When Mr. Murphy no longer needed her, God would provide again.

The tap-tapping on the roof didn't wake Hazel right away. Instead, it worked its way into her dreams. She was a child again, huddled against the side of a building, knees to her chest, trying desperately, ineffectively to stay dry in the rain. Her stomach sank as she knew that no matter how quick the shower or extended the storm, her thin dress would be soaked in minutes and sticking to her skin for hours afterward, even after the rain stopped. And yet...her clothes still felt dry. How could that be?

She came awake, and with a contented sigh, she remembered where she was, that she was safe and warm, no longer the girl whose family lived in alleyways or abandoned buildings.

Rain couldn't invade this home. Yesterday, Mr. Murphy had fixed the roof. She had no worries in this cozy little cabin. The walls were patched; the floors were clean. She had firewood and food and several new pieces of furniture, with more on the way as soon as they were made. She could barely even believe how blessed she felt. Everything in the cabin was hers to use, and all she had to do was care for and teach one child. Granted, Louie would be a challenge. But he was well-spoken and thoughtful. And any boy whose heart held that much love for an animal who constantly tried to leave was a good child. Or at least had a good heart.

She wasn't so sure about Archie.

But Louie and Archie were tomorrow's responsibility. Today was church. As much as she looked forward to worship, this would be the first time since she came to town that she would be forced to see Benjamin. She knew she couldn't avoid it forever, but her stomach twisted with dread at the thought of facing the man who had jilted and humiliated her.

She tried to push away that worry by focusing on the thought of church. As a child, she had been drawn by the bells and beautiful singing, but when she was very young, she hadn't thought she'd be allowed to attend services. Certainly, there was no adult to take her, and she was too shy to enter herself, intimidated by the large buildings and solemn, even stern faces of the men and women going in and out.

When she was ten years old, she had found God in the kind smile and generosity of Miss Hastings, the teacher at the Mission of Mercy school in a one-room shack close to the waterfront. She was the one who had first brought Hazel to a church service and had let her know she was welcome there. And before long, she was dragging her sister to the mission church each Sunday.

Once Hazel moved to Boston to become the nanny for the Wells children, she had accompanied her employers each week, taking her place with others of her class. Their church building was far grander than the one where she'd first pledged herself to God, but it hadn't felt quite as welcoming. She wondered what church services would be like here in Tucker Springs.

With a sigh, she pushed back the quilt and sat up slowly as her muscles tensed and protested. Hazel was fairly certain she had never experienced the sort of muscle ache that she felt now as she slid from the bed and moved in short, halting steps, every movement agony. Shivering, she quickly slipped into her dressing gown and pulled on a pair of house shoes she'd received as a gift from the Wellses' cook last Christmas. She straightened her bed to get her body moving. Movement added warmth and stretched the stiffness from her body. Then she made her way into the cold living room.

Her memory provided the step-by-step instructions as she attended the unfamiliar task of building a fire. Painfully, carefully, she placed kindling and a log on the red coals. At least she wouldn't have to start from nothing. She held her breath as the kindling caught, then burned out, then caught again. Finally, the dry log produced some sparks and the fire grew. The room began to warm. The sun was just rising, so there was plenty of time for her to try to start a fire in the cookstove. Mr. Murphy had brought coffee he'd ground in the store. Early Sunday mornings were her days to sit with

Mr. Wells's discarded newspapers from the past week and catch up on whatever was happening in the city and the country at large. She did this while sipping coffee. Of course, she had never been the one to brew the stuff, but she'd seen it done plenty of times.

While the coffee boiled, Hazel cut a slice of bread from the loaf that Miz Caroline had brought over the day before. She slathered it with butter and set the plate on the table, then went to the bookshelf for the last newspaper she had purchased just before leaving Boston—true, she had read it through a couple of times, but surprisingly she found something she had skipped over or forgotten each time she picked it up. Hazel was just pouring her coffee when a knock at the door gave her a start. It was much too early for Mr. Murphy to arrive to take her to church, wasn't it?

And yet, when she opened the door, there he was. Handsome even while shivering on the porch with rain rolling off his shoulders. "Mr. Murphy!" She opened the door wider. "Come in, please."

His gaze swept her from head to toe, and he shook his head. "I best not." He smiled. "Don't want to start any gossip."

Suddenly conscious that she was still wearing her dressing gown, she suppressed a gasp. "Of course! Is everything all right?" She glanced over his shoulder at the empty wagon. "Where's Louie?"

"Don't worry. He's at home with Wyatt. I just came to tell you there won't be a service this morning."

A strange combination of relief and disappointment mingled through her. "I see."

"The reverend was building a fire in the stove to warm the church, and part of the roof caved right in on him. Doc says he's got a concussion and a couple of broken ribs."

"Mercy! Will he be okay?"

Mr. Murphy nodded. "His…daughter and her husband are looking after him."

Inwardly, she smiled. He was trying to keep from directly mentioning Benjamin and Ivy. She debated whether or not she should mention that she was well aware that Benjamin's wife was the reverend's daughter. Before she could speak, a gust of icy wind sliced through the thin layers of her dressing gown, and she shivered.

Mr. Murphy frowned. "You're freezing," he said. "I'll be going so you can close the door and get warm." He turned, then paused. "Do you have everything you need for today?"

Hazel nodded, trying not to allow him to see her teeth chattering. Mercy, it was cold for late October.

"Then I'll see you tomorrow."

Hazel closed the door, shutting out the cold wind but holding on to the warm feeling in her heart. It was an odd circumstance for someone to care that she had everything she needed, let alone ask after her well-being.

By the time she finished her slice of buttered bread, Hazel had talked herself down to earth. After all, Mr. Murphy was her employer and had promised to provide for her needs. It was only natural he would ensure she had what she required.

Hazel was beginning to believe that maybe there

was something to Benjamin's love of his town. Though she still believed "charming" was a bit far-fetched, his assessment of the generosity, kindness and caring of the townsfolk was true. At least where the Averys and Mr. Murphy were concerned. She had her doubts about the folks who had threatened to boycott, but even those people had indirectly come to her assistance. If not for their petition, it was doubtful that Mr. Murphy would have hired her to help with Louie. She had to say that all in all, the Lord had most definitely turned her mourning into—if not dancing, at least—hope.

Like the apostle Paul, she would be content with whatever life brought to her and not ask for more.

Ezra glanced at the clock in the corner. Relieved to see it was lunchtime, he set the money box on the shelf beneath the counter and hung his apron on the peg behind him. A steady stream of customers had been in and out of the store all morning, and so far, he hadn't heard one complaint about Louie. Reason to be grateful.

Though the mud persisted, the sun was shining, and its rays were like strong arms lifting his spirits. His smiles came easily, even for Mrs. Green, who had spent a full thirty minutes badgering him about getting an interview with Miss O'Brien for her newspaper, particularly now that she had become a victim of the thief. He finally forbade her from making a beeline to the cabin. With a huff, she'd left the store five minutes ago without making a purchase.

Just as he shrugged into his coat and was about to close up and head over to the café for lunch, a disheveled man walked in. He seemed nervous, clutching his battered hat tightly between his hands. He was tall with a long beard and hair that obviously hadn't seen a pair of shears in some time, and he appeared so thin a strong gust of wind just might blow him off his feet. Ezra took careful note of him. They didn't get many strangers in town on days when the stagecoach didn't run. Especially strangers in such poor condition.

"How can I help you?"

The man cleared his throat. "Name's Jackson. Miles Jackson. I'm looking for work."

Ezra's heart sank even as it went out to the fellow. If he'd shown up during harvest season, he'd have had more work than he could manage. But now... Ezra shook his head. "I don't know of anyone hiring just now." He looked the man over again. Disappointment clouded his face, and Ezra noticed sunken cheeks beneath his thick beard.

"Well, thank you just the same." His thin shoulders slumped, and as he turned, Ezra could see the outline of his shoulder blades even through his threadbare coat.

I was a stranger, and ye took me not in. The words of Jesus had never seemed more appropriate than now.

"Wait just a second while I lock up. I'm headed to the café for lunch. I'd be honored to buy you a meal."

Fire flashed in the blue eyes that stared back at him. "Mister, I ain't asking for charity. I said I was looking for work, and that's exactly what I mean. If you can't help me there, then I thank you for your time and I'll be on my way."

Ezra held up his palms and stepped back. "Sorry to

offend." Ezra tried to come up with something he could pay this man to do so that he could get a meal inside him. "I just remembered that I've been needing to…" He looked around, trying to find something he'd been needing to do.

The man shook his head. "Like I said, I don't take charity. But thank you just the same."

Ezra nodded as the man slipped back into the cool afternoon. The man's dignity might be all he owned while he starved to death if he didn't accept help soon.

Ezra was about to close up and head over to the café for lunch when a figure caught his eye through the large front window. Miss O'Brien shivered outside the window as Mr. Jackson tipped his hat and walked down the boardwalk.

Ezra stepped outside. "Miss O'Brien? Everything all right?" Her hand nervously clutched a locket at her throat.

She rushed to meet him. "Oh, Mr. Murphy. I've lost him."

"Louie?"

"Who else?" She gulped in and blew out a cloudy breath.

Shrugging out of his coat, Ezra slipped it around her shoulders. "Calm down. Tell me what happened."

"Thank you." She pulled the coat more closely around her. "I left Louie writing his letters…"

"You left him?" Ezra frowned. If he'd wanted to leave Louie alone, he wouldn't have needed to hire a nanny in the first place.

"Well, yes." Her tone seemed to have reached a

stage of exasperation. "Only for a minute, to visit the necessary. But when I came back, he was gone!"

Swallowing hard, Ezra nodded. "Well, let's go find Louie."

Ezra's stomach sank as he worried that all his worst suspicions had been confirmed. Miss O'Brien wasn't able to handle Louie after all. If they found him bothering one of the people who had signed the original petition, this would just prove that even having a nanny wasn't enough to keep Louie under control. He'd hoped that Miss O'Brien's arrival and need for work was providence, bringing him what he required. He should have known that things never worked out that way for him.

Chapter Seven

"**A**rchie!"

Ezra jerked his head around at the sound of Louie's frantic cry. "For mercy's sake…" Well, at least they wouldn't have to search high and low for the boy.

"Pa! Get him!" Louie screamed.

Archie dodged Louie and made a dash for Miss O'Brien.

"Archie! Stop!" he commanded.

The terrified canine did not stop. Rather, he dashed right toward Miss O'Brien in his attempt to avoid Louie's grubby grasp. Miss O'Brien started to bend down to grab the animal, but Louie, eyes intent on nothing but his dog, swerved to try to make a grab of his own and ended up colliding directly with her. Had she been standing upright, she likely could have taken the blow, but bent down as she was, with the muddy ground slick and unstable under her feet, she tumbled over in a heap.

Ezra felt as if time was slowing down as he watched the collision, helpless to prevent it. Then time sped back up again abruptly when he heard Miss O'Brien's cry of pain. He rushed over to help her and found that she'd landed awkwardly on one arm, possibly injuring it.

The other arm was wrapped around Archie. She'd caught him after all.

"You got him!"

Ezra crouched over her, wanting to help but not sure what to do. "Are you hurt?"

"A little," she said, sitting in the street, her breath coming in deep gulps.

Ezra could see the pain in her eyes as she pressed the frightened, whimpering animal close.

Louie held out his chubby arms. "Give him to me."

She gave an emphatic shake of her head. "I think not," she said. "The poor thing is frightened half to death."

The boy's face scrunched with indignation. "You give me my dog. Pa!"

"Louie Murphy," Ezra said, exasperation shooting through him. "Don't let me hear you yelling at a lady. And besides, don't you think you owe her an apology? You knocked her to the ground, and now she's hurt!"

Louie did have the grace to look shamefaced at that. "I…I'm sorry I knocked you down, Miss Hazel. Honest, I am. It weren't on purpose—I just didn't see you there."

"I accept your apology," Miss O'Brien said with remarkable grace for a woman still lying in mud. "I believe you when you say you didn't mean any harm. But Louie, we're going to have to work on noticing things around you when you chase after Archie. I believe I'm not the first person who's gotten hurt because you weren't paying attention."

"I ain't never knocked nobody down before," Louie protested, looking offended at the suggestion.

"But when you opened the hog pens and the animals got out, some of those hogs got hurt before they could be brought home, didn't they?"

"They…" Louie started to argue, then paused, turning to Ezra. "Did they, Pa?"

"They did," Ezra confirmed, a little awed at what he was seeing. Had he really never explained to Louie the consequences of his actions? Was this what his boy had needed to hear in order to understand? "But we can talk about the hogs later," he added. "Miss O'Brien is hurt right now. Go stand in front of the café and wait while I help Miss O'Brien."

"But what about Archie?"

"Best to leave him with me for now, to keep him calm," Miss O'Brien interjected.

Louie seemed despondent at that. "How come he's so calm with you? He ain't never like that with me."

"Well, how would you like it if someone three times your size or more was constantly chasing you down, grabbing you when you didn't want to be held?" Miss O'Brien pointed out. "You wouldn't like that at all, Louie. Am I right?"

As if in response, Archie sighed and rested his furry head against her chest.

Louie frowned down at the nestling dog. "Just don't forget he's mine. You can't have him."

Focusing on the more important matter at hand, Ezra

reached down to pull Miss O'Brien up, but he realized she was favoring one arm and holding on to Archie with the other. He bent and slipped his arm around her back, then searched her eyes. "May I lift you?"

His face was so close to hers—almost like a prelude to a kiss. He swallowed hard as she wordlessly nodded without breaking their gaze.

Moving as carefully as he could, he lifted her by her waist. When she was on her feet, he kept one arm around her and led her back to the boardwalk.

"Can I have Archie now?"

Miss O'Brien shook her head. "Not until we are all three cleaned up."

Her expression softened at the dejected dip of Louie's lip. "Louie," she said. "It's clear to me that you love this dog. I am aware that you are not being intentionally unkind to him."

"He's the best dog alive, that's why."

"Well, we won't argue that point for now. But if you don't want him to run away all the time, you'll have to start respecting his boundaries."

Louie frowned and looked at her through narrowed eyes. "What's that?"

Miss O'Brien adjusted Archie, who snugged closer to her and gave a deep, contented sigh. She sucked in a sharp breath as she moved her other arm to support the dog, clearly in pain.

Ezra stepped closer and reached for Archie, but she shook her head without breaking her eye contact with Louie. "For instance, if he doesn't want you to hold him, put him down. He is a living creature, not a toy."

"But if I put him down, he runs off."

Hazel shrugged. "You can't force someone or something to stay when they don't want to. The best thing you can do for this dog is to let him run when he wants to. He'll come back to you when he's ready—which will probably be a lot sooner if you stop scaring the life out of him by chasing him and screaming after him. Can you just give it a try?"

With a deep sigh that indicated Louie felt completely and utterly put out with the whole situation, he nevertheless—surprisingly—nodded. "I reckon. Can I have him now?"

A small smile stretched Miss O'Brien's lips. "No, you may not have him just yet. Not until we are all properly cleaned up."

"I have to be getting back to the store," Ezra said. "Do you want me to take Louie and Archie with me for the rest of the day?"

She shook her head. "That won't be necessary." A grimace of pain accompanied her words. He was just about to insist when Jennie stepped outside. "Come on, Hazel. Let's go back to the cabin and get you cleaned up." She leveled a gaze at Louie. "You follow, and don't you make a lick of trouble."

"Aw, Miss Jennie. She won't give me Archie."

"Serves you right."

"Stop by the doc's office on the way so he can look at Miss O'Brien's arm," Ezra told Jennie.

"Oh, that isn't—" Miss O'Brien protested, but Jennie didn't let her finish.

"Already planned to."

Clearly defeated, Louie tagged along behind the two women as Jennie headed them down the boardwalk. Ezra watched in silent awe. He was beginning to realize that having Miss O'Brien in their lives had already changed so much in just a few days.

He was more hopeful now that she might truly be able to get through to Louie. And as an added bonus, not the least of the creatures that had been affected by her presence in Tucker Springs, Archie might finally get some peace.

Even though Hazel had originally protested needing Jennie's help, she was grateful the other woman had insisted. According to Dr. Kehoe, her shoulder had likely dislocated temporarily—but it had fixed itself by sliding back into place on its own. It would be sore, and she would have to rest it, but the injury wasn't serious. He had tied up Hazel's arm with a large square cloth. After instructing her to try not to move it for a couple of days, he gave her a packet of laudanum for the pain.

She walked out of the examination room to find Jennie waiting, chatting with the doctor's wife. They had left Louie on the cold porch with a tied-up Archie.

"Does she need to come back, Doc?" Jennie asked, wrapping a shawl around Hazel's shoulders.

The red-faced, jovial physician shook his head. "I only wish all my patients were such easy cases to fix." He turned to Hazel. "Just do as I instructed and keep the arm tied up even when you retire for the night. There is only enough medicine for a couple of nights, so mind how often you take it."

Hazel nodded. "Thank you. Do I..." She thought about the minuscule amount of money tucked inside her reticule but knew the doctor needed to be paid. "Your fee?"

"Don't tell her," Jennie said ushering her toward the door. "Bill it to Ezra Murphy. His boy is the one who knocked her into the mud—even if it was an accident."

When the doctor looked dismayed at the words, Hazel hastened to add, "He truly didn't see me. We've had a talk about paying attention to our surroundings—and not chasing after dogs that don't want to be caught. I think the message sank in."

Mrs. Kehoe's eyes twinkled. "It sounds as though young Louie Murphy may have found his match. I was pleased to hear Ezra had hired you." She patted Hazel's arm. "You'll be an asset to this community."

"Well, if I can go more than a day or two without ending up in the mud, we might all have the chance to find out for certain." Hazel allowed a laugh at herself.

The woman's pleasant laughter joined Hazel's. "Will we see you at church on Sunday?"

"Yes, ma'am. If the reverend is sufficiently recovered."

"Well, thank you both for your help." Jennie opened the door. "I had best get my friend here home and settled in so I can go help Ma at the café."

Hazel followed her friend out the door after another quiet thank-you to the doctor and his wife.

Louie stood quickly as they stepped onto the porch. His eyes settled on Hazel's sling and widened. "Is it broke?"

"No," Hazel said, shaking her head. "Just a little sore. But I will be limited for the next few days, which means you will help me around the cabin."

He frowned. "Am I living with you now?" He said it as though he considered the very idea a punishment for this morning's transgressions.

"No. You'll just help with the chores I am unable to do."

"Like what?" He held on to Archie and turned away when Jennie reached for him. "Hey, respect my bounders."

Jennie's brow furrowed. "Boy, what are you talking about?"

With a scoff and a shake of his head, he rolled his eyes. "It means don't get too close when I don't want you to. My bounders." He gave Hazel a glance. "I don't think Miss Jennie's as smart as you."

Despite the lift in Hazel's heart at the camaraderie with the child, she knew her purpose for remaining in Tucker Springs included more than just keeping the boy out of trouble. He clearly needed a lot of instruction. "Louie, Miss Jennie is very accomplished. And smart."

To Louie's credit, he kept the dog close but not too tight, and Archie wasn't wiggling for freedom as they walked back to the cabin.

"I don't know about that, Miss Hazel. She didn't know about bounders."

Hazel opened her mouth to try again, but Jennie held up her hand. "Allow me." Then she turned back to Louie. "For your information, little guy, I went as far in public school as was possible. As far as you will go, for that matter—if Miss Stewart ever deems you worthy of attending again."

"I don't want to go. Miss Hazel can teach me lots more."

"Like bounders, you mean?"

"Yep."

She cast a sidelong glance at Hazel. "May I?"

Hazel nodded. "Be my guest."

"I'd wager that Miss Hazel didn't use the word *bounders*. I would guess, rather, that she said *boundaries*."

"No." Louie gave a sharp intake of air. "Oh. Yeah."

"Louie," Hazel said, turning to look at him. "You owe Miss Jennie an apology for the disrespectful way that you spoke to her."

"I do?"

"I'm afraid so. It's unkind to say that someone's not smart. And you should always apologize if you've said or done something to hurt someone's feelings—especially someone who has always been very good to you, as I know Miss Jennie has. Please, let's remedy the issue before we arrive at the cabin. It'll be one less thing to attend to this afternoon."

"I'm sorry for saying you ain't as smart as Miss Hazel." He paused, then apparently hadn't finished with what he wanted to say. He turned to Hazel. "Is it okay if I keep thinking she's not as smart as you are as long as I don't tell her so?"

Jennie guffawed. "I'm probably not as educated or as intelligent as your nanny. I'll give you that one all for free." She shook her head. "Just watch how you talk to me, little man, or I'll string you up by your toes like a piece of meat."

Louie giggled. "And roast me on a spit like one of Mr. Bohannon's pigs?"

"You better believe it!"

When they arrived back at the cabin, the distinct sound of clucking reached Hazel's ears. "What on earth? When did I get chickens?"

Jennie shrugged, chuckling. "Your guess is as good as mine."

Louie groaned. "I hate chickens!"

Hazel cast a sidelong glance at Jennie and grinned.

Jennie grinned back, nodding. "Sounds like we just figured out Louie's chores."

Chapter Eight

Miz Caroline grabbed Hazel's arm the second she walked into the bustling café later that week with Louie at her side. "Oh, Hazel. I'm so glad you're here." She set two heaping plates of bread on two respective tables. "Come with me. I need a big favor. Wait!"

Hazel stopped and stared at the frazzled woman. "Yes?"

"How is that arm? Can you carry a crate of food?"

"It's just a bit sore. But I'm fine. Where did all these people come from, anyway?" She followed Miz Caroline's heavy steps into the kitchen.

"It's festival week, not to mention the men are taking turns today fixing the church roof after what happened to the reverend."

"Festival week?"

"Yes, we usually have our harvest festival the second week in October. But this year, all the rain postponed it. I voted we cancel it altogether this year. But I got outvoted, so here we are just days before the festival, and it's chaotic around here."

"Oh no! I wonder why Louie hasn't mentioned the festival."

"Who knows what that child is thinking?"

Lifting a crate filled with food, Miz Caroline shoved it into Hazel's arms. The smell of wafted to her nose, and her stomach growled.

"Caroline," Mr. Will hollered. "Stop blathering and get these plates out to the Bohannons. You're getting backed up!"

With a huff, she turned to her husband. "I'm getting things out as fast as I can."

"Where's Bess?" His bellow echoed off the walls.

"I'm here, Pa. They can hear you a mile away."

"Stop making eyes at Charles Lowe and help your ma."

The pretty girl's cheeks bloomed under her father's correction. She grabbed a plate in each hand and left the kitchen.

"Miz Caroline," Hazel said, glancing from wall to wall. "Where is Jennie?"

"Oh, of all the days for that daughter of mine to wake up too sick to get out of bed." She shook her head. "Bess tries, bless her heart. You'd think with ten children, I'd have plenty of help here."

"Oh no. Poor Jennie. What can I do to help out?" Hazel hated that her new friend was ill. But that explained the crate. "Shall Louie and I run this food out to your place and check on her?"

"What?" Miz Caroline grabbed up a plate and rested it far back on her long arms. Then she loaded up two more plates and grabbed another with her free hand.

"No, no. She'll be fine. Likely just the sniffles. This crate isn't for her—it's for the reverend."

Alarm seized Hazel's stomach. "The reverend? You mean take this to the parsonage?" The parsonage where Benjamin and Ivy Gordon lived with Reverend Harper.

"Oh, Hazel. Don't stare at me like I've asked you to dig up a body. Ben's working on the church with Clay Willow, and Ivy is putting up apples with Gilly Bauer. They're baking streusel or something for the festival on Saturday. Like some of us have time to bake anything to enter into the contest." She shook her head without waiting for Hazel to agree to the delivery.

Feeling a tug on the arm of her dress, she looked down into a pair of narrowed brown eyes. "I reckon we ain't eating for a while?" Louie asked.

Hazel shook her head. She had been looking forward to a nice lunch herself. She'd tried to fry Louie a slice of ham to eat along with the last of the corn muffins and beans she still had from Saturday, but she'd burned the meat too badly for the child to even pretend to eat.

Ezra entered the café as they walked out of the kitchen. He frowned in confusion even as his lips curved into a smile when he spied them. "What are you two doing here?"

"She burned lunch."

Hazel gasped. "Louis Murphy! That was supposed to be our secret."

Louie shrugged, but Hazel couldn't help but notice the look that passed between father and son. A knowing sort of look that embarrassed her. Apparently, her poor cooking skills were already a topic of conversation between the two of them.

She shook her head and let out a laugh. "At least Archie wasn't too proud to eat my pitiful attempt to make an edible meal."

Ezra chuckled but looked curiously at the crate. "May I help?"

"I've got this, but would you mind awfully if I ask you to keep Louie with you and get him some lunch?"

"I'd be happy to. What about you?"

"Miz Caroline asked me to take this to the reverend."

His eyes widened. "Oh? And you're going to?"

Clearly, she wasn't as much of a closed book as she'd hoped to be, if he could see that she was uncomfortable with the idea. Hazel wasn't sure how she felt about a stranger being able to read her as well as Mr. Murphy did. As uncomfortable as she was with the idea that he was scrutinizing her motives, there was an odd bit of happiness at the thought of someone paying such close attention to her thoughts and feelings. She shrugged. "Miz Caroline assured me that the reverend is alone today, so there is no danger of running into anyone I'd rather avoid for now."

"Hazel!" Miz Caroline brushed by her. "Either take the food to the reverend or don't, but, honey, please don't just stand there in the way. I might run you clean over."

"I'm going right this second."

Without another word, she walked toward the door. The banker, Mr. Lowe, tipped his bowler hat and held the door as she breathed a quick thank-you and headed toward the church at the edge of town. The smell of baking wafted to her from the crate, a much more pleasant aroma than the stench of Mr. Bohannon's hogs, which still lingered faintly in the air even days after he removed the animals from the middle of town.

It wasn't much farther to the church, and Hazel enjoyed the cool autumn day as she walked the rest of the way to the parsonage. She noticed several men on the roof. Her stomach dropped as she saw Benjamin looking at her. Hazel watched in horror as he startled, losing his grip on his hammer, which thudded on the roof and began to slide.

"Move out of the way!" She heard the voice, but for the life of her, Hazel couldn't take her gaze away from the hammer that had picked up speed on the slanted roof and was coming right toward her.

Strong arms grabbed her and pulled her back just as the hammer landed, with a thud, in the dirt.

"Are you all right?"

Hazel nodded, trying to catch her breath as she imagined what a hammer might have done to her head if someone hadn't hurried to save her.

She frowned. Who was that someone, anyway? She looked up—way up—into a pair of concerned brown eyes. Not beautiful, soft, large brown eyes rimmed with thick eyelashes like Mr. Murphy's, but still kind. "Thank you." She drew in a shaky breath and expelled it. "I don't know what got into me."

"Well, I'm just glad I was here." The man took off his hat. His brown hair was a bit thin, and Hazel guessed him to be late thirties to early forties. "Clay Willow."

"It's nice to meet you, Mr. Willow. I'm Hazel O'Brien."

"Likewise, Miss O'Brien."

In the awkwardness that followed, Hazel surprised herself by saying, "Call me Hazel. I mean, the first time you laid eyes on me, you saved my neck."

"My honor. And I have a confession to make…"

"I see…"

"It's not the first time I've laid eyes on you. I own the mill across the street and just down a little from the general store and Avery's Café." His eyes traveled to her hair. "It's hard to miss you. No one else around here has hair like that."

Long ago, her red hair was a source of embarrassment and annoyance if anyone mentioned it, but Hazel had resigned herself to being, if not unique, certainly not commonplace, so she gave a small laugh. "I'm sure it is. Well, Mr. Willow, I'm on a mission of mercy to the reverend, so I'll say goodbye, but thank you again for saving me. I don't know how to repay you."

His eyes twinkled, and he gave her a crooked grin. "If I can make a suggestion, I know how you could repay me."

"Oh?" Hazel asked. Guarded, she narrowed her gaze. "How's that?"

"First, call me Clay, and I won't feel so awkward about calling you Hazel. Even though I did just save your pretty head."

Hazel laughed, though the "pretty" comment sent a flush across her cheeks. "Very well, Clay. But truly, I must go. I don't want to keep the reverend waiting for his lunch."

"I'll walk with you," Clay said.

And he did without waiting for agreement from Hazel. Still, she wasn't offended. He seemed like a nice man.

"So that second thing you could do to repay me…"

"Yes?" she asked, again guarded as his voice trailed off.

"I would be honored to escort you to the festival on Saturday." He hesitated for a split second before continuing. "That is, if you and Ezra aren't…"

"Why, no. Mr. Murphy hasn't said a word. But I am not required to look after Louie on Saturdays."

"I see. I don't want to step on another man's territory, if you get my meaning?"

"Oh!" His *meaning* was suddenly abundantly clear. "First of all, Mr. Willow, I am no one's *territory* to be stepped on or otherwise. And second of all, Mr. Murphy is my employer and nothing more."

"Then you are free to accompany me?"

Exasperated, she gave a huff. "Of course I am free to accompany you, Mr. Willow. Didn't I just say so?"

"Good! I'll see you Saturday at eight thirty. You bring us lunch. Did I mention I have two children?"

Movement from the corner of her eye caught Hazel's attention before she could tell Clay that while she was free to accompany him, she wasn't sure she had any desire to do so, no matter how grateful she was for his help earlier. Pushing her out of the way of injury didn't entitle him to order her to cook for him and his family. While he spoke, she shot her gaze to the movement, a flash of hair the same color as hers. A man ducking behind the church. He stopped, and she met his gaze.

He wasn't exactly the way she remembered him, so she couldn't be sure. It was preposterous to even think about it. But was it... "Pa?"

"That's right, I'm a pa."

Annoyed, Hazel jerked her attention back to the man who had stepped in front of her.

"I best get back to work on the church before Ben drops another hammer."

"All right," Hazel said, glancing around him, trying to see the man again.

"So, Saturday at eight thirty?"

Oh, would he just go away? "Yes, yes. Fine. I'll see you then, Mr. Willow."

"Clay."

"Yes, yes. Goodbye, Clay."

It wasn't until she had delivered the reverend's lunch and was walking back toward the café to collect Louie that she realized she had agreed to allow that man to escort her to the festival. But then again, if other folks were assuming there was more to her relationship with Mr. Murphy than what it was, perhaps this would stop any rumors before they could start to fly.

Ezra and Louie were still eating lunch and discussing the harvest festival when Miss O'Brien returned to the café. It seemed Louie remembered last year, but not the year before. Ezra stood and held a seat for her. "Miz Caroline boxed up some lunch and a couple of apple fritters for you to take back. She said it's her treat to thank you for taking the food to the reverend."

"Thank you, Mr. Murphy," she said, a little breathlessly.

"Everything all right?"

She nodded. "I'm afraid I've been rather sedentary since coming here. It felt good to walk around, but I'm a bit out of practice. When I worked for the Wells family, the children and I walked every day for exercise—per Mr. Wells's orders." She laughed. "I can't tell you the number of times Jacob Wells—he's just a year older than you are, Louie—would start a game of tag, and of course they always wanted me to be the one to chase after them."

Her smile froze, and it appeared as though her eyes suddenly shimmered. Ezra drew in a sharp breath as he realized how much she truly loved the children she had once tended. How could she have left them behind?

He glanced at Louie. The boy's gaze was on his nanny in sort of a wondrous pondering of the story she had just told. Was he picturing himself with siblings running after Miss O'Brien, getting attached to her the way the Wells children had? Was it a good thing he was doing here? Letting this woman, who would be leaving in the spring, into his son's heart? A son who longed for a mother.

"What else did those children do?"

"Well, let's see. We played ball. And we read books. Lots and lots of books. And of course, there were lessons. And they loved to sing songs." Her eyes lit up as she spoke.

"Did they feed chickens with you?"

Ezra realized with a start that Louie was jealous listening to her talk about the Wells children with such familiarity and tenderness.

Miss O'Brien grinned. "Chickens! Decidedly not. Only the cook handled chicken, and she certainly didn't feed them."

Louie's eyes grew wide. "What did she do with them?"

"Can you guess?"

"Did she cook them?"

"Yes, she did."

"Miss Hazel?" Louie's brown eyes filled with concern as he frowned.

"Yes?"

"Are you going to cook our chickens?"

Ezra caught his breath at the look of affection that swept across the nanny's face. This woman honestly liked Louie. It wasn't an act to encourage courtship on his part, as he'd observed with more than one woman. He waited to hear the answer to Louie's question.

"Dear boy, not one of our chickens will see the inside of a pot."

"Promise?"

"Louie, I do not need to promise to keep my word to you. You can trust me. Our chickens are going to be the fattest, most spoiled pet chickens anyone has ever seen." She laughed. "They will be like three fat queens sitting on their thrones. And if they deign to offer us eggs, we will thank them for their kind benevolence and back away as befitting royal subjects."

Ezra chuckled at the absurd description. "Then it's a

good thing your cold cellar is about to be loaded down with fresh pork."

"Pork?"

"Sure, it's just about hog-killing time. Several of the farmers take turns helping each other out. As a matter of fact, Robert Bohannon was first this year and he donated a couple of pigs to be roasted tomorrow for the festival."

Louie nodded vigorously. "The very best food is when Mr. Bohannon roasts a pig out on the spit." He frowned, narrowing his eyes. "You know what a spit is? I ain't talking about the kind that comes out of your mouth."

"Yes, I'm fully aware of the difference between the two. And for the record, one of them is disgusting and quite inappropriate to talk about—or demonstrate—in polite company. Particularly when you are eating." Her eyes twinkled even as her voice had shifted to a less teasing tone.

He frowned. "Oh! You probably mean the kind that comes out of your mouth."

"Precisely."

He hesitated, frowning, then drew in a breath. "What would you call polite company?" He pursed his lips and rocked back on two legs in the chair. Ezra was about to tell him to set the chair straight, but he didn't want to interrupt.

"Anywhere you are required to be on your best behavior. In other words, where you are expected to use your manners. Like school, as you've already discovered, and, for instance, an eating establishment."

He frowned. "What's an eating 'stablishment?'"

"Anywhere you eat in public and pay for it." She grinned. "Like this one."

"But I don't pay to eat here."

Ezra chuckled. "That's because I do. Fix your chair."

Louie seemed to take that in stride but he dropped his chair down on all four legs. He turned back to Miss O'Brien. "What about church?"

"Most definitely, church is a place for your best manners."

His eyes narrowed, and he pursed his lips before he heaved a sigh and found her gaze. "Henry Avery and me are supposed to have a spittin' contest after church on Sunday. But I reckon we can go back behind the church so no one sees us."

Miss O'Brien's face suddenly went pale. "I—I don't think you should go behind the church alone. Perhaps another venue for the spitting contest would be better."

"I don't see where."

"The festival, perhaps?"

Louie seemed to consider the suggestion. "I reckon I'll have to see what Henry has to say about that." He leveled a sincere gaze at her. "But I can't make any promises, except if we have to do it Sunday, we'll go in back where no one sees us bein' impolite."

"Well—" She smiled. "I agree going behind the church would be more appropriate than the alternative, so no one sees the disgusting game. Are you certain a contest of that sort is absolutely necessary?"

He nodded, the expression on his face somber. "It is. Henry challenged me. He'll call me a lily-livered coward if I don't show up." He breathed in a sigh—one that sounded long-suffering and made Hazel's lips turn upward. "He can't beat me, you know. I'm the town champion."

"The Tucker Springs champion spitter?"

He grinned proudly, once again pushing back on two chair legs. "Yep. Fannie Willow came close to beating me last summer at the Independence Day celebration, but I won, and she had to give me two cents her pa gave her for peppermint. Boy, did she bawl like a baby." He laughed and wiggled in the chair, nearly losing his balance.

Ezra reached over and steadied the chair. "Keep it on the floor before you knock it over."

"Yes, Pa."

Ezra sucked in his breath. Louie had been uncommonly well-behaved the last couple of days. What was Miss O'Brien doing to make the boy so compliant?

"Fannie Willow? Is she related to a man named Clay?"

Ezra's head shot up at the widower's name. "How do you know Clay Willow?"

"Why, I don't, really."

A wave of pink spread over her face. She was blushing over Clay Willow's name?

"Then..."

"Oh, well. If you must know, he pushed me out of the way before Benjamin Gordon's hammer fell on my head."

Ezra's throat went dry at the thought of her being

in harm's way. His ire rose. "Ben threw his hammer at you?"

"Obviously not. It fell from the roof where he was working."

Relieved, he smiled at his foolish jump to a faulty conclusion. "Then I suppose I should thank Clay for keeping you safe."

"I already did, obviously. But if you must, you can thank him at the festival. I will be…" She averted her gaze and let her words trail off. Ezra felt an odd sense that something wasn't quite right. But if she didn't want to share it with him, he wouldn't pressure her to do so. He was just her employer—he had no right to know her private business, as long as it didn't impact Louie.

"Mr. Clay is Fannie Willow's pa." Louie, clearly oblivious to the tense undertones of the previous couple of minutes, picked up where he and Miss O'Brien had left off. "And she's mighty pretty, but I still ain't gonna let her win a spitting contest."

Miss O'Brien reached over and pushed away a lock of hair from his eyes. "And any girl worth your attention wouldn't want you to lose on purpose. She would want to win fair and square. Although I must say, I have never seen a girl enter a spitting contest."

"Well, she's been wanting my hunting knife for a long time, and I told her she could have it if she won."

Talk about contests, and about what they could expect to see at the festival, got them through the rest of the meal. After they finished, Ezra was walking with Miss O'Brien and Louie along the boardwalk that would take them back to the cabin and him to the store when

Miss Tucker's carriage flashed by, nearly tipping on two wheels as it sped through town. "Mercy! What was that all about, I wonder?" Miss O'Brien said.

Ezra frowned. "That's Miss Tucker's carriage. But Smith's not driving it. That's odd."

"Why is that odd?" Miss O'Brien asked.

"Because Miss Tucker doesn't allow anyone else behind the reins. Smith has been her driver, butler, server, everything except her lady's maid and cook, for as long as I can remember. And his wife, Millie, does the cooking and helps tend to her personal needs."

"I hope nothing is wrong. I quite like Miss Tucker."

"You've met her?" Ezra knew he hadn't been with her every second, but when would she have had the opportunity? She hadn't even had a chance to attend church yet. But then, she was not being forthcoming about Clay, either. She might have many secrets that would surprise him.

"We rode together on the stagecoach." She smiled. "She told me she would remember me in a few years, when she is riding through town and sees a passel of redheaded children. That was less than a week ago."

"A lot can happen in a week."

She sighed. "It certainly can." They came to a halt in front of the entrance to the store.

"Well, we better get back to the cabin," Miss O'Brien stated. "Louie still has his sums to do today. Then he has to clean out the queens' throne room."

Louie laughed. Then he groaned as he realized what was in store.

Ezra grinned. "The chicken coop?"

"If that's what you wish to call it. At the palace, we will use its proper name." She grinned. "Shall we go, Prince Louie?"

"Do princes clean throne rooms?"

"Only the ones who want one of Miz Caroline's apple fritters."

He listened to the sound of laughter as she walked away and couldn't help but wish he was going with them.

Chapter Nine

Saturday finally rolled around, and Ezra breathed a sigh of relief as he watched Louie rush off to find Henry Avery at the festival. It had been a long week of anticipation and preparation. Though the temperature was a bit colder than usual for the harvest festival, the three-week delay hadn't seemed to discourage the day's turn-out. Wagons dotted the fields at Tillman's orchard, and a baseball game was already underway. The women would bring pies and jams to enter into contests, and there would be games and livestock for judging. Robert Bohannon had donated two hogs to be roasted. All in all, it would be a fine day. He had to grin as he remembered the entire spit conversation he'd had with Hazel and Louie. While he tried to remember to be respectful and formal when speaking to her, in the privacy of his thoughts, he was finding it harder and harder to think of Hazel as Miss O'Brien.

As far as he was concerned, the only flaw in the otherwise enjoyable day was Clay Willow. If he was being honest, it was not even the man himself who bothered him. The forty-year-old widower with two small children was a fine man, as far as Ezra knew from their limited interactions. He certainly couldn't fault the man for initiative. Willow did not let any grass grow under his feet before making the most of the fact that there was a new single woman in town. He had apparently invited Miss O'Brien to attend today's festivities with him and his children. When Ezra had casually asked her what time she would be ready for Louie and him to collect her to visit the festival together, her face had flushed and she'd told him in a soft voice that she already had an escort. Putting two and two together, he now understood her hesitation to discuss Clay at lunch the other day.

The thought had occurred to Ezra that he might want to court her. But he wasn't altogether certain what was proper what with her living in his cabin and taking care of his son. He wanted to avoid all appearance of evil, like the Bible instructed. But then, the Bible also mentioned that it was a good thing for a man to find a wife. Apparently, Clay thought the same thing and Ezra had waited too long.

So now here he stood pretending to observe the festival but actually inspecting the crowd for the only woman in town with red hair.

He spied them over by the target practice booth. He himself had donated a few doodads as prizes for the children who knocked down all the targets. He walked over just as Fannie Willow, Clay's six-year-old daughter, won the target practice. Her squeal of excitement brought a grin to his face, especially when she selected a doll from the shelf. "Pa, look!" she said. "It's the one you always said we can't afford."

Clay smiled at his daughter and patted her head, but it was clear the words embarrassed him. Especially said in front of a woman he was courting. "She's a beautiful doll," Hazel said. "Your pa must have taught you how to shoot like that."

Her words immediately brightened Clay's countenance. And by the time Ezra closed the short distance, Clay's smile had returned. "My late wife, Emily, made me promise to teach our daughter how to shoot. She said a woman can't always depend on a man to defend her."

"She sounds like she was a very wise woman." She looked down at Fannie and touched the girl's shoulder. "I know your mother would be very proud of your accomplishment today."

"Yes, ma'am." The girl beamed at Hazel, clearly pleased with the praise, before she turned to her pa. "I'm going to go show Clarie!"

Ezra's throat grew tight as he watched Miss O'Brien with another man's child. He had assumed her attention and affection toward Louie were indications of a special attachment. But perhaps she was fond of all children equally.

She smiled as he approached. "Good afternoon, Mr. Murphy. Clay's daughter just won the lovely doll you donated. Did you see?"

It was beginning to chafe the way Hazel felt free to call other men by their first names but persisted in calling him Mister. Still, he forced himself to smile politely. "I did. She's a good shot."

Clay chuckled. "She tried to get Hazel to take a shot."

Miss O'Brien laughed, as well. "I've never even held a gun—I'd be more likely to shoot my own foot than to hit a target."

Why did Clay just spout off the name *Hazel* just like that, as though they hadn't just met?

"We are going to watch the baseball game," she said. "Would you care to join us, Mr. Murphy? Louie said he intends to play. Apparently, he is going to be the one to throw the ball to the batter. I believe he said it is called being the pitcher."

It was difficult to be annoyed with her when she was choosing to go and encourage Louie even on her day off. "Yes, he loves pitching. He tosses anything with even the hint of a round shape at the fence posts. He hits whatever he's aiming at about every time."

They chatted for another minute about the rules of baseball. Hazel had little understanding of the game, but she had a quick mind and grasped the rules easily once they were explained. It would have almost been a pleasant conversation if he hadn't been irked by the way Clay hovered at her elbow. When the couple—if they could be called that—invited him again to head over to the field where the game would be played, Ezra demurred.

"I'll be over in a few minutes. I want to speak to the sheriff first."

He watched as they walked away together. Clay offered his arm…and Hazel put her hand in the crook of his elbow.

"Oh, you are not at all happy with that scene."

The sound of Jennie's voice drew his head around. She stood with a candied apple in her hand and a grin on her lips. He was just annoyed enough, he wouldn't inform her that she had a spot of red on her nose. "Don't be ridiculous. I thought you were sick."

"I got better. Sorry to disappoint you." She smirked. "If you were any more jealous of Clay at this moment, your face would be the color of Gilly Bauer's pea soup."

He scowled. She was right, of course, but Ezra had no intention of admitting that he was starting to think of Miss O'Brien as a little more than Louie's nanny. "You're insane."

"I heard Miss Joy say that Mrs. Kehoe told her that Clay's ma came in to have a tooth pulled by the doc yesterday, and she said that Clay was looking for a wife and thought Hazel was just about the prettiest thing he'd ever laid his eyes on."

"What of it?"

"What indeed?" She laughed and turned as Micah came upon them and handed her a drink. "Did you give Ezra the good news?"

Jennie blushed and shook her head. "Not yet."

Ezra looked from Jennie to Micah. "What good news?"

A grin spread across Micah's face. "Jennie agreed to become my wife." He took her hand. "Her pa gave his blessing last night."

Ezra shook Micah's hand then engulfed Jennie in a bear hug, lifting her off her feet.

"Ugh. I can't breathe," she complained.

Ezra set her down and grinned. "Congratulations. When's the big day?"

"As soon as I can get my dress made," Jennie said. "And Micah wants to catch the thief first, so that nothing interferes with our day."

Ezra nodded soberly and addressed the sheriff.

"Not to throw a wet blanket on your good news, but any news about who waylaid Smith at Miss Tucker's?" Apparently, the sixty-year-old butler had come upon the thief breaking in through one of the upstairs windows. He had been shoved back hard enough to fall down the stairs. Thankfully, Mrs. Smith had found him not long after, and he'd received immediate medical care. His concussion and broken leg were serious injuries, but he was expected to make a nearly full recovery, given enough time.

"It's just awful," Jennie said. "He was unconscious until last night. Doc Kehoe said that at Smith's age, he'll be laid up for a long time."

Micah shook his head. "No leads so far. I've sent word as far as Iowa City about all the things that have been stolen, but if the thief is still around here, it's unlikely he's tried to resell anything—there would be too great a chance of the stolen items being recognized."

Ezra sighed, disappointed that there wasn't more news. "I think I'll go tell Haz—Miss O'Brien about Smith. She knows Miss Tucker and has been concerned."

When he turned, he saw Miss O'Brien speaking to a belligerent Louie. The boy stomped off and she looked flabbergasted as she looked after him, shaking her head, her hands on her hips. Clay stepped up and said something to her. She touched his arm but shook her head and followed Louie.

Ezra caught Clay's stormy gaze as he turned away from her. Clay scowled at him then continued watching the game.

Hazel caught up to Louie easily despite his attempt to escape. "Louie!" He stopped and turned, his brown eyes flashing. "You must go back to the game."

"No!" He stomped the ground with his boot, then kicked the loose dirt with this toe. "You saw. They won't let me pitch."

"I'm sure they want someone bigger. Your time will come, Louie."

He sneered. "Aw, what do you know? You're just a girl."

She shrugged. "Perhaps, but you are being a very sore sport. I'm disappointed in your behavior. I thought you were better than this."

"Everything okay here?"

Hazel turned to see Mr. Murphy had joined them. "Not exactly. But we are discussing the situation."

"Well?" He turned to Louie. "What happened? Why aren't you playing the game?"

Louie clamped his lips together as he looked at his pa, clearly trying to decide if he wanted to risk sharing the details. "It's a dumb game. I got tired of it." He was avoiding eye contact, squirming as though he had ants in his pants. Even if she hadn't seen it happen, she would have known he was lying, which only compounded Hazel's disappointment. Bad behavior was never acceptable—but lying about it only added another wrong on top of the pile. Hazel gathered in a breath and exhaled. She didn't want to tattle on the child. She had hoped he would be forthcoming with his father and tell him what had occurred, the way he had behaved. But if he would not be forthright, then she would have to be. She assumed Mr. Murphy would ask her and turned expectantly. Instead, he nodded. "Well, I reckon it's not a game for everyone. There's a target shoot over there. Fannie won a doll."

Louie scowled. "I don't want a doll."

Ezra chuckled. "I didn't suppose you did. But it might interest you to know that I saw a set of painted soldiers as a prize. You liked the ones Miz Caroline ordered for Henry's birthday, right?"

Louie's eyes brightened, and he grinned broadly. "I'm going to win 'em!"

Ezra chuckled as he watched the boy run back toward the target shoot.

Exasperated, Hazel shook her head. Was the man really not going to follow up, ask what happened, address the problem of Louie's temper and his poor behavior? Apparently not. Mr. Murphy was still grinning when he turned back to her. As he met her gaze, his smile disappeared. "What? Are you angry?"

With a huff, Hazel turned and walked away. "Angry? Why should I be angry? The boy made a spectacle of himself by shouting at Mr. Rubles for refusing to let him pitch."

Mr. Murphy's brow furrowed. "Did he say why Louie couldn't pitch? He's pretty good."

Shrugging, and disappointed that he was focusing on Mr. Rubles rather than Louie's inappropriate reaction, Hazel hesitated before responding. She might be the nanny and not the mother, but if she were to remain Louie's nanny, Ezra needed to be aware of her beliefs about indulging tantrums. "The other players are older. Bigger. I'm sure Mr. Rubles didn't want Louie to be hurt. He offered to let him play outfield, and he even said he can bat. Louie's response was to throw a fit, yell at Mr. Rubles and storm away. And then just now, when you asked him about it, he lied—badly and transparently—but you let him get away with it."

Mr. Murphy's face reddened. "Oh. Well, maybe I can talk to him later."

"Yes, I suppose that's better than nothing." Hazel spun on her heel and started to walk away.

"Wait. Hazel! What is it?" She felt his hand wrap around her arm to stop her. "I said I'd talk to him."

With a sigh, she turned. "Mr. Murphy, the time to discipline is in the moment. Good character isn't born into a person, it is grown. I hope you do speak to Louie later, but allowing him to behave so poorly and then rewarding him with another game, without making him explain what happened or helping him see how his earlier behavior was wrong, is simply not the way a man of character is grown."

From a grove of apple trees at the edge of the field that Mr. Tillman had cleared for the festival came a familiar, mocking laugh. She shot a look over Ezra's shoulder. A flash of movement and then a man's back as he walked away caught her attention. The red hair on the retreating man's head sent a wave of dread and nearly panic through her. Surely not— *Oh, please, Lord. Don't let it be Pa.* He had always said she couldn't go far enough to hide from him if he truly wanted to find her. Had he made good on that? If so, why on earth did he want to find her? Or were her eyes playing tricks on her, showing her what she feared most to see? Yes, surely that had to be it. What on Earth would Pa be doing out here?

"Hazel," Ezra said.

His voice brought her gaze back to his.

"I know you disagree with my parenting style. But Louie is my son. I've been raising him without a mother. Maybe you could show some compassion."

She let out a tired sigh. "I do have compassion—for Louie, most of all. I know what it is to be a motherless child, and I have great compassion for him on that score. But I also have compassion for those who must endure the antics and tantrums of that child. Compassion for the people who must endure him when he becomes a man without learning how to behave. And I have compassion for you, Mr. Murphy."

"Me?"

His voice still held an edge, so Hazel chose her words carefully.

"I have compassion for your situation as you raise him alone. But I also have compassion for you because you worry so much that Louie will not know he is loved by you."

"Doesn't every parent?"

Her mind flashed to the red-haired mystery man. "Not all. But the good ones do want their children to know they are loved."

"Well, then?"

"I've seen you with Louie. I've seen the way you hesitate to correct him, hesitate to do anything to cause him to frown. It's commendable that you want his happiness above all, but I fear you're shortchanging him in the long run by not teaching him the consequences of his actions now, while he's young enough to change. If he does not learn now how to control the behaviors that anger or alienate people, then his future will be bleak indeed. He'll struggle to hold on to friends, to find honorable work, to be a member of a true community if he does not learn to govern his temper and his tongue. If he does not learn from *you* that those behaviors are not acceptable. God disciplines those He loves."

Hazel hesitated, then realized that even if it meant she would lose the position as Louie's nanny, Mr. Murphy must know what she believed about the situation. "You may not believe it is my place, and perhaps it is not, but a parent doesn't show love through indulgences, but by discipline."

"So, you think I should yell at him or beat him? Treat him the way my pa…"

Hazel narrowed her gaze, wishing she had the courage to ask him to finish his sentence, but the meaning was all too clear. His father had been too harsh, so he was the opposite, too lenient. "I would never encourage the mistreatment of a child. *Any* child. But there must be consequences of some sort for bad behavior. That fact is just part of life. If I do wrong, I am corrected. If I steal, wouldn't I go to jail?"

Mr. Murphy scoffed. "You are comparing a six-year-old behaving badly in a game to a thief?"

"You know I am not. I'm saying children must be taught to behave well even in situations they don't like so that when they grow up, they don't feel they have the right to behave badly and get away with it." She narrowed her gaze. "Wouldn't you agree?"

"Pa!" Louie stomped toward them, red-faced.

"You didn't win the soldiers?"

"No. I missed."

"Well, maybe you'll get them for Christmas." He reached into his pocket and pulled out a couple of coins. "Here, go get an apple fritter from Miss Jennie's booth."

Hazel knew it would be useless to argue further, so she nodded and excused herself. She wished she could just as easily excuse her thoughts from Louie and his stubborn pa, but the rest of the day she found herself replaying how she might have handled it differently and whether she'd ever truly be able to teach Louie if his father also refused to learn.

Chapter Ten

A week after the festival, it seemed as though God had snapped His fingers, turning the air from cool to cold. Louie's lessons continued at a rapid pace. Though the boy hadn't apologized for his poor behavior on the day of the festival, he had been obedient in their time together and not only did his chores but threw himself into his schoolwork. He was learning at a steady rate above other children Hazel had taught.

They had settled into a routine where Louie had clear, consistent responsibilities and knew the consequences if he shirked them. Once he'd fully understood that throwing a fit didn't ease the punishment but actually increased it, the tantrums had stopped. He'd also relaxed a bit after learning that Hazel would not turn her own temper on him, even when he misbehaved.

She had no idea how he fared at home, as since the festival, Mr. Murphy rarely spoke beyond pleasantries unless there was something of relevance to say.

On Wednesday morning almost three weeks after her

arrival, Hazel went about her morning routine, fixing breakfast—through Miz Caroline's detailed instructions and recipes, she had learned to make flapjacks, biscuits, eggs the way Louie liked them, bacon, ham and apple muffins. Normally, Louie arrived when she was almost finished cooking. That way he had a warm breakfast that was still fresh. But this morning, the eggs, ham and biscuits were finished, and he still hadn't arrived. She spooned his food onto his favorite plate and set it next to the stove to stay warm.

She added a log to the fireplace and gave it a nudge with the poker to give herself something to do while she waited, and still they had not arrived. She shoved away images of some disaster—a house fire or an injury. Her ears stayed alert, listening for Archie's bark. The dog had made himself at home. He didn't even mind his baths anymore, and if Hazel were honest, she agreed with Louie: Archie was just the best dog in the world.

She glanced at the clock again. If they didn't show themselves in five minutes, she was going to find them.

Finally, at half past eight, she heard the telltale bark and flew to the door. Archie shot inside the second she flung the door open. Louie stomped in after him without a word to her. Not even "good morning." And his cheeks were streaked with tears. "What happened?"

Her heart sped up as Ezra walked to the door. His face was clouded over and tense with anger. "Mr. Murphy?"

He scowled. "Will you stop calling me Mr. Murphy? It's getting ridiculous. You do know I have a first name, just like *Clay*, for instance. And *Wyatt*."

Tilting her head, Hazel narrowed her gaze and looked up into his stormy eyes. Without a word, she snatched her heavy shawl from the hook by the door and walked out onto the porch, motioning for him to accompany her.

Clearly taking her cue, Ezra paused. "I'm leaving, now, Louie. I love you."

Stone-cold silence responded. Although Hazel's instinct was to insist that Louie return the endearing words, she had determined to stop trying to force the proper relationship she wanted them to display. Ezra was the child's father, after all.

With a heavy sigh, he stepped out onto the porch. "I'm sorry I snapped at you."

Hazel reached around him and pulled the door closed. "*Mr.* Murphy," she said with emphasis. "I didn't know my use of your name annoyed you. And yes, I am fully aware that you have a first name, just like Clay and Wyatt. And Micah, the sheriff, and Chester, the blacksmith. But those men are not my employers. You are free to call me Hazel if you choose. But as I am in your employ, it would be improper for me to call you Ezra." Even if she had started to think of him that way, in the privacy of her own thoughts. She lifted her eyebrows and met his gaze, and when her eyes briefly drifted to his soft, full mouth, she pressed her lips together and forced her eyes upward, but it was too late. He had noticed. Hazel's cheeks bloomed under his scrutiny, and she saw him flush, as well.

"I have to get to the store. I'm already late," he said abruptly.

"I understand. But before you leave, please tell me what happened with Louie this morning."

"I found a stash of food in a potato sack under his bed. I can't convince him to tell me why he had it—or why he kept it hidden. Do you think you could try to get it out of him?"

"I'll try." Her first two months at the Wellses' house, she had hidden food. But Louie's reasons surely weren't the same as hers had been. She'd stored food because she had known what it was to be hungry and had feared it happening again. And she stopped storing it when the children's maid discovered it and told her that food under the bed would draw rats.

He nodded. "If you can figure it out, I'd be glad to hear your findings. He cried when I took the bag from him. But there were canned goods, candy, bread that Miz Caroline baked yesterday and sent home. It makes no sense to me at all." A brisk wind fell across the porch. Hazel shivered and pulled the shawl closer about her. The gesture didn't go unnoticed by Ezra. He took two steps toward her and, reaching around, grabbed the latch.

"Wait." She placed her hand over his to stop the door from opening. He was too close—she couldn't think. "Mr. Murphy, I have the door." He stepped back, thankfully. Trying to ignore the tension between them, she gathered a shuddering breath. "I don't know why a child as well cared for as Louie would store food away, but I'll do my best to discover his reason. I'm sure he believes it is prudent."

Ezra narrowed his gaze. "I expected you to suggest discipline."

Stung, Hazel met his gaze head-on. "Well, it may be needed by you, but I have no cause for complaint. He didn't take food from me. Even so, I would never punish a child without getting to the reason for his behavior in the first place. I may be strict, but I am not unjust, nor am I a bully."

A sheepish smile tipped the corners of his lips. "I'm sorry. That wasn't fair, was it?"

It was a very lovely smile. Perhaps that was why she felt herself softening, wanting to extend an olive branch. "Mr. Murphy, I'm sorry you have had a difficult morning. Would you care to eat breakfast here with Louie?"

He hesitated, and Hazel's cheeks warmed. "Of course. I'm sure the Averys are expecting you."

A maddening smile tilted his lips. "If I weren't running so late, I would be pleased to stay and eat, *Hazel*. But the truth is that I won't even have time to stop for breakfast today. It's time to open the store."

Hazel smiled. Apparently, Ezra had decided to accept her invitation to use her first name.

"And by the way, *Hazel*. Louie says your cooking is getting really good."

"He does?"

He nodded. "I guess all those recipes from Miz Caroline are paying off."

That and a couple of hands-on lessons in the café. Still, Hazel's heart lifted at the praise. She tried not to show the way her heart was also lifting at the sound of her name spoken so sweetly.

Ezra's smile turned teasing as he leaned in to add, "He said he doesn't give his lunch to Archie hardly ever anymore."

"To Archie!" She planted her hands onto her hips. "No wonder that dog is getting so fat."

"I best be going." He smiled and winked at her. "Hazel. Oh, by the way. Tillman was in the store yesterday. He said there are more fresh apples on the ground from the wind we had over the weekend. He'd be pleased for all the ladies wanting to put up more apples to ride on out and pick them up off the ground so they don't rot."

"Oh, that would be wonderful. Miz Caroline promised to show me how to dry apples for pies over the winter. If you don't mind, Louie and I will go this afternoon."

"Sounds good. Head over to the livery whenever you're ready, and they'll hitch up my wagon for you."

She opened her mouth to protest that they could walk, but he held up his hand. "I insist."

Louie was already eating when she got back into the warm kitchen. "Oh, good. You found your plate. I was worried about you since you weren't here at the usual time."

He shrugged. "You ain't mad that I helped myself?"

Usually, she didn't allow him to get things without asking. But in this case, she had set the plate out for him. And she had been outside. "You clearly knew the plate was yours, so no, I'm not angry." She refrained from asking why, if he had thought she might be mad, he had taken the plate anyway.

"So, if food is yours and you take it, that ain't stealing, right?"

Caution made her still for a moment, remembering what Ezra had said about the hidden food. She had a feeling he was trying to make a point and wanted her on his side. Sometimes, Louie's intelligence was a challenge. "Well, that food on your plate is yours and it was obvious it was intended for you, so when you took it from the stove, no, it wasn't stealing." She narrowed her gaze and poured water into the pot to warm for dishes. "Why are you talking about stealing?"

He shrugged. "I don't know."

"I think you do. Won't you tell me what is troubling you?"

"May I just eat?"

Hazel bit back a smile. It was a calculated question on his part. She had been trying to convince him to use "may" instead of "can" when he asked permission. She decided to let the matter drop. He would tell her when he was ready.

By noon, he had completed all the lessons for the day and had cleaned out the coop. Though for the first time since they'd made their mysterious appearance, the queens hadn't produced one single egg among the three of them. Hazel determined to ask someone if it could be the drop in temperature disrupting their laying. As a matter of fact, the temperature seemed to have dropped even from this morning, and she wasn't keen on the idea of riding in the cold wagon for apples, after all.

But as she glanced at Louie, who was lying on his

stomach in front of the fire, running his fingers over the lines in the floor, she suddenly made a decision.

Hazel grabbed her coat and bonnet and tossed Louie his coat. "Wear your gloves," she said pulling on her own.

He frowned. "Did I do something wrong, Miss Hazel?"

"You, Mr. Murphy, did nothing wrong. You've been an excellent scholar this morning, and we've finished your lessons early in the day, so we are going on a jaunt."

"A jaunt?"

"An adventure. Grab those two baskets from the corner and follow me, please."

Louie slid into his coat, shoved his hat on his head and grabbed the baskets as she'd instructed.

Hazel still hadn't talked to Louie again about the bag of food he'd collected. But a jaunt seemed a good opportunity to discuss troubling things.

Ezra had just finished counting the dime books on the display for his monthly inventory when the bell jangled above the door. He looked up as the sheriff sauntered down the aisle. "What can I do for you, Micah?"

Absent his usual smile, Micah heaved a sigh and pulled off his hat as he approached the display. He glanced around and noticed Mrs. Green and Miss Joy staring without even attempting to pretend indifference. He lowered his voice to just above a whisper. "I was hoping you'd come with me."

"Where?"

"The thief tried to hit Miss Tucker's place again."

"Tried?"

The sheriff offered a wry grin. "Apparently, she ran him off."

"She? You don't mean Miss Tucker?"

"That's what James Rubles said."

Chester Rubles's son had been helping with the horses and other heavier tasks at Tucker's place with Smith laid up. Ezra frowned. "Did James say what the man looked like?"

"It happened last night, while he was at home. James showed up a little bit ago to clean out the barn and saw the mess. He came into town straightaway to report it."

Ezra had been so intent on what the sheriff had to say he had completely forgotten about the two sisters. But they had inched their way closer and closer. Mrs. Green had that look on her face that meant she was looking for a bit of "news" to print in her paper.

"Well, can you get away and come with me out to the old lady's house? She likes you a lot better than she does me."

"Don't tell me you're afraid of a seventy-year-old woman."

The corners of Micah's eyes crinkled. "Terrified. She's never much cared for me."

"Well, you did break into her chicken coop and set them free."

"I was ten. It was a dare. What was I supposed to do?"

"Jeremiah's helping out today, so I can leave for a while." Ezra untied his apron and hung it on the peg behind the counter before calling over his clerk to explain that he needed to step away for a while.

Mrs. Green pounced the second they reached the door. "So, Sheriff, what can you tell me about the robbery at the Tucker house?"

"Not a thing," Micah said. "We won't know any more than you do until we go out there. It might have been a misunderstanding."

"Or a simple prank by a schoolboy," Ezra said with a chuckle. "Say, if someone dared him."

"Fine," Mrs. Green said with a huff. "I'll accompany you."

"Sister!" Miss Joy chided. "Let the sheriff do his job."

"My readers deserve to know if there's been another theft."

Micah touched the woman on the arm as he looked down into her rosy face. "Mrs. Green, I appreciate your dedication to keeping the community informed. However, I wouldn't dream of risking your safety. With the thief running loose still, we just don't know what we'll be running into. But I give you my word, the instant I have a suspect in custody, I'll give you an exclusive interview and let you be the one to inform the readers of the *Chronicle*."

"Sister, that's a very generous offer." Miss Joy smiled. "If we ever decide to elect a mayor in Tucker Springs, I think you would be the obvious candidate, Sheriff."

Mrs. Green huffed. "If anyone is going to be the first

mayor of this town, it'll be Mr. Green." She narrowed her gaze. "I'll be holding you to that promise, Sheriff."

"Should we take your wagon?" Micah asked.

Ezra groaned as they stepped out of the store. "Oh, I left the wagon for Hazel to take Louie to get apples."

"First names, huh?"

"Just me. She won't budge on calling me Ezra, but she doesn't mind if I call her by her first name."

Micah shook his head. "Women are a mystery."

"That they are. I ordered some new furniture from Wyatt for the cabin. When I dropped it off the other evening, you would have thought I had given her a mansion like Miss Tucker's. I thought she was going to cry."

Micah chuckled. "Jennie teared up when I picked her some yellow wildflowers and brought them to her. Turns out she wasn't being sentimental, though. The flowers made her nose run." He motioned to Ezra. "Come on over to the livery with me. I'm sure we can borrow a horse for you."

As they headed down the boardwalk, Ezra gave Micah a sidelong glance. "Are you really going to give Mrs. Green an interview after you arrest the thief or thieves?"

A wry grin spread across Micah's face. "My mayoral opponent's wife? If only I hadn't promised before I entered the race, now I'm bound by my word."

It didn't take long for them to get to the livery and rent some horses. Soon, they were on the road to Miss Tucker's home.

The wind whipped across Ezra's neck, a cold gust with an almost icy feel to it. He pulled his collar up closer to his ears. "Is it just me, or does it feel colder than it did this morning?"

"Maybe."

"I hope Hazel and Louie bundled up riding out to Tillman's. She's not used to Iowa winters. I wonder if she's prepared." He turned his gaze to Micah to find his old friend watching him with a knowing look. "What? I'm just concerned."

"Sure, sure. It's just nice to see you show such… *concern* for a woman. To be honest, I'm just glad you never had eyes for my Jennie."

Ezra wanted to laugh out loud. To him, the idea of a romantic relationship with Jennie was absurd. "Jennie has always been like a sister to me. And if John had come back—without Marie and Louie, of course—she would have been my sister in truth instead of just in spirit." Or would she have been? Everyone in town had expected it, but they'd been awfully young. She was only fifteen when he sneaked off to join up. And he was only eighteen. Maybe it had been puppy love rather than the kind of devotion you could build a lifetime on. But they'd never had a chance to find out. And for whatever reason, John had married Marie, instead.

"I won't speak ill of the dead. But John was plumb crazy marrying Marie when he knew Jennie was back here waiting for him, praying for him every night. I mean, Marie was good-looking and all, but she sure wasn't Jennie."

"I won't argue with you there," Ezra said. Jennie was one of the best people he knew. When she became a mother someday, he knew she'd never turn her back on her child the way Marie had. She would sooner cut off her right arm than do anything to hurt Louie. He was starting to believe that Hazel was the same.

"And I don't mind a woman with ambitions for herself. I ain't one of those men that feels like if a woman works she's making him look like an unfit provider."

"I'm happy you two are getting married. It's a good match."

Micah grinned and nodded. "I couldn't agree more."

Ezra laughed, and a cloud billowed from his lips. The temperature was most definitely falling. Again, his thoughts went to Hazel. He knew Louie had a warm coat, scarf and gloves. But Ezra wondered about her.

Miss Tucker was sitting on the porch, rocking in a white wicker chair, a shotgun lying across her lap. For the first time since he'd known her, she wasn't wearing a fancy getup. She wore a simple linsey-woolsey gown with no frills or ribbon or silks and satins. Even her signature pearls were absent.

"I hope that shotgun isn't for my benefit," Micah said.

"No, it is not," she scowled. "But what are you doing here?"

"We heard there was a bit of commotion last night. Want to tell me what happened?"

"No need. I ran him off."

Micah and Ezra exchanged a look. "That's admirable, Miss Tucker," Ezra said diplomatically. "But unless you tied him up and tossed him in the cellar, he's still running free."

"Believe you me, I could just as easily catch that

scoundrel as your so-called sheriff here." She glared at Micah. "Once a thief, always a thief, as far as I'm concerned."

This was getting them nowhere, and every time the wind whipped through the long porch, it sliced into Ezra. He had no doubt that even with a heavy coat and a thick quilt over her lap, Miss Tucker was feeling the cold even more than he was.

"Now, Miss Tucker," he said. "Micah's been the sheriff for five years."

"That was not my doing. I said when you people elected him, that you'd rue the day. Well, I reckon you're ruing it now, aren't you?" She leveled that stern gaze at him, and the only thing Ezra was ruing was standing up for Micah in the first place and gaining her sharp tongue. But no, he wouldn't cower before a few harsh words. He was a grown man. They both were. "Miss Tucker," he said. "Now, I have to say with all due respect—Sheriff Lane is no thief. But the man who attacked your home is very much a thief. He is also violent, and I don't want him coming back here and hurting you. Look what he did to Smith. So, don't you think you need to tell us anything you can remember about the thief? That way we can go after him."

"You do not have to tell me what that man did. Smith has been with me for forty years, and he's…" Her voice trembled, and she cleared her throat, furiously blinking back tears. "Why do you think I'm waiting right here? That man will be back. This big house is like a moth to a flame for every ne'er-do-well and petty thief in the territory. But I can promise you this, the next time he shows up, I won't miss." She pointed at a spot just beyond the porch. Ezra followed the length of her gnarled finger, and his eyes grew wide. She'd shot the head right off the statue old Mr. Tucker had erected of the great George Washington.

The door opened, and Mrs. Smith, the sweet white-haired wife of Miss Tucker's ever-present servant, stood in the doorway. Miss Tucker turned, her expression a sudden wash of worry. "What is it, Millie? Is Smith all right? Does he need me?"

A gentle but clearly exhausted smile spread across the woman's face. "No, ma'am. But he wanted me to tell you to stop being…I'm so sorry, ma'am, but these are his exact words…to stop being ridiculous and get yourself in the house before you freeze to death."

Ezra turned to Micah, and his friend was struggling not to smirk.

"I suppose he's right." Miss Tucker turned a sharp gaze to Micah. "Young man, you find out who did this, or, I vow, I will use all of my influence to get you removed from your position."

"I'll do my best, Miss Tucker. I promise. But I need some information from you. Did you see what he looked like?"

Miss Tucker scowled. "Well, obviously I am not a bat. I cannot see in the dark. If I could, I would not have desecrated the image of poor Papa's favorite president, now would I? But I can recall that he was a tall man and very thin. Like President Lincoln—rest his blessed soul."

"All right." Ezra turned to Mrs. Smith and smiled. "How is Smith holding up, ma'am?"

She shook her head. "He is very grateful to be alive and very frustrated that he is not tending to Miss Tucker."

Miss Tucker waved away the words. "I'm not a garden—I don't need to be tended to. There's nothing I cannot do without until he's well enough to provide it, and if he finds there are some tasks he cannot handle anymore, then what of it? You and Smith are family, and this is your home for as long as you wish. I don't care if he never walks again. Now you go and tell him to stop fretting. I am going to come inside as soon as these men leave."

When Mrs. Smith returned to the house, Miss Tucker looked between Ezra and Micah. "Please let it be known discreetly that I am looking for some additional help. I am afraid Smith will not be able to return to service in the role he has held thus far. As such, I've decided to put him in charge of my entire estate. Even if he is able to walk again, he will no longer have the strength to do the outdoor chores and drive me hither and yon. And Millie is getting on, too. I am prepared to make her my housekeeper in charge of my household and hire someone else to handle the cleaning. Please ask that woman who runs the paper if she will take a break from her ridiculous gossip and print something of relevance for a change. She may send the bill to the manager of my estate."

"Smith?" Micah asked.

"Well, what on earth have I been flapping my jaw about if you even have to ask?"

"Yes, ma'am. Sorry."

Her expression softened as did her tone. "Sheriff, find the man who hurt my friend. That is all that matters."

Chapter Eleven

"Apple pie." Louie grinned, showing the gap where his two front teeth were starting to peek through. "That's my favorite."

Hazel smiled. "How about apple cider?"

Louie nodded. "I've only had that once—at the harvest fair."

"What else?"

"Apple fritters. Miss Jennie's are the best I've had."

"Agreed!"

"Your turn." Louie nudged her. "What's something else you make with apples?" The conversation continued from there for a few minutes more, Hazel turning it into an impromptu spelling lesson as she had Louie try to spell each delicacy they discussed.

The Tillman farm was seven miles from town and stretched out with acres and acres of apple trees. Hazel's arms ached by the time she reined in the horses and wrapped the leather straps around the brake the way that Ezra had shown her.

Louie and Archie took off at a run the second their feet touched the ground. Hazel grabbed the baskets from the back of the wagon and headed for the rows of apples. Excitement fluttered in her stomach. The only time she'd picked out her own apples was at the market in the city. And that had been baskets of fruit set in carts outside—from which they had had to steal in order to eat. As a child, she and her sister had a routine. One would distract the vendor while the other grabbed as much from the carts as they could before the vendor caught on. During the seasons where fruit was readily available, they always ate well.

"Louie!" she called out as she lost sight of the boy in the rows and rows of trees. "Come and help fill the baskets."

She carefully inspected each apple for bruising or little squirmy passengers. The first basket was nearly halfway filled when she heard Archie bark, though he and his boy remained out of sight. She shivered and looked around.

"Louie, come help fill the baskets," she called again. "It's getting colder. Let's hurry so we can get home where it's warm." *Home.* The very thought of her cozy little cabin gave her a sense of peace and joy. In that moment, Hazel knew without a doubt that she would be happy living in Tucker Springs, in her cabin, taking care of Louie for the rest of her life. And for just a flicker of a moment, she saw Ezra as part of that life. Not just as the father of the boy in her charge. But something more. Something she didn't dare even allow her heart to hope for.

She shoved the dream from her mind as the reality of Louie and Archie reached her, both panting from running. She and Louie picked out the best apples they could find and had them loaded in the wagon in just a half hour. "I don't know about you," she said as she climbed into the seat and took up the reins, "but I'm ready to get inside to a warm fire."

Louie nodded, pulling Archie close—the way she had noticed he sometimes did when he was troubled.

"Something wrong?"

He shrugged.

"Does this have anything to do with the bag of food your pa found?"

Louie turned his gaze on her as she flicked the reins and the horses started to walk forward. "Miss Hazel?"

"Yes?"

"It's going to be extra cold tonight, ain't it?"

"Yes, it seems that way. But you don't have to worry, Louie. Your pa will see to it you are warm and safe in your home."

He nodded. "I wish everyone could be warm at night."

Hazel's stomach twisted and alarm seized her as an image of her and Rose shivering against the side of a building flew across her memory. "I do, too, Louie."

Silence fell between them for the next couple of miles until finally Louie spoke. "If a boy knows about another boy who sleeps outside even in the cold and doesn't have very much food to eat…what do you think that boy oughtta do?"

Hazel hesitated briefly. She was pretty sure that she

was about to learn the reason behind the sack full of food, and she didn't want to say anything wrong. Still… Louie had to learn not to be deceitful, even when he was trying to do the right thing. "Do you need to tell me something? Do you know a boy who has to sleep in the cold?"

"I don't want to 'tray a trust."

"Betray a trust?"

He nodded.

"I see. Well, I'll leave it up to you, but I don't think telling something out of true concern is betraying a trust." When she saw that he didn't understand, she tried again. "If someone tells you a secret, and that secret is that they're hurt or scared, then I'd think that finding someone who can help them is more important than keeping the secret. Don't you?"

He fell silent and appeared to be considering her words. Disappointment blew across her as icy as the wind as they drove the rest of the way home in silence. "Miss Hazel?" Louie asked as she pulled on the reins, halting the horses in front of the cabin. "Is lying out of true concern a bad thing?"

Warning bells jangled in her brain. This was a bit trickier than giving away another boy's secret. With a quick prayer for wisdom, she drew a breath. "Louie, I think maybe it's time for you to tell what you know. Why were you hiding food in that sack?"

"If I do, are you going to tell Pa?"

"Probably. As I said, I think helping someone is more important than keeping a secret. And telling your father means he'd be able to help, too." She climbed down as he hopped down from the other side. "Bring in those apples, please. And we can discuss this in the house."

She heard his quick intake of breath and cast a sharp glance at him. He stared out into the woods. She followed his gaze. "What is it?"

"It's Pa."

Hazel's heart picked up speed as she turned to see Ezra waving as he walked up the lane.

There weren't too many times over the last few years that anyone besides Louie had given Ezra's heart a lift just by their presence. Hazel did that. True, she had lightened his load a great deal by agreeing to stay in Tucker Springs. But he was beginning to feel more than just gratitude. And as he watched her instructing Louie at the back of the wagon, he gave himself over to a dream where he was coming home to them—where the three of them were a family. What would it be like if he had made the sort of proposal Ben Gordon and so many others—his step-pa, for instance—had made to bring women out West? In places where men outnumbered women two to one, it was often necessary for men and women to make an arrangement based less on romance and more on good, common sense and mutual convenience. His own ma had done that when his true pa had died. He thought of the ring she'd shown him the day she had married Ephraim Murphy. A ruby set inside a heart. "Your pa gave me this the day he married me. Ephraim won't want me to wear it anymore, and I don't want to dishonor him by doing so. I will put it away for you so that when you find the woman you love enough to spend your life with, you can give it to her. She'll love it as much as I always have. And she'll love you as long as she lives—the way I will always have a special love for your pa."

"Hello, Ezra. Is it that time already?" Hazel's tone seemed distracted, so he could only assume that was the reason she had used his first name at last.

"It's not quite our usual quitting time, but Jeremiah's been minding the store most of the afternoon while I went with Micah to speak with Miss Tucker. I stopped in and asked him to close up. I thought I might help you and Louie carry in apples."

She smiled. "I must say, you have impeccable timing."

As he took a basket of apples, he glanced at Louie, who had turned his back and was walking with Archie toward the chicken coop. With the boy out of earshot, he told her about his trip out to Miss Tucker's. "The woman doesn't have much faith in the sheriff to find the thief."

"Poor Micah, still paying for the sins of his youth." She smirked.

"He can't seem to convince her that he's mended his ways in the past seventeen years. She staunchly believes once a thief, always a thief."

"She does?" He'd meant the words as a joke, but Hazel's whisper of a question made it seem like she'd taken it all too seriously. Ezra felt a beat of concern.

"Old folks are notional, and Miss Tucker has always been set in her ways," he said carefully, trying to gauge what had caused the shift in her mood. "I've never known anyone quite so stubborn."

"I very much enjoyed her company during the stage-coach ride. I have been meaning to visit."

He was just about to say he would be happy to ride out to Miss Tucker's with her sometime when she looked over his shoulder and frowned. "What on earth is he doing?"

Ezra turned just as she started to walk around him. He followed. "Louie?" The boy jumped and stopped dead in his tracks, then slowly turned. His coat was unbuttoned, and apples fell from his shirt and rolled across the ground. Incredulous, Ezra watched as another little boy and an even smaller girl stepped from behind a tree and dropped to the ground, snatching up the apples. They stood, each holding several apples in their arms.

"Louie," Ezra said, forcing his voice to stay calm. "Explain this, please."

They reached the three children, and Louie looked up, his eyes riddled with guilt. "He's my new friend, Kent," Louie said. He picked two apples off the ground and set them in Kent's arms.

"Hello, Kent," Hazel said softly. She glanced over at the little girl. "And who is this?"

The little girl's head was bare except for brown curls, no scarf or hat. Her enormous eyes looked up, made even wider by fear. She dropped the apples and stepped behind Kent.

"That's Janey," Louie said. "She's Kent's sister."

"I see." Hazel smiled down at the children. "Do you go to school, Kent?"

"Pa says we can't."

"Oh? Why not?"

Louie glanced from Hazel to Ezra. "Pa, we can't tell anyone about this," Louie pleaded. "Kent's pa don't want no one to know they're living in the woods."

Ezra touched the small of Hazel's back, and she turned, meeting his gaze. He knew they must be thinking the same thing. How far back in the woods was this family of squatters living? How long had Louie known about them? Were they up to no good? Was that why they didn't want anyone to know they were there?

During a time when the folks in and around Tucker Springs were being robbed and poor Mr. Smith had been injured so badly, it was inexcusable that Louie should keep this secret. Of course, he had no way of knowing about the robberies, because Ezra and Hazel had both hidden the truth so that he didn't become afraid.

Ezra studied the brown-haired little boy who looked to be about Louie's age. The girl he guessed to be three, perhaps four. They were painfully thin, with pale skin. Another concern shot through him. Were they ill?

The little girl reached around and grabbed an apple from her brother's arms. Ezra heard a crunch as she took a bite.

Hazel took in a sudden breath. "Are you children hungry?" she asked.

Kent turned a soulful gaze to Hazel. "Sorry, ma'am, Janey shouldn't have just took an apple like that. She ain't learned much manners." He stepped forward and arched his body, offering the apples. "Louie said we could have 'em, but I reckon they're yours. Here, you can have 'em back."

Hazel met Louie's gaze. "Why don't you bring your

friends inside so they can get warm? And it's past time for our afternoon snack." She winked at Janey. "In some countries it's called 'tea.'"

The little girl started to follow, but Kent grabbed her by the shoulder and held on to her. "No, thank you. We best get going."

"You don't want to come in for some corn muffins with honey and some milk? That's what Louie enjoys between lunch and supper."

But Kent was resolute. "I reckon we ought not stay, ma'am."

Little Janey looked, with longing, toward the cabin and sighed before speaking for the first time. "We ought not, ma'am." The words sounded rote, as if she'd said them many times before.

Ezra stared off into the woods. If Hazel could convince the children to go inside to get warm and fill their obviously empty bellies, he would go into the woods and find the children's father. Or perhaps he should go fetch Micah and they could search for the stolen items together.

"Maybe if I spoke to your parents? If they said it was all right, would you come and have a snack with us?"

"Pa wouldn't like it. We don't take no charity."

"But if I talked to him…" Hazel tried again.

"We're not s'posed to tell nobody where we're stayin'."

Hazel's lips thinned, and though she kept her voice calm and even for the children's sake, Ezra could tell she was getting frustrated. "Now you listen here, children. I want to know where you live. If you do not tell me, I'll follow you every step of the way until we reach your home."

"Aw, ma'am. My pa's going to wear me out with the switch if you do that."

Ezra put his hand on Louie's shoulder. "Louie? We need to know if this is why you were saving food in the bag. Were you planning to give the food to Kent and Janey?"

Louie looked down at his feet but nodded. "Yes, Pa."

"We ain't asking for no charity, sir." Kent glared at Louie. "And I reckon he took it upon hisself to take food. I sure never asked him to."

"It's fine. We have plenty to share. But I am afraid I do have to insist that you tell me where you live."

The child inhaled a shaky breath and blew it out in a puff of cloudy air. "Pa was sure right. I shouldn't have ever got myself a friend."

Poor Louie looked miserable. His expression dropped, and his brown eyes filled with tears. "Sorry, Kent. I didn't mean to get you in trouble."

Kent's frown softened a little at that, and his resolve seemed to weaken. "We used to live in a house back in Texas," he said, offering the words like an apology. He shrugged thin shoulders. "We was headed West, but the wagon broke. My pa said we'd just have to stick it out here until he can save enough for an axle."

Ezra thought back to the man—Jackson, was it—who had come into the store looking for work.

"Your name is Kent...what?"

"Jackson, sir." The boy stepped forward and offered

his hand like a grown man. The gesture went to Ezra's heart, and he took hold of the small, ice-cold hand.

"Children?" The sound of a woman calling from the woods made Kent and Janey both jump and back away from Hazel and Ezra.

"It's Ma!" Janey said.

Before they could do or say anything else, a woman appeared.

"Oh!" Hazel said.

Ezra turned to her, concerned. She leaned in close to him, keeping her eyes on the woman who was approaching her children. "That's one of the gowns that was stolen from my trunk," she said, barely above a whisper.

Anger flared inside Ezra. So, Jackson *was* the one responsible for the thefts in the area. How foolish did a man have to be to give one of the stolen items away to his wife? No wonder he kept his children away from other children.

"Keep her here if you can," he whispered back. "I'm going to find Micah."

"Hello," Hazel said, walking forward. "You must be Kent and Janey's mother."

The woman regarded her with suspicion. "I will just gather my children and go," she said. "I'm so sorry they bothered you."

Ezra forced himself to smile at her. "I believe I met your husband. Jackson, is it? I'm Ezra Murphy. I own the general store in town."

She had an arm around each of the children as she nodded. "Yes, he mentioned that he'd spoken to you.

It's nice to meet you." She glanced between Hazel and Ezra. "Well, we best be going. Come, children."

"Wait," Hazel said. "I was just about to give Louie something to eat. I'd be happy if you and the children would join us. It isn't much, just some corn cakes and honey and some of these apples. Have you eaten any? They are sweet as sugar." She winked at Janey, and the little girl giggled.

"I'm sure you're very kind," the woman said, sounding like she was working up to a refusal.

"Please don't say no," Hazel said softly. "I can see that the children could use a good meal."

"My husband would not be pleased." She gathered a breath. "We do not accept charity."

"Mrs. Jackson, please." There was an urgency in Hazel's tone that Ezra had never heard before. "I know what it's like to be hungry—so hungry that the ache in the pit of your stomach won't go away no matter how much water you drink or how much you try to pretend you've just eaten a full meal. No child should feel that way. Please don't ask me to stand by and do nothing while that's happening."

The other woman's eyes filled with tears, and she nodded. "Very well. The children may eat, but I can't."

"Well," Ezra said, "I'll get the apples unloaded for you, then I'll head back to town."

Hazel nodded, her eyes filled with uncertainty. But Ezra wasn't uncertain at all. As he left them all inside, he only hoped Hazel could keep Mrs. Jackson and her children there at the cabin so that the children didn't have to see their pa arrested.

It didn't take long for him to find the sheriff and tell him the story. They rode out through the woods, hoping to find the stranger—or at least his camp. There was enough of a reason for Micah to search their things whether the man was present or not.

As they approached the smoky smell of a campfire not even half a mile from Hazel's cabin, Ezra could barely conceal a groan. Mrs. Jackson and her children were already back at the camp. They sat on a log near the fire, wrapped together in a quilt.

Fear shot to Mrs. Jackson's eyes as she straightened up from the fire and darted a gaze to her husband. Miles Jackson wore a confused frown and stepped close to his wife, sliding a protective arm about her. "Can I help you, fellows?" He nodded at Ezra. "Murphy, do you have work for me?"

Ezra felt a wave of confusion. The man's eyes held a look of hope, and his voice sounded almost pleading. Why would a man guilty of thievery care so much about finding honest work? Was this an attempt to fool them into thinking he was innocent?

Micah glanced at the children. "Ma'am, can you take them inside the wagon?"

The man gripped her tighter. "Don't go nowhere, Maude. You young'uns just stay put."

Ezra sighed. He'd been hoping to avoid this. "Have it your way, then," he told the man before turning to Mrs. Jackson. "Ma'am, I'm afraid the dress you are wearing was stolen from the woman who just fed your children."

A look of utter horror covered the woman's face.

Either she was the best actress in the entire world or she had no idea that the dress she wore was stolen.

"But that isn't possible…"

Clearly, Micah felt the same way about the woman's reaction. His voice was gentle as he spoke. "May I ask where you got the dress?"

Her gaze darted to her husband.

"I gave it to her," he admitted. "But it was given to me."

"By whom?"

He shook his head. "I don't know who the man was. He shared our fire one night and when I woke up, there was the dress. I figured he noticed her other dress had a tear and left it in payment."

"What did the man look like?"

"It was dark and cold, and I was just up in the night tending the fire. His collar was turned up high and his hat was down low. I wouldn't recognize him if I passed him on the street."

"Well, here's my dilemma, mister," Micah said. "I'm the sheriff of Tucker Springs. That stolen dress was part of a string of thefts that included two attempts to rob a certain home. One of those times, a man was hurt badly."

"Well, that wasn't me. Like I said, a man left the dress. I told her she could have it since the man had left and there wasn't any way to give it back. But if it was stolen, then she'll return it."

"Of course I will!" The woman's eyes beseeched. "I'll go take it off right this second and you can return it to Miss O'Brien. Just don't arrest my husband. Please, we'll be on our way. We can just walk to the nearest town or the one after that."

Kent turned his sunken, wide eyes on Ezra. "Please don't take my pa."

Micah drew a deep breath and exhaled. "I'm truly sorry, Mr. Jackson, but I'll need you to come to the jail with me until the judge sorts it all out."

"You'll have to shoot me before I let you take me away like a no-good thief in front of my children."

"You'd rather them see you get shot? Rather die than even try to clear your name?" Micah asked, gripping his Colt.

The woman touched her husband's arm. "They know you didn't do this, Miles. Let's take it a step at a time."

The man glared at them both, his expression full of anger so fierce, Ezra almost took a step back.

"Where's your horses?"

The man scowled. "I had to sell them a few weeks back. Ask the man at your livery. He bought them."

Ezra climbed out of his saddle and handed the reins to Jackson. "Take it. I'll walk back to the cabin. My wagon is there." He turned to Micah. "Can you take the horse back to the livery?"

He gave a curt nod as he kept his firm gaze on Miles Jackson. Ezra knew he had to do one more thing before he could leave. "Mrs. Jackson, the woman you met this afternoon is kind and would be happy to give you and your children warm shelter tonight. No one will blame you for your husband's misdeeds."

She turned her back to him without a word. Sorrow

filled him at the thought of them staying in the cold, run-down wagon.

Wanting to distance himself from the heartbreaking sight as quickly as possible, he cut through the woods, taking a shortcut to the cabin. The wind whipped up, carrying the cries of the children as Micah took their father away.

Chapter Twelve

Hazel flopped over in her bed and punched at the straw tick mattress. She had slept on it in perfect comfort ever since the day she had moved in. But there was no rest for her tonight. Not when all she could see when she closed her eyes were the gaunt little faces of the children who had come out of the woods. And the worry that shrouded Mrs. Jackson like a veil. And now her husband was in jail. What would happen to them? In her mind's eye, Hazel could vividly imagine the sheriff leading Mr. Jackson away. Then that scene faded, and she recalled Mr. Wells saying he was going to call the constable to get to the bottom of the missing pearl pin. And Mrs. Wells crying and begging him not to. Hazel closed her eyes and prayed fervently for the Jackson family.

Why was it so much easier to pray for this family than it was to pray for herself? She had given her heart to Jesus when she was ten, and she had learned early on to give grace to others. But sometimes extending that grace to herself was beyond her abilities. Maybe it was because she hadn't been able to fully leave the evils of her childhood behind. Even after Miss Hastings helped her and Rose get away from their father, he had not disappeared from their lives. He had found them and stayed near them, lurking in the dark corners, taking advantage of their weaknesses and pressing them to come back and help him with his criminal schemes. It was as if seeing them move away from the way he raised them had angered him, and he wanted to drag them back down into the dark with him.

"Hazel, honey, your light shows your pa's darkness for what it is. And he cannot stomach that," Miss Hastings had told her one day when Hazel was railing against the fact that he could never just let go of her and Rose and let them live their own lives.

Once she was employed by the Wells family, Hazel had vowed to separate herself completely from her father. When a maid position came open at the Wellses', Hazel had talked Rose into joining her so the sisters could finally leave their pa behind once and for all. But somehow Pa had drawn Rose back into his web again. Hazel still had no idea how he had convinced Rose to steal Mrs. Wells's pearl pin, but that had been the beginning of the end for both sisters.

Hazel threw off the heavy quilt and her dark thoughts with one quick motion and stood. The sky outside was still not light, but she knew what she was going to do. She had two and a half hours before Ezra would be there with Louie, and before he arrived, she had a mission.

She dressed and quickly tended to her morning duties. When she opened the door to dump her morning wash water, her gaze rested on something on the doorstep. A wave of dread washed over her as she recognized the dress Mrs. Jackson had been wearing the day before. It was folded neatly and had been placed carefully in front of the door. She set the water down and picked up the gown, running her hand over the costly but worn material. This was by far the oldest of the dresses that had been stolen, but still much finer than anything Mrs. Jackson likely had ever owned.

When Ezra stopped by to get Louie yesterday, she had asked him what had happened when Mr. Jackson was arrested. He told her that both man and wife had protested his innocence. He might have believed Mr. Jackson if not for the proof of the dress, but he did believe Mrs. Jackson completely when she said she had not known the dress was stolen. The sheriff had searched the tiny wagon and found no sign of any other stolen goods, including the remaining dresses. It was possible he had already sold them, but if so, why was his family still so hungry and living in such conditions?

As her mind replayed meeting the Jackson children, it was the eyes that she couldn't escape. Large— almost too large—and sunken in. They reminded Hazel of Rose's eyes during their childhoods. Eyes that begged her to make the ache in their stomachs go away. Part of her wanted to shake her head and will the images from her mind. But she couldn't do that. Otherwise, she'd be no better than the crowds of people walking along the streets, ignoring the cries of the hungry and wretched. Spitting out the word *charity* as they might an oath.

She'd once heard a woman on the street say, "Charity is another word for love. When God opens your eyes, He expects you to see, and when you see, He expects you to do. And that's true religion." She had said it in response to Hazel's thanks as she handed her some bread and a block of cheese. Hazel had only been ten years old, but she'd never forgotten. That was the reason she had sought the solace of the mission and, to her undying gratitude, had found Miss Hastings.

Hazel knew what had to happen. She was going to bring Mrs. Jackson and the children back to the cabin to stay until things could be figured out. She had room, and Ezra surely would not mind. Louie had already become friends with the children, and he would enjoy sharing his lessons with them.

She headed toward the woods, but the sound of a wagon brought her up short. Could Ezra be early? She spun around and stared at the Averys' wagon. Miz Caroline was at the reins, and Gilly Bauer and Ivy Gordon were beside her. The three ladies carefully stepped down and walked across the yard toward where she stood. Hazel noticed Ivy positioned herself the farthest away from her.

"Where are you going?" Miz Caroline asked.

"I might ask you the same thing." Hazel smiled to take the edge off her words. She was not completely sure she was ready to share her plan.

"We are going to bring Mrs. Jackson home with us." She looked at Gilly and Ivy. "With whichever of us she will go with, that is. These two stopped at the café this morning as I was hitching the horses back up to the wagon. It turns out, none of us slept well for thinking of that poor woman and those precious children all alone."

Hazel gave a somber nod. "I confess I had the same kind of night. I, too, am going to see if she will bring the children and come back to the cabin with me."

The women began moving down the narrow path as they spoke.

Gilly nodded toward Hazel's hands. "Are you taking her a dress?"

Before she could answer, Ivy gasped then said hesitantly, "Is that the dress that was stolen from your trunk? Micah told Ben she was wearing one of your dresses and that is how they knew Mr. Jackson is the thief."

Hazel nodded. "It is."

Miz Caroline frowned deeply. "Do you mean to tell me," she said, indignation edging her voice, which had lifted in volume, "that Micah and Ezra made that poor woman change into a different dress so they could return that to you?"

"No, ma'am," Hazel said. "It was on my doorstep when I got up this morning."

Gilly clicked her tongue, her face clouded over with sorrow. "Poor woman. She had no idea what her husband was up to."

"What shame she must have felt," Ivy said, her voice soft with sympathy.

Hazel looked at the tall woman, and her heart stirred with compassion. How many times had she turned the other way when she had come close to meeting Ivy Gordon on the boardwalk? And even at church, she had avoided the Gordons like the plague. And perhaps Benjamin deserved some of that, but did Ivy? Hazel looked across at Ivy, who was walking on the other side of Miz Caroline. "I am sure she felt deep shame, but she shouldn't have. It wasn't her fault."

Hazel couldn't be sure, but she thought she saw Miz Caroline cast her an approving look. Before anyone could say more, they came into the clearing. Directly ahead, a wagon sat askew, the axel clearly bent and one wheel lying on the ground. The tiny flicker of a campfire was still smoldering beside it. They could hear a child crying inside.

Miz Caroline stepped up and knocked on the side of the wagon. "Hello the camp."

Moments later, Mrs. Jackson stepped out. The dress she wore was the most threadbare garment Hazel had ever seen someone actually wear. And considering her childhood, that was saying a lot.

Maude's eyes were wide as they shifted between them. Clearly, she was nervous. Hazel couldn't blame her. Their last visitors had hauled her husband away.

"H-hello." Her voice was thick with unshed tears, tears she had undoubtedly been holding back for her children's sake. Dark circles under her eyes spoke of a night more sleepless than any of theirs. "May I help you?"

"I'm Caroline Avery. You must be Mrs. Jackson."

"Maude. Yes." Her chin rose as she bolstered whatever dignity she had in reserve. Hazel understood. When you had nothing left but your dignity, you held on to it all the harder.

Miz Caroline made the introductions of the others as smoothly and graciously as if they were all there for a sewing circle or canning day. "And you know Hazel," she finished up.

Hazel stepped forward with the dress. "I would love for you to keep this."

The woman's pale face flushed red. "We do not take charity, but thank you." She choked out one more trembly sentence. "And my husband did not steal that."

Miz Caroline stepped closer and put her arm around the woman's shoulders. "Honey, where did you get the dress?"

"A stranger left it on the ground outside our wagon. Miles said it was probably payment in exchange for sleeping by our fire."

"What did this stranger look like?" Hazel asked, recalling the red-haired man she had seen at the festival.

Maude shook her head. "I never saw him. It was after we were in bed. But when my husband got up to tend the fire in the night, he could see the silhouette of him as he slept on the ground." Tears filled her eyes, and she looked at them. "We are Christian people. We would never take something that is not ours. Miles would rather die." She fixed each of them with a look of such utter certainty that Hazel had no doubt that she believed every single word. "And I would, too. Anyone who knows us knows that." Her shoulders slumped, and a sob escaped her lips. "But no one here knows us."

Miz Caroline stepped forward. "We may not know you, honey. But we are sisters through the Lord. And we are here to help you any way we can."

Hazel nodded, and she saw Gilly and Ivy do the same.

Miz Caroline glanced back at them and then at Maude. "May we pray with you, Maude?"

Maude nodded, and the women drew closer together. Gilly stepped between Miz Caroline and Maude. Ivy gave Hazel an apologetic glance before stepping in between her and Maude and completing the circle.

Without prompting, they all clasped hands, and Miz Caroline began to speak. "Our Holy Father in Heaven, we stand in awe of Your holiness. But we thank You for Jesus and for allowing us to come boldly before Your throne in prayer. Please be with the Jacksons, Lord. Please let the truth be known. Protect this family and bless them."

Miz Caroline paused as if considering her plea carefully, then continued. "Please be with the five of us gathered here today, Lord. We ask that You bind us together through our common love for You. Please keep us all safe and close to You all the days of our lives. We humbly ask this in Jesus's holy name."

When they finished, they stood in silence for a minute, then Hazel held the dress out again.

This time Maude took it. "Thank you."

"You're welcome."

"We would like—"

"Ben and I—"

"Would you—"

The women all stopped and looked at each other and smiled.

Miz Caroline took the lead again. "As you might have guessed, we would all like for you and the children to come stay in our homes until Mr. Jackson is cleared."

Maude gasped. "I could not possibly do that. We do not take charity."

"Charity is another word for love, you know," Hazel said softly. "A kind woman reminded me of that when I was young and in need of help."

Gilly nodded. "Hazel is right. And you would not refuse love, would you?"

Maude's eyes filled with tears again, and she shook her head. "When you put it like that, I cannot refuse."

"Good." Miz Caroline motioned to Gilly and Ivy. "How about you two help her get the children ready to go?" She looked at the sun, still low in the sky but growing brighter by the moment, and turned to Hazel. "You best be getting back to the cabin. Ezra will be arriving with Louie soon."

"Yes, ma'am." Hazel started to ask whose house Maude and the children would be going to, but she knew the answer. The Avery children would be a balm for the Jackson children as sure as Miz Caroline would be for Maude.

She couldn't imagine where they would put the three of them, but she had a feeling Miz Caroline had it all worked out.

She turned and walked back down the tiny forest path. Her mind and heart were filled with the providence of God. His hand was in the big things, but it was in the small, everyday things, too, and that fact made both the good and the bad of life so much easier to bear.

Ezra frowned as he drove down the lane to the cabin, noting there was already a wagon in the yard. Recognizing the Averys' wagon, he pulled back on the reins and stopped his horses next to it.

Before he could even wonder which Avery had stopped by, Hazel stepped from the woods and into the cabin clearing. She threw her hand up in an easy wave, and he waved back, feeling the grin spread across his face at the sight of her. "Is everything okay?" he called as she got closer.

"Yes, better than okay," she said. "Would you like to come in for breakfast with Louie and me and I will tell you all about it?"

"Sure."

Her eyes widened. "Wonderful. That will give you a chance to see the new table and chairs in use." She smiled as she mentioned the furniture Wyatt had finished a few days ago. Ezra returned her smile.

Louie scrambled down and set Archie on the ground while Ezra situated the reins.

Hazel ruffled Louie's hair. "Louie, if you want to run inside and set the table and wash up for breakfast, we'll be right in."

Louie bounded to the cabin, Archie hot on his heels. Ezra swung into an easy step next to Hazel. "Why is the Averys' wagon here?"

He listened as she told him about the five women and their early-morning meeting. "I'm glad to know they'll be safe at the Averys'. It was hard to sleep, thinking about what would happen to the woman and her children."

"I was going to invite them to stay at the cabin. Although I guess I should have asked you first."

He smiled at her. "As far as I'm concerned, as long as you are Louie's nanny, the cabin belongs to you—you're free to invite anyone you please."

As they entered the cabin, Louie came out of Hazel's bedroom and Ezra could see guilt all over his face. "What were you doing in there, Louie?" He tried to keep his voice level and calm, a method he had learned from Hazel, but he still asked the hard question, even though he worried he wouldn't like the answer. Facing confrontations with his son was something he'd learned from Hazel, too.

Louie's face flushed redder. He shook his head. "Nothing."

One of his hands was clenched while the other hung free at his side. Before he could speak, Hazel did.

"What do you have in your hand, Louie?" She sounded as calm as though she might be asking him what he wanted for breakfast.

"Nothing."

She frowned. "Is it something that belongs to me?"

Louie looked like he was going to bolt. But finally, he nodded.

"Show me."

He unfurled his fingers to reveal a heart-shaped locket. Ezra couldn't be sure, but it looked like it was made of real gold.

"Louie, do you know that it is wrong to steal?" Hazel asked, her voice trembling.

Ezra stared at her. In all the times he had seen her correct Louie, he had never seen her lose her temper.

But as he watched her take a deep breath, he knew she was fighting to get her anger under control.

"Yes, ma'am, I do. It's one of the ten 'mandments."

Her face relaxed a little. "Ten commandments. You are right. Then why do you have my locket?"

His face was pale, and his lip started to tremble. "I was just looking at it, Miss Hazel, I promise."

"So why do you have it in your hand?"

"'Cause I had just picked it up and I heard you and Pa come in and I forgot I was holdin' it."

She took another deep breath. "Do you think it is right for you to go through my things?"

"No, ma'am."

She looked at him and waited.

Tears filled his eyes, and he held the locket out to her. "I'm sorry, Miss Hazel."

She nodded and took it. "I forgive you, Louie."

He threw his arms around her waist.

She hugged him tightly. "I need you to listen to me."

"Okay." The word was muffled.

"Look in my eyes, honey."

He raised his teary gaze to hers.

"I care for you very much, and I don't want you to grow up to be a thief or a pilferer. Now, I never specifically said that you shouldn't go through my things, so you aren't in trouble for it this time. But if you ever go through my things again, there will be consequences." She smiled gently at Louie, and even though she wasn't looking toward him, Ezra felt his lips tilting up. "Do you understand?"

"Yes, ma'am." Louie still wasn't smiling.

"Okay then, run see if the queens have any more eggs for us, and I will get the skillet hot and start with the two we have." She pulled the cast iron skillet down and turned back toward the cookstove.

Ezra smiled at her use of the ridiculous nickname for the three chickens. She was very sensible but somehow still managed to make things fun.

Louie started for the door, then came back and tugged on Ezra's shirt.

"What is it, son?" Ezra asked. "What's wrong?"

"I have a 'fession to make."

"A confession?"

Louie nodded and kept his gaze on the floor.

"What is it?"

"There was a man at the festival."

"A man?"

Louie nodded. "He came up to me when I missed and didn't win the soldiers."

"He came up to you? What did he want?"

Louie took a step back, his eyes clouding with indecision. "I don't want to get in trouble."

Ezra reached out and put his hand on his son's shoulder. "Tell me the truth now and you won't be."

"He said he'd give me a prize—those soldiers I wanted—if I got Miss Hazel's gold locket and put it in the chicken coop under Maisie."

Hazel gasped, and Ezra heard something drop, but before he could look over to make sure she was all right, Louie had flung himself at Ezra, his body shaking with sobs as remorse overwhelmed him.

Ezra sank into a chair and held his son close while

fierce anger shot through him—not at his son, but at the man who had approached him. Someone had dared waylay his son at a festival and put ideas of thievery in his head? He looked across at Hazel, who stood at the stove, her face as white as a ghost. A busted egg lay at her feet, but she stared at the floor as though the mess weren't there.

"I am sorry for lying, Pa. And sorry for listening to that man."

He pushed Louie back gently so he could look him in the eye. "I forgive you, son. It is always the best thing to tell the truth, and I am proud of you for speaking up. Now, you stay with Miss Hazel, and I am going to tell the sheriff what the man said."

"Will Sheriff Micah arrest him?" Louie's tears had stopped, and his eyes sparkled with excitement.

"He already did, son."

"Louie." Hazel spoke from behind him, and her voice was strained. "What did the man look like?"

Louie frowned. "Kind of skinny. And mean-looking. But smiley."

"What about his hair?"

Louie looked confused. "What about it?"

"Was it like mine?"

Ezra turned his head to look at her. What was she getting at?

Louie laughed. "No, silly. He was a boy. Not a girl."

"I mean—" Hazel stopped. "Never mind."

Ezra pushed to his feet. "I have to go see Micah." And Mr. Jackson. Ezra was far from a violent man, but that thief should be glad he was behind bars.

"Louie, after you tell your pa goodbye, don't forget that you still need to run out to the coop and see if the queens left us any eggs."

Ezra lingered on the porch because he could tell she wanted to talk privately. When Louie was out of earshot, he turned to her.

"Hazel, I better not stay for breakfast. I want to get to Micah. But I hope breakfast is something we can do another time."

"That would be nice." She seemed distracted, and he found himself wondering if he had misread her feelings. "How would Mr. Jackson know about my locket?"

"He probably saw you with it on."

"I don't see how. When could he have possibly seen me?"

"I don't know. Maybe in town." Suddenly the memory rushed back to him. He snapped his fingers. "I know when! The day that man came in my store, claiming he was looking for work. You were out on the boardwalk looking for Louie. I saw you clutching your necklace like you do when you are nervous. He tipped his hat to you. So, he must have seen it, too."

She blew out her breath as if she had been holding it. "Of course, that must have been it." A cloud passed over her face, and she lifted her gaze to him. "Oh, poor Maude. She was so sure her husband was innocent."

"Well, she probably will be better off in the long run with that scoundrel in prison and all of you women surrounding her and the children. She'll be like a new woman."

"I suppose," Hazel said with a sigh. "Sometimes even the best women love the worst men. But I'm not sure…"

Ezra could see in her face how conflicted she was. Even with a frown creasing her brow, she was so pretty it was difficult to look away. He swallowed hard, and as much as he hated to leave, he knew he needed to let Micah know what Louie had told him. "Well," he said, walking to the door, "I'll be back later to get Louie."

She followed him to the door and held it open for him as he stepped outside. She looked back over her shoulder and joined him on the porch, letting the door close behind her. As if she was rushing before she lost her courage, she reached out and squeezed his hand. "Thank you for almost joining us for breakfast…Ezra."

He turned his hand in hers so he could squeeze hers, too. "Thank you for almost cooking breakfast for me, Hazel."

She headed back into the house, but not until he saw that she was grinning as broadly as he had been all morning.

Chapter Thirteen

Strangely, the brief exchange with Hazel had made Ezra's heart pound but had calmed his emotions. But he felt his anger rising again as he neared the jail. Stealing was a terrible enough thing, but it could be understood, if not excused, if the man had done that because his family was hungry. But deceiving a child into stealing for him was another thing entirely.

He stepped inside the door of the jail.

Micah looked up from the desk where he was going through the mail that had come in on the stagecoach. "Hi, Ezra. What can I do for you today?"

Ezra glanced over at the cell where Miles Jackson sat on the floor with his back against the wall. "I need to talk to your prisoner."

"By the look on your face, I don't think it would be good to let you inside the cell. But you can talk to him through the bars." Micah put the mail down. "What happened?"

"I'll tell you what happened." He pointed at Miles.

"He cornered my son at the festival and told him to steal a gold locket from Hazel."

The prisoner's head jerked up. "That's a lie! We weren't anywhere near the festival, even though my children begged to go. I knew I couldn't buy anything for them there and didn't want them to be disappointed. But even if I'd gone, I'd never try to get a child to do something like that." The fire went out of his eyes. "Stealing is a sin. I'd never do that—nor would I ask anyone else to, especially not a child, so help me God." He dropped his gaze back to the floor. "I know you ain't never going to believe me, but it is true."

"Just like I don't believe someone just left the dress for you," Ezra half yelled, frustrated that this man was still protesting his innocence in spite of all the evidence of his guilt. "You think we should believe that?"

Mr. Jackson nodded, a grim look on his face, as if he knew what he was going to say wouldn't be believed. "I told you what happened. A man slept by my fire. The next morning, I found the dress on the ground outside my wagon."

"Since when do people pay a fee for sharing a fire on a cold night?" Micah asked.

Mr. Jackson's face flamed red. "Of course, I never would have demanded or even expected payment for using our fire. No Christian man would." He dropped his gaze again. "I thought maybe he had seen how tattered Maude's dress was and was repaying kindness with kindness," he mumbled. "That would keep it from being charity." He met Ezra's eyes again. "And would allow me to give my wife something she needed badly and that I could not provide without being a beggar."

Ezra stared at him. He seemed so sincere. Was Miles Jackson that good at lying? Or had they arrested the wrong man? He needed to clear his head. He nodded at Micah and walked out of the jail without another word.

As he stepped out the door, a man pushed himself off the jail wall he had been leaning against. Ezra glanced over and met the cold green eyes of a tall redheaded man. The man sneered as he scrutinized Ezra. Then he scoffed, tossed a cigar butt on the ground, turned and walked away.

Ezra knew he'd just been insulted, and it had felt personal somehow, though he was sure he'd never met the man.

Ezra started to walk back toward his store, then turned to look at the man again. He was heading into an alleyway between the livery and the leather shop, and something about his sneaky manner gave Ezra pause. He reversed his path and followed the man. He had no clear idea of what he would do if he caught up with him but felt compelled to follow. The more he thought about it, the more it seemed like the man had been eavesdropping outside the jail. Picking up the pace a little to match his quickening heartbeat, he closed the distance between them.

As Ezra approached the stranger, the man turned around and faced him. "You lookin' for a fight?" the older man snarled, shoving his hands into his pockets.

Ezra held his hands up, palms forward. "No, sir. I just hadn't seen you around town before."

"Is that against the law?"

"No." Ezra stuck out his hand. "I am Ezra Murphy."

"Good fer you." The man looked down at Ezra. "You want me to give you a prize?"

"What did you say?" Ezra's mind went to Louie's "'fession" of a tall man offering to give him a prize.

"I said, do you expect a prize for telling me your name?"

"No, but I do expect you to tell me your name."

"Then you can keep on expecting." Without warning, the man pulled something out of his pocket and threw it at Ezra.

Ezra threw up his hand to block his face. Something bounced off his arm, and he realized the man had bolted for the woods at the back of town. Ezra barely caught a glimpse of him disappearing into the trees. He looked down at the ground and shook his head. The dangerous object he had protected himself from was nothing more than an empty tobacco tin. Clearly it had been used as a distraction technique. That was the sort of move a person of low moral character would make, and Ezra was annoyed that he'd fallen for it.

He headed back to the sheriff's office. Micah was still there, and Ezra ignored the prisoner in the cell as he told him what had happened.

Micah emitted a low whistle. "You think he's the thief?"

Miles Jackson sat up straight and looked like he wanted to say something, but he kept his mouth shut.

"I think he's involved, at least." Ezra jerked his head toward Miles. "They could be in cahoots."

"I ain't in cahoots with no one," Miles protested. He jumped to his feet. "I'm innocent."

Micah stood. "Miles, you may be telling the truth. But I can't release you on a maybe. The fact of the matter is you're getting three square meals in here, and that's more than you were getting on the outside."

"But my family—"

Ezra held up his hand. "Your family is with the Averys. They're being well taken care of and well fed."

"And well loved," Micah added.

Miles sank back down on the floor.

Ezra walked over to the cell and looked him in the eye. "We will do our best to find out the truth. If you're innocent, you will be set free."

Miles nodded. "That's all I can ask for now, I guess."

Micah cleared his throat. "Let's keep this information about the redheaded man between the three of us. The women in town have grown mighty fond of your wife, Jackson. I don't want them storming the jail for your release while we're trying to get to the bottom of this."

Miles nodded.

As Ezra left the jail, he wondered if a guilty man would be so agreeable to those terms.

It had been a little over a week since that moment between Hazel and Ezra at her cabin door. Neither of them had mentioned the tender exchange since it happened, but she had continued to call him Ezra unless they were in front of Louie. She glanced at the beautiful table and chairs where Louie sat doing his lessons.

Ezra had been so excited about bringing in the new furniture. Had that just been an act of kindness? Or was he growing to care for her as she undoubtedly was for him? She couldn't help but think—and hope—the latter. And yet another part of her said that he deserved someone better, someone who had been raised going to church instead of thieving on the streets.

She had always struggled with feeling unworthy. Miss Hastings had encouraged her to see her worth to both God and mankind, but she couldn't quite shake the old doubts. She dreaded the moment she would have to tell Ezra about her past, but she knew she would have to before much longer. He deserved to know the full truth before their relationship went any further.

The sound of footsteps on the porch jerked her back to the present. She walked to the door and opened it. No one was there. She frowned. She had been almost certain she had heard someone. "I'll be right back," she said over her shoulder to Louie.

As she stepped onto the porch, closing the door behind her, she could see Ezra's wagon at the other end of the lane, heading her way. He was supposed to pick up Louie early today, because they were going out to the Averys' to help Mr. Will get ready for their turn at hog butchering tomorrow. But that did not explain the footsteps she thought she'd heard.

She walked all the way around the cabin, but still, there was no one there. The hair on the back of her neck stood up. Cautiously, she stepped to the outhouse, reaching for the handle, then yanked the door open. Empty.

When she reached the front porch again, Ezra was

just pulling into the yard. He jumped down and hurried toward her, the smile on his face seeming to hold much more than kindness.

"How was Louie today?"

"Oh, he was fine." She smiled. "Excited about the hog killing."

She pushed the door open, but Louie was nowhere to be found. Had he heard his pa outside and run to hide as he sometimes did? She heard Archie whine from inside her bedroom and went to push open the door. She could feel Ezra right behind her.

Her eyes widened, and she gasped. Louie stood at her dressing table covered in white powder from head to toe. Her powder—expensive, a gift from Mrs. Wells. The sweet scent filled the air, and flecks of the powder covered the floor and dressing table.

At her gasp, Louie turned around. "Look, Miss Hazel, I'm a ghost!" He gave a mischievous laugh. For a moment she was speechless. Then, oblivious to the tension in the room, he looked past her, and his grin widened. "Pa, I'm a ghost. Whooooo." He waved his hands in the air.

"Louie! Stop. This isn't funny." Ezra's voice was sharp. "You had no right to get into Miss Hazel's powder. And look at the mess you have made."

The boy's face fell as if he'd just realized that no one else was laughing. "Archie came in here growling, and I followed him. Then I saw the powder and I wanted to play ghost. Remember, Pa? Like we did with the flour?"

"I'm disappointed, Louie," Hazel said without waiting for Ezra to respond. "I thought you understood that my things are off limits."

Hazel looked at Ezra, and he gave her a sheepish grimace. "A couple of months ago, we were trying to make bread and it wasn't turning out. We ended up playing with the flour." He shrugged. "At the time it seemed funny. I guess it was a bad idea."

"No, that was a fine idea. Because the flour was yours and you were an adult in charge." She turned back to Louie. "But this was a bad idea, Louie. Can you think of why?"

She stood quietly, and when Ezra looked like he would fill the silence, she gave him a pleading glance. He clamped his lips together and nodded.

Louie also nodded. "Because it doesn't belong to me," he grumbled. "It was fun, though."

"Well, Louie," she said. "I hope the fun was worth it. Do you remember what I said would happen if you got into my things again?"

Louie looked uncomfortable and dropped his gaze as he answered. "That there would be consequences."

"That's right. So tomorrow, if your pa agrees, instead of going to the Averys' for the hog butchering, you will come here to clean up this mess."

Louie gasped.

Ezra also drew in his breath behind her. "But he looks forward—"

She turned to face him, trying her best to silently convey how important this was.

His eyes met hers, and in that gaze, she revealed all she believed about the importance of them standing firm together on this. Louie had come so far since that first day when she had ended up in the mud. But he needed a united front and consistency if they were to work together raising him with an understanding of right and wrong.

He looked at his son. "Well, son, I guess you'll have to miss out on the hog butchering. A man fixes what he messes up, as best he can. You can't replace the powder you wasted, but you can clean it off the floor and table."

Louie's face crumpled, and tears made rapid tracks through his powder-covered face. "Please don't make me miss the butchering, Pa. Please."

"It's not up for discussion, Louie. Now tell Miss Hazel you are sorry and that you will see her in the morning."

Louie still had tears streaming down his face, but he looked her in the eye. "I'm sorry, Miss Hazel. I won't get in your things again." He glanced back at his pa as if still hoping he would change his mind. Apparently reading the staunch look on Ezra's face, he turned back to her with a heavy sigh. "I'll see you in the morning."

She felt compassion for him, but she knew now was not the time to give in. "I don't think it will take you all day to clean up the mess, Louie. Perhaps we can catch a ride out to the farm with Miss Jennie after the lunch rush at the café, if that is okay with your pa."

Ezra nodded. "That sounds like a fine idea."

"If we don't go until after lunch, I will miss the chocolate cake. Pa, couldn't I clean it up after the butchering?"

"No arguing, son." Ezra's voice was kind but firm,

and even though she knew it was ridiculous for her to feel such, Hazel was so proud of him. "Now we had better get going. Thanks to your shenanigans, we will have to drive back to our house and get you cleaned up. I will be late to help Mr. Will."

Hazel cleared her throat. "Of course, the other option is to go as you are. Louie here will certainly be the most pleasant-smelling boy at dinner." She glanced up at Ezra. "Don't you think?"

Louie balked. "You think I'm going smelling like a lady? Pa, tell her. I got this all over me."

Ezra chuckled. "And you're the one who put it there, son. Miss Hazel is right. Most of the powder will blow off on the way there. Just the smell will linger."

Hazel closed the door behind them and leaned against it, smiling. She had wondered if Ezra was ever going to be able to stand firm with Louie, but he'd done beautifully. She couldn't help but think he had changed because he trusted her and valued her opinion. That was a wonderful feeling.

She walked back over to the bedroom door. It would be hard to leave that mess until morning. But she would. A knock sounded at the front door.

She ran over to open it. "Did you forget—"

"You?" Her breath caught in her throat as she stared into a familiar face, but definitely not Ezra's. "What are you doing here?"

Chapter Fourteen

Like something out of a dream—and not necessarily a good one—Hazel stared, slack-jawed at her sister shivering on her doorstep. She repeated the question. "Rose, what are you doing here?"

Rose frowned, and though her teeth were chattering, she cocked her head defiantly. "Are you going to leave me standing on the porch to freeze to death?"

"Maybe I should." But Hazel stepped back and let her in.

Once inside, Rose shrugged out of her worn coat. She took off her hat—a man's hat—and hung it on the peg by the door, then turned. Her gaze met Hazel's, and all the defiance of a moment ago melted. She just looked so tired and beaten that Hazel felt a stirring of sympathy.

"Hazey, I really am sorry."

"About what?" Hazel huffed. "And don't try to get around me with that old nickname. I am a grown woman, and my name is Hazel, not Hazey."

Rose nodded, sadness evident in her blue eyes.

"About letting him talk me into stealing the pin. He really did convince me he was going to hurt Mrs. Wells to get it if I didn't get it for him—"

Hazel held up her hand. "We are not talking about that again. Why are you here?"

Rose walked over to the fireplace and turned, closing her eyes. "Oh, Hazel. It's so nice to be warm. This place is beautiful. How long do you get to live here?"

"It's mine."

Her eyes widened. "He gave it to you?"

"He...whom?"

"Don't pretend you don't know who I'm talking about. The handsome shopkeeper."

Despite all of the emotions mixing together into a swarm of confusion, Hazel felt warmth flood her cheeks at the description of Ezra and the implication. "He didn't give it to me outright. But it's mine for as long as I'm looking after Louie." She leveled a gaze at her untrustworthy sister. "Any discussion about Ezra or Louie Murphy is off-limits. I won't have it. Is that clear?"

In response, Rose just pointed to one of the hand-carved rocking chairs that Ezra had surprised her with. "May we sit down and talk?"

Hazel sighed before she walked into the sitting area, added a log to the fire, then sank into the chair across from Rose. "Talk, then."

"I... He..."

"He?" Hazel drew in her breath sharply. "Is he here?"

Rose nodded.

"In Tucker Springs?"

Rose nodded again.

Down deep she had suspected that Pa was in town. Then she'd convinced herself the man Louie described had to have been Miles Jackson. Hazel's stomach clenched into a tight knot, the way it always did at any thought of her pa. "When did you arrive?"

"Me?"

"Both of you."

Rose shook her head. "I came because he was already here. I wanted to warn you."

Questions were swirling in her head like a twister. She hardly knew where to start. "How long has he been here?"

"I don't know for sure."

"Guess."

"Right after you arrived, I imagine." Rose twisted a white handkerchief into a tiny ball like Hazel had seen her do a hundred times before.

"How did he know I was here?"

Rose kept her gaze on the handkerchief and didn't speak.

Hazel heard the answer loud and clear in her silence. "You told him? Why would you do that?" She had only told Rose about Benjamin and his letters and Tucker Springs because her sister had cried until she was sick over ruining Hazel's life and had been distraught about what Hazel would do.

"I didn't mean to. He cornered me and was saying all sorts of horrible things about you. Finally, I got so mad that I told him you had gone to be a fine lady in Tucker Springs, Iowa, and probably be best friends with the richest lady in Iowa, who had a whole town named after her. And that he and I would never amount to anything more than we already were."

Hazel groaned. She could see that exact conversation in her mind's eye. Their pa was a master of manipulation. He had always taken pride in his ability to convince people to give him information or money or even food. And Rose, with her too-open heart, had always been an easy target for him.

"How long have you been here?"

"I came in on the stagecoach."

Hazel narrowed her eyes. The stagecoach ran Monday and Thursday. Today was Friday. "Which day?"

"Yesterday."

"How come no one mentioned seeing someone new in town?" She knew from experience this town noticed when a new woman came to town.

"I thought about how much attention that would bring to you, so I bribed the driver to let me off at the outskirts of town."

"And it took you a day and a half to walk here?" Hazel could always tell when Rose was being less than straightforward. And right now she wasn't lying, but she was definitely withholding information.

"No. I didn't come straight here. I went looking for Pa. There's no saloon or dance hall, so it took a while. But I found him."

Hazel felt her face tighten, but she nodded. "Of course you did."

"Hazel, I wish you could understand. I am done with him. But I am the one who gave him this opportunity to hurt you, and I wanted to stop him before he could do any more damage."

"What did he say?"

"He said I better get back on the stagecoach and head home unless I was here to help him. And that when he was done here, he would be taking you back East where you belong."

Hazel felt anger flare up inside her chest. She prayed for God to calm her. Pa liked it when she lost her temper—it made her easier to manipulate. She leaned forward and studied her sister's face, more gaunt than she had remembered. "Rosie, where did you spend the night?"

Rose's face flushed again. "Out in your chicken coop."

"And you stayed out there all day? Did Louie see you?"

She shook her head. "I hid behind the hay when he came out."

She was glad Louie hadn't gotten a scare from a strange woman in the chicken coop. Especially right after a man had stopped him at the festival— The truth hit her in the middle of that thought. Her pa. Her pa had been the mean-looking but smiley man who had bribed Louie to steal her locket. Guilt struck her hard. Had she allowed Louie to be put in danger?

"What is it?" Rose's face was concerned.

For a few seconds, Hazel had forgotten her sister was even there. She told Rose briefly about the festival and their pa's bribing of Louie.

"He has always wanted your locket."

"Yes, he has. But you're never to give it to him," Hazel reminded her sister. "Even if he threatens to hurt me to get it."

"How are you always so strong?"

Hazel sighed. "It is not my own strength, Rose. My strength comes from the Lord."

"I try to draw strength from Him, too. But even now that I'm an adult, Pa makes me feel weak and helpless."

"Did he hurt you, Rosie?"

Her sister shook her head. "Not really. Just his normal tricks. Acting like he was going to hit me but stopping an inch from my face. Then laughing."

Hazel shuddered. "He is evil."

"I know," Rose agreed, sounding more sad than scared.

That night as they got ready for bed, Hazel wondered what she would tell Ezra tomorrow when he showed up with Louie. She knew the answer as soon as she wondered—she would tell him the truth. No matter how much it hurt.

When she said her prayers, to her surprise, she thanked God for bringing Rose to her. They needed each other.

Ezra glanced over at his son riding beside him on the wagon. Louie had dealt with Henry Avery's teasing about the powder smell better than Ezra had expected. He even overheard the boys talking about how it was wrong to get into other people's things. Hazel had a way of influencing everyone around her for the good. Louie was quiet this morning, and Ezra knew he was thinking about what he would miss at the Averys' while he was at the cabin cleaning up the powder mess.

He hadn't told Louie, of course, but after Ezra left him with Hazel, he didn't plan to go straight to the Averys'. He and Micah were going to go looking for the red-haired man. Miles Jackson had sat in that jail long enough for crimes he may not have committed. With the sheriff along, he hoped they would find the man's lair, and he especially hoped the stolen items would be there so Micah could arrest the real thief and hold him for trial until the judge came through town. And get Mr. Jackson back to his family. He had spent a lot of sleepless nights imagining himself locked up away from Louie. And Hazel.

He pulled the wagon into the yard at the cabin and jumped down. Louie scrambled down with Archie tucked against him. The dog squirmed to get down and ran off to do his business. Ezra looked over at Louie. "You be respectful to Miss Hazel. It is not her fault that you are missing the hog butchering."

"I know it's not, Pa. I won't be mean."

Ezra smiled. He still could hardly believe how far Louie had come, thanks to Hazel.

They stepped up on the porch, and he knocked on the door. Often, Hazel opened it immediately, like she had been watching for them. But when a few minutes passed and she still hadn't come to the door, he knocked again. Still no answer. Archie wandered back, wagging his tail in anticipation of seeing Hazel. He paced in front of the door. Jumped up. Paused and started barking, his whole body tensed.

"Hold on, Archie. Be patient," Ezra said the words, but the dog's reaction concerned him a little.

Louie scratched his head. "Maybe she's visiting the queens."

"Go on and check the coop." As the boy dashed off to do just that, Ezra knocked again. Still, there was no answer.

The sound of indignant clucking and flapping rose into the frigid air. Louie came running back out of the chicken coop, Archie on his heels. The dog hadn't stopped barking since he'd started. "She ain't in here, Pa." A glance over at the outhouse showed it wasn't occupied.

Ezra glanced toward the woods. Had she gone to the Jacksons' wagon? He couldn't imagine why she would. Had there been an emergency? His throat went dry at the thought of her alone here, hurt or worse. He and Louie walked back up to the door.

He knocked again. He tried the knob but found that it was locked. He knocked again. "Hazel?"

He heard something fall inside, and the door cracked open. Archie began to twirl on his hind legs, barking and trying to squeeze in through the small opening as Hazel peeked out. Her face was pale and her hair was disheveled. "Ezra. I'm sorry, but I'm not feeling quite myself today."

Louie grabbed Archie and held him tightly against his chest.

Alarm shot through Ezra. "You're sick? I'll go get the doc!"

Her eyes widened and she shook her head. "No, no.

This just isn't a good time. Can you go ahead and take Louie with you to the Averys'?"

"But I have to clean up the powder, Miss Hazel." Louie moved toward the door as if he were going to push on in.

"No!" Her tone was harsh. Louie stopped short, his brow furrowed in response to the tone he'd never heard from her before. He pressed Archie closer. When she spoke again, her voice sounded calm. "I can already see that you are willing to take responsibility for your actions, and that is what counts. I'm proud of you." She looked at Ezra with pleading eyes. "Please go on and don't worry about me."

Ezra hesitated, studying her pale face. "Do you have a fever?" He reached forward, but she leaned back before he could press his palm to her forehead. Something wasn't right. She was behaving too strangely for this to be a simple illness. But short of forcing his way into a young woman's house against her will, Ezra couldn't fathom what to do.

She shut the door, and he heard her lock it behind her.

He put his arm around Louie's shoulders as they walked back to the wagon. "Looks like you will get to be there for the beginning of the hog butchering after all."

Louie didn't seem relieved. "I'm worried about Miss Hazel, Pa. She ain't never raised her voice to me before. She must be really sick." His countenance dropped, and he practically whispered, "Do you think she don't like me anymore since I spilled all her pretty powder? Maybe she really liked that stuff."

"Miss O'Brien was certainly not behaving like herself. There's no question about that. But don't ever think she doesn't like you." He placed his hand on Louie's head. "She loves you very much. Okay?"

"Sure, Pa." Louie nodded, but his eyes still looked troubled.

Back in the wagon, he turned toward the Averys'. He would be late to meet Micah, but he needed Louie somewhere safe while they looked, and he no longer had to worry—as he might have a month or two ago— that Louie would make trouble if Ezra wasn't there to watch him. As he pulled back out on the path to town, he couldn't shake the feeling that the woman who had wrought that change was in terrible trouble.

Chapter Fifteen

"You ain't as dumb as I thought you were." Pa scoffed as they listened to Ezra's horses clip-clopping down the road away from the cabin.

"I have never been dumb," Hazel said to the man who held her trembling sister by her hair. "And neither is Rose."

"You are so high and mighty, thinking you're better than your old pa. Ever since that old lady Hastings filled your mind with Jesus saving you." He sneered as he said the precious name. "And God loving you." He laughed, mocking the very thought that anyone could love her. "But you ain't no better than me. You lied to that man and little boy to save your own hide."

"I did it to protect them."

"And I did all those things over the years to protect you and your ungrateful sister from starving to death. Everything I have ever done was for you."

"Not a bit of that is true. It was never for us. We ate from trash bins or kind vendors. And we stole from fruit stands. You sacrificed nothing." A mirthless laugh escaped Hazel's lips. "Nothing you have ever done is to serve anyone but you. I wish you could see that and change your ways. God's grace is big enough even for you."

He loosened his grip on Rose's hair and pushed her away from him, rising to his feet. "Change my ways? My ways could make us rich. If you two would come to your senses and join me, we could take enough from that rich old biddy up on the hill to live free and easy for the rest of our lives."

"I'd never be happy living 'free and easy' on stolen money," Rose said as she jumped up and crossed the room, putting some distance between herself and Pa.

Hazel stared openmouthed at her sister. She had never seen Rose stand up to their pa. Knowing what it felt like to be standing alone, she knew Rose needed and deserved her support. "I feel exactly the same."

"Yer both fools." Pa spat out the words. "I'm the father of a couple of mindless so-called good Samaritans."

"There is no doubt that we came from your union with our mother," Rose stated. "But you are not our father in any way that counts."

"That's true." Hazel crossed the room to stand near her sister. She linked their arms. "We have one Father, and He is watching over us and taking care of us like you never did."

Pa's face grew so red that Hazel thought he might have a stroke. "Get me that locket and whatever else you have that is worth anything and I'll be moving on without you two worthless girls. But if you try to tell anyone about me, I'll come back and make you sorry."

Visibly frightened of his anger, Rose dropped Hazel's arm and took a step back.

There was no question in Hazel's mind that the minute he was gone, she and Rose were going to the sheriff. "You are not getting my locket, Pa." She hadn't put it on yet this morning, and for whatever the reason, some instinct had led her to put it under her mattress when she went to bed last night.

"Is that so?" He moved toward her.

Swallowing hard, Hazel stood her ground and nodded.

He narrowed his eyes to a pair of dangerous green slits. He reminded her of the snake in the garden, and for a long time that's what he'd been. Cajoling, convincing, manipulating. But no longer. "I will have that locket if I have to tear this place apart to get it, daughter. Or I might just shake you until you tell me where it is."

"Don't you touch her." Hazel glanced at Rose and saw she was holding the cast iron skillet in her hands.

"What are you gonna do about it, girlie?" Pa scoffed.

Suddenly a loud knock echoed through the cabin. "Hazel, let me in right now!"

She made a dash for the door, scrambling to reach the lock before her father reached her. "Ezra, watch out!"

Ezra pushed the door open just as Pa shoved Hazel out of the way and barreled out. Hazel fell backward and landed with a thud. Surprise filled Ezra's eyes as Rose set the iron skillet down on the table and ran over to help her up. They reached for her at the same time.

She saw Ezra staring at her, tenderness and concern etched on his face. "Hazel, are you all right?"

She nodded, rubbing her shoulder where she'd landed. Gathering a deep breath, she met his gaze. "Ezra, this is my sister, Rose."

She could see good manners warring with shock and curiosity in his expression. "Your sister?"

Hazel turned to her trembling sister. "You were brave, Rosie. I'm proud of you. Will you be all right if I speak to Ezra alone?"

Rose nodded, offering Ezra a tentative smile. "It was very nice meeting you, Mr. Murphy."

"Likewise." Despite his polite tone, Hazel noted the confusion still clouding his expression as Rose went into Hazel's bedroom and closed the door. "She doesn't look like you," he said as if distracted.

"She has our mother's coloring and features. I always wanted black hair and blue eyes. But the Lord didn't see fit for me to have those."

"Who was that man? Why was he here? Was he trying to rob you? Or..." He looked her over as if reassuring himself she was unharmed. "Are you sure he didn't hurt you?"

"I am sure." She put her hand on his arm. "I know you want to go straight to Micah, but please wait just for a few minutes so I can tell you everything."

"But that man..."

"That man is my pa." Shame coursed through Hazel. Ezra stared at her, slack-jawed.

"I'm sorry. When Rose showed up yesterday after you and Louie left for the Averys', she told me that my pa really was in town. I was going to tell you this morning. But right before you got here, I unlocked the door to go outside and do my chores, and Pa was lurking on the porch. He pushed his way in. When you knocked, he threatened to hurt Rose or Louie if I told you what was going on."

"What did you mean by when you realized your pa 'really' was in town?"

This was harder than she thought it would be, but she was determined not to make any excuses or leave anything out. She told him about seeing a flash of a red-haired man who looked like her pa around town. "I thought I saw him twice. But I wasn't sure. And both times, I was speaking to someone else, so I couldn't run after him to check."

Ezra was silent for a minute. When he finally spoke, his words were slow and measured. "You asked Louie if the man who bribed him had hair like yours. You knew it was your pa."

"No! I had a fleeting thought that it might be. But I convinced myself that it wasn't possible. I have never known my father to be anywhere besides New York and Boston."

"How can that man possibly be your father?"

She met Ezra's gaze, and for a brief second, she saw incredulity in his eyes, but just as quickly the suspicion returned.

She shook her head. "I'm sorry, Ezra. Let me start at the beginning, and I promise not to leave anything out."

She told him her life story. About living in alleyways and abandoned buildings. Her father's gambling, thieving and drinking. Her and Rose resorting to theft as well, just to keep from starving. She told him about finding Miss Hastings and meeting Jesus. That she had worked for the Wellses until Rose had stolen from them and they let her go even though she had promised they could take the cost from her pay for however long it took. Even if it meant she never saw another penny for her labor. That the reason she had written to Benjamin Gordon in the first place was because she wanted to get away from her pa and even Rose once and for all. She was weeping by the time she finished.

Ezra had listened without speaking. And when she fell silent, he still didn't speak.

"Ezra, say something. Can't you forgive me?"

He gathered a heavy breath and exhaled as he pushed to his feet. "I have to go tell Micah about all of this. We need to find that man before he hurts anyone else. And we have to release an innocent man from jail so he can return to his family." The accusation, though not spoken, was nevertheless present in his tone. He believed this was all her fault.

"I truly am sorry. If I had known my pa was here, I would have told you."

Ezra's eyes flitted to the cabin. "What part does your sister play in all of this?"

"She came to warn me that Pa was here. And to confess that, in anger at him, she had told him I was coming to Tucker Springs."

He nodded. "I will be back to talk to you after I talk to Micah." He walked away without even glancing back at her.

She could barely force her feet to move to carry her to the closest chair. How had this happened? She had thought Tucker Springs would be a new beginning for her. And the longer she'd stayed, the more she'd hoped that she and Ezra and Louie might become a family.

But that hope was gone now. She remembered how he looked at her after he found out who she really was. "Oh, Lord," she cried. "Will I never be free from my past?"

The quarter of a mile he walked in the brisk November air did nothing to cool his anger at Hazel for her part in keeping a guilty man free and an innocent man locked up. As Ezra walked toward the jailhouse, he understood the term *bittersweet*. If he'd had any doubt before today, he knew now that he loved Hazel. When that man—her pa, he now knew—had shoved her back so hard that she fell, he'd been frightened beyond anything he'd ever felt. And that was why it hurt so much to know that there was no future for them together.

Because she had deceived him, and now he would never be able to fully trust her again. The pain he felt was like a dagger, slicing away at his heart. Why had it taken knowing that she hadn't been forthcoming about her past to make him realize that he loved her? If she had just revealed her suspicion in the first place, from the first time she thought she had seen her father, then perhaps Louie would never have been approached and nearly tempted into theft by that vile man. Certainly, she could have spared Miles Jackson the shame of being arrested in front of his wife and children. And if they'd known whom they were looking for, her father could have been captured long ago and put in jail where he belonged.

When Ezra thought of those cold green eyes he'd stared into that day outside the jail, he shuddered. They were the dead, unfeeling eyes of the man who could leave an innocent father and husband to take his punishment. And Hazel had allowed it all, just by keeping silent.

As a Christian man, he would forgive her. What choice did he have? And he knew she would never knowingly have allowed Louie to be placed in harm's way. But forgiving her, as his faith required, wasn't the same as opening himself up to trusting her again. He couldn't take a chance that Louie might be hurt again by a so-called mother.

When Marie had come to town almost six years earlier with Louie in her arms, she had seemed as though she wanted to settle into small-town life, raise Louie among the good, solid folks who were so strong and honest, pillars of the earth. But in the end, she wanted excitement and wealth more—enough that she'd stolen from him, and even worse, left Louie home alone in order to make her escape when she'd chosen to run off. By all appearances, Marie had only left the baby alone for a few minutes, timing her escape with when she knew Ezra would be getting home from the store. But what if he had been delayed? And what if Hazel's pa had decided to do more than just bribe Louie? What if the man had hurt his boy in some way?

He couldn't take that chance again—not with his son's heart. Not with his own. Louie already had a strong love for Hazel. But once he explained it to his son, surely Louie would understand that this meant she could never be his ma. At least Ezra had never declared his love to her, nor made any promises.

As he thought about the future and the family he might have had, he took a moment to mourn the loss. Then his thoughts turned to the jailhouse and the man inside who already had a family that he was struggling to provide for. Miles Jackson, a decent and honorable Christian who had only tried to live honestly, had found himself beaten down by life again and again. What would he do once Micah let him go? How would he care for his family? Given his abhorrence at the idea of accepting charity, he'd never agree to stay at the Averys'. And when he returned to that broken-down wagon, his wife and children would go with him. With winter upon them, and the snow coming any day now, they would never survive.

He stared across the street at the paper office and remembered the advertisement Miss Tucker had placed.

He hesitated for a beat. Then turned and walked back toward his wagon. After all, Jackson was currently somewhere safe and warm—and after waiting this long, he could wait a few more minutes.

Less than an hour later, he pulled into the long lane that led up to Tucker House. He was relieved to see that Miss Tucker was no longer keeping vigil on the porch with her shotgun and lap blanket.

Mrs. Smith smiled as she opened the door. "Ezra," she said. "It's so lovely to see you. Is Miss Tucker expecting you?"

"No, ma'am. But it's very important that I speak with her." He stepped inside and closed the door. "How is Smith?"

"Very out of sorts, if I might be honest." She folded her hands like a prayer. "But he's alive, so I won't complain about his attitude."

"Well, it's a relief to everyone that he's recovering."

She motioned toward the sofa. "You have yourself a seat right there in the parlor, and I'll go see if Miss Tucker is receiving guests."

Ezra looked around the elegant room. Truth be told, the Tucker house was probably the most elegant home he'd ever seen. The thought of Miles Jackson moving through these spaces, taking the place of Smith, who had always seemed so haughty and regal, brought a grin to his lips.

"And what, may I ask, do you find amusing, Ezra Murphy?"

Ezra stood. "Nothing is amusing. How are you, Miss Tucker?"

The elderly woman moved forward, supported by a wooden cane. "Getting older and wiser by the day— and, unfortunately, in need of more support than my legs are capable of at times. You are not here for pleasantries, so do not waste my time, please."

She sat down and motioned with her cane for him to do the same.

While some folks were put off by Miss Tucker's bluntness, Ezra found the honesty refreshing most of the time. At least she wasn't manipulative. She said what she meant.

"I want to tell you something about the man Micah arrested last week."

"The thief? Go on."

"That's just it, Miss Tucker." He leaned forward. "Thing is, the man in jail isn't the thief."

She scowled. "I knew that sheriff wasn't worth his salt. But no one listens to me. Do they? I just buy all the new schoolbooks and pay for church roofs and such. And now we are back at the beginning."

"Not exactly. We do know who the thief is."

"Well, good, then he will be arrested."

Ezra dreaded the next thing he had to tell her, but he had no choice. "He escaped. But," he hurried on, "the good news is that he isn't likely to ever come back to this area again." Once Mrs. Green got word of the true thief's description, she'd let the whole town know in short order what to look for, and it wouldn't be safe to be a redheaded man anywhere within twenty miles.

"And I suppose that is supposed to make up for the sheriff's incompetence?" Her voice trembled. "And what of poor Smith? Where's the justice for him?"

"I understand, Miss Tucker, and I wish I could catch the man myself." Ezra squeezed the brim of his hat until his hands ached. He loosened his grip and looked the old lady in the eye. "But there's another reason I've come to speak to you."

"Another reason?" Indignation dripped from her lips. "What other reason could there possibly be?"

"It's in regard to the advertisement you placed for a couple to live and work here."

"Is the general store doing so poorly that you're

looking for a new trade, Ezra? No one actually took their business to Jamesburg, did they? I thought with Miss O'Brien's help that little rapscallion of yours was doing quite nicely. And I hear he's smart as a whip. That doesn't surprise me. You and your brother were both bright."

"Thank you, ma'am. But no, the store is getting along well. Better than last year, as a matter of fact. And there's been no more talk of losing customers."

"I see. Well, the position is intended for a man and wife. I find it more pleasant that way. Smith and Millie have served well in this household, but they are getting too old to do what must be done."

Ezra couldn't resist a smirk. Smith and Millie were definitely getting on in years, but neither were even in the same decade as Miss Tucker. "I believe I might have the couple you're looking for."

She lifted her brow. "Oh? And pray tell, who might these people be?"

"I would like for you to consider Miles and Maude Jackson."

"The name is familiar, but I can't place where I've heard of..." Her voice trailed away, her words replaced by a sharp intake of breath. "Have you lost your mind? And I just said how bright you were. Clearly, I misjudged you entirely."

"May I ask why you object? You haven't even met them."

"Well, if you think it's because he was arrested, it isn't. I don't care if a person is accused, just if they're guilty. I won't condemn him for being misjudged—

especially by that fool of a sheriff. That could happen to anyone. But Ezra, those people have children. Children! Mercy me. I cannot have Smith or Millie worried about tripping over children's toys, nor can I imagine the constant din of hearing them running hither and yon."

"Well, I can assure you that no one will be tripping over toys, because they simply do not have any. They are much too poor. When I found the children and wife, they were so thin I could see their collarbones."

"Oh, those poor children." Miss Tucker and Ezra both turned toward the door to find Mrs. Smith, her hand pressed to her chest, head shaking.

Closing her eyes, then opening them again, Miss Tucker scowled and shook her head. "See what you've done?" She gave a huff. "Well, bring them on out here so that I may meet them. But I make no promises."

"May I bring them this afternoon?"

"Bring them to lunch. At least I can observe their table manners that way."

Ezra's heart sank. What was he thinking? These poor failed farmers from Texas were never going to be refined enough for Miss Tucker. "Ma'am, I think I have wasted your time. I am sorry."

"Now, wait just a minute, Ezra Murphy. I will be the judge of whether or not my time has been wasted."

"I can assure you, they will not have the table manners you'd find appropriate."

She narrowed her gaze and studied him for a few seconds.

"For mercy's sake, Viola Tucker." Mrs. Smith stepped farther into the room. "If their manners are lacking, they can be taught. The children, anyway. And when will they be eating at your dining room table?"

"Just bring them for lunch today," Miss Tucker said to Ezra.

Two hours later, Miles Jackson was a free man, Maude Jackson and the children were reunited with their husband and father, and both Miles and Maude were employed.

Miss Tucker became instantly besotted with Kent Jackson's intelligence and wit, and Mrs. Smith scooped up Janey and claimed her as the granddaughter she'd always wanted.

Once more, that sense that life was both bitter and sweet overwhelmed him. As wonderful as it had been to see the Jackson family well settled, he now had a much more unpleasant task at hand. His thoughts turned to Hazel at the cabin, and with a sense of dread, he turned his wagon in that direction. He hated to, but he knew what had to be done.

Chapter Sixteen

For the third time that day, Hazel heard a knock on the cabin door. She had been cleaning like a madwoman, trying desperately to erase any memory of her horrible pa from the tiny cabin she loved so much. Rose had helped for a while, but she had finally gone to lie down for a spell. More to get away from the tension in the air than out of a real need to rest, Hazel suspected.

She paused for a breath before she opened the door, wanting to put off the reckoning she knew was coming.

"Hazel?" She heard the alarm in Ezra's voice through the door and realized he might think she had delayed in answering because her father had come back.

She flung the door open.

Ezra stood on the doorstep looking more somber than she had ever seen him.

"Did you find him?"

He shook his head. "No. I got Miles out of jail and took him and Maude and the children out to Miss Tucker's."

"Miss Tucker's?"

She listened in amazement as he told her how the Jacksons had come to be employed by Miss Tucker.

"That was a good thing you did, Ezra." He frowned and she flinched, gathering that it was no longer proper for her to use his first name. "Mr. Murphy."

"It was the least I could do after what they have been through because of…"

"Because of me," she finished for him.

"Because of your pa. But yes, partly because you weren't truthful with me."

Would Miles's arrest really have been prevented if she'd said that she'd seen her father? No one had witnessed Pa committing any crimes by that point, whereas Maude had been seen wearing her gown. A gown that had most definitely been stolen, even if the thief hadn't been Maude's husband after all. It had been an honest conclusion that a homeless man might steal to feed his family. But clearly, that wasn't Ezra's focus right now.

"You can't forgive me?" she asked, the last word catching in her throat. She already knew the answer.

But he surprised her. "I forgive you."

She stepped toward him. "Oh, Ezra—"

He held up his hand as if warding her off. "I forgive you, Hazel. But that doesn't change the truth." He took her by the arms and looked down into her eyes. "There are two things I can't abide. Thievery—"

"I didn't steal anything, Ezra. I despise thievery."

"—and lying."

Her breath whooshed out of her, and she felt tears sting her eyes. "When I deceived you this morning, I was trying to protect you and Louie. Not to mention Rose."

He ran his fingers through his hair. "I don't mean this morning. I mean all the opportunities you had to tell me the truth about your pa, about your past, and how you chose not to do so. Holding back the truth is just as much of a lie as saying the words."

Hazel's legs kept trying to buckle even though the last thing she wanted to do was faint. She had no doubt that this time Ezra would let her fall rather than catch her in his strong arms. She stumbled to a chair and sank into it. Neither of them spoke for a few seconds.

When she finally looked up at him, she could see a new emotion in his face. One she had come to know well in her childhood. Pity.

He sat down across from her. "Hazel. Since we never spoke openly about it, I cannot know for sure whether you were ever open to a relationship between us that would have been more than just employee and employer. But I was. I had given my heart to the idea that we would be a family."

She nodded. "Yes," she admitted, "me, too."

"It's hard to let that go, but we have to forget what might have been and move on. I won't put Louie in the position of having another ma that puts her needs and wants above his, and I can't trust you not to do that."

His words were like little poison arrows, and Hazel could feel them piercing her heart and soul. "What do you mean another mother? I was under the impression Louie's mother was dead."

He took in a slow breath and exhaled. "She is. But

she had already abandoned him. We got word that she died of illness a couple of years later."

"I'm so sorry. But you could trust me. I would never leave you and Louie."

She instinctively reached her hand toward his, and he covered it with his and pushed it away.

"No. I couldn't."

"So we can never have more than a professional relationship?" She heard the pain in her voice at the thought.

Ezra pushed to his feet and motioned for her to remain seated. "Actually, what I came to tell you is that I think our professional relationship should end, too. I can't have a person like that in Louie's life at all."

She gasped. She had been fairly certain that she had lost any chance of having his love. But it had never occurred to her that she would lose her job, too. "Oh no." The words, part lament and part plea, escaped her mouth of their own volition.

She saw what looked like a shimmer of tears in his eyes and told herself that above everything else, she must not make this harder on him. She had brought this on herself. He shouldn't have to suffer for it. She squared her shoulders. "I will begin packing."

"No." His voice was firm. "You—" he glanced toward the bedroom "—and Rose, if you'd like, may stay in the cabin until spring."

"What about a nanny for Louie?"

"Louie will go with me to work and do his schoolwork in the storeroom. He's getting old enough to help me some around the store. Miss Stewart has indicated that she will welcome him back to school in January."

Hazel felt an unfamiliar emotion shoot through her. Jealousy. She had heard enough local gossip to know that the only thing that had kept the pretty teacher from setting her cap for Ezra had been his horribly behaved son. Now that Louie had improved so much, she was fairly certain Miss Stewart would like nothing better than to become his new mama. Just as suddenly as the thought came, she knew she could not stay here until spring and watch Ezra court and possibly even marry someone else. "I will be out of the cabin by the first of the new year."

"Don't be hasty, Hazel. I'm the one changing the terms of our agreement. I won't throw you onto the street. Or force you to leave before you have the chance to secure another position. Besides, I know Jennie will want you to attend her wedding. Please, stay until spring."

Years of habit brought her shoulders back. She had nothing left but her dignity—so she would hold all the tighter to it now, just as she had so many times before. "No, thank you. I'll do fine on my own."

He looked like he would argue, then clenched his jaw. "Suit yourself, then. You don't have to get up. I will see myself out."

And just like that, love walked out the door of the little cabin. Hazel buried her face in her hands and sobbed.

Ezra watched as Jennie and Micah walked arm in arm down the aisle of the church, Mr. and Mrs. Lane. He was happy for his friends, but his heart felt just a little raw at the sight. Especially when Hazel rose and walked out after them. The guests were all invited to a dinner celebration out at the Averys', and most would attend.

He heard a sigh next to him and turned to see Reverend Harper wiping a tear.

"Everything all right, sir?"

The preacher nodded and smiled. "I have had the privilege of being the instrument of God as He joined together over two hundred couples during my time as a minister, and I always find it to be such an extraordinary blessing. The joining of two lives. That couple came into the church this morning as two individuals. Now, they are one."

"I've just never understood that part of marriage." Ezra searched the reverend's face, longing for the peace that radiated from him. "How can two people who are so different—like Jennie and Micah, for instance—suddenly become one person?"

"Ah," the reverend said. "That is the mystery, isn't it?"

"I suppose it is."

"If I had to guess, I'd say that your question isn't necessarily about the happy new couple, is it?" He inclined his head toward Hazel, who had stopped at the door to speak with Miss Tucker. She was radiant in a gown of shimmering blue.

Ezra forced himself to look away and turned back to the reverend. "You mean Miss O'Brien?"

The man of God chuckled. "I thought the two of you had a certain spark between you. And she certainly worked wonders with Louie. Love does that, doesn't it?"

Ezra frowned. "I don't understand. Love does what?"

"It works wonders."

"I'm not following you, sir."

The reverend smiled patiently. "Love can make two people into one. It can turn a little boy from terrorizing the community to being polite and useful." He nodded toward the door, where Miz Caroline had handed Louie a crate to carry. "And when a woman knows she is loved, she can turn loose of all of the shame she feels about her past and hold her head high."

"You know about Miss O'Brien's past?" Ezra asked. Though they had let the townspeople know what the true thief looked like, they'd been careful to limit the number of people who knew that the man was Hazel... Miss O'Brien's father. There were those in town who might have judged her harshly for it.

He nodded. "I hear things." Likely from Micah— though Ezra supposed there was no harm in it. The reverend certainly wasn't a gossip. That was why it always felt so safe to confide in him.

"I just wish her love for Louie had kept her from lying to me and putting my son in danger."

"She put Louie in danger?"

"Well, her silence about her suspicions did."

"I see." The reverend smiled and patted Ezra's shoulder as though he were no more than Louie's age. "I'll be sorry to see Miss O'Brien leave town. We'll be a poorer town without her contribution."

Ezra shook his head as he walked out of the building. His gaze instinctively searched for and found Hazel. Clay Willow towered over her as she shivered in the cold air with only her shawl. The woman always walked outside without her coat. Indignation flared against Clay. A gentleman would offer her his coat or at least go inside and get hers.

With a huff, Ezra stomped back inside the church and located Hazel's coat hanging on a peg. He stuffed his hands inside the pockets to be assured she had gloves and then headed back outside. He walked up to the inconsiderate man and the freezing woman and slipped her coat around her shoulders, holding on as she slid her arms inside without a word. "You're always half-frozen."

Her wide green eyes found his. They seemed hopeful. "Thank you, Mr. Murphy."

He scowled. "Ezra."

She nodded. "Ezra," she repeated softly.

Clay spoke up abruptly. "We had best be heading out to the Averys', Hazel."

Ezra lifted his gaze to Clay. "I'll see the two of you out there." He knew Hazel well enough to recognize the disappointment in her eyes at that. Perhaps she had thought the offer of his first name was a sign that he had changed his mind—but he hadn't. He could not trust a woman who had put his son in harm's way with her silence.

Ezra's eyes narrowed as he watched them walk away. Clay strutted like a peacock toward his wagon, his massive hand spanning Hazel's back possessively. Jealousy surged through Ezra that he knew he had no right to feel.

As he walked toward his own wagon, he saw a figure coming from the church. He turned and frowned as he saw Rose looking toward the retreating wagon, her hand shading her eyes. Suspicion clouded his mind, and he stomped toward her.

Her expression turned to relief. "Oh, Mr. Murphy, am I glad someone is still here."

"Is that so?" He barged ahead, his ire only growing. "What were you doing in there all alone? Looking for the offering plate?"

Rose's eyes grew wide and she gasped. "You think I would steal from God?"

"And she *wasn't* alone." The reverend stepped onto the porch and shut the door behind him. "She and I were discussing a matter."

Heat seared Ezra's face even as he told himself that it was an honest mistake. The girl was an admitted thief. And not like Hazel, who had run away from her father and refused to steal another thing when she was ten years old. This girl had stolen for her father not more than six months ago. But clearly she had not been up to anything untoward this time, and he had accused her to her face.

"Well, I apologize for the misunderstanding."

"I understand." Her eyes sought his. "Will you tell my sister I am sorry I couldn't attend the dinner?"

"Is she expecting you?"

"I am sure she assumed I had already gone. Several people offered to take us out there."

"I'm afraid it was my fault." Reverend Harper said. "I do have a tendency to run on. I wasn't planning to attend the dinner." He looked pointedly at Ezra. "I suppose I could be persuaded to escort a pretty girl if absolutely necessary. It will take me just a few minutes to hitch the buggy."

"Rose," Ezra said. "I truly am sorry for misjudging the situation. I would be honored if you would allow me to escort you to the Averys'."

Rose narrowed her gaze. "Mr. Murphy, thank you for the apology, and, yes, you're right that you misjudged the situation. From what I have been able to gather about you, you often make others pay for your wrong opinions." She turned to the reverend. "Sir, thank you for taking the time to answer my questions." Her eyes and lips were soft as she smiled at the aging minister. "You're a man who lives the life he professes."

Ezra squirmed a little under her obvious implication. "My wagon is this way."

She glared at him. "The only reason I'm riding with you is because I promised to help with the dinner so Jennie can be the honored bride she deserves to be."

She jerked her arm away as he tried to help her into the wagon. Ezra knew better than to speak. Surprisingly, as they approached the Averys' home twenty minutes later, Rose was the one who broke the silence. She turned to him. "Ezra Murphy, I want to say something to you."

He gave her a guarded nod. "Go ahead."

"I know you're a good man. I can see it. And my sister would not care so much for you if you were anything like our pa." She turned herself straight. "But I don't believe you're as intelligent as everyone thinks you are. Because if you were, you would move mountains to convince her that you are sorry for breaking her heart."

Ezra pulled on the reins to halt the horses. He wrapped the reins and set the brake and turned to reply, but she had already made her way down from the seat and was walking away.

Wyatt walked toward him, his head turned to watch the dark-haired beauty. He turned back to Ezra as she disappeared into the house. A low whistle made its way through his lips. "They sure do grow them pretty back East."

"I suppose."

"Clay seems to think so. He won't leave Hazel's side. I'd be surprised if she makes it to Christmas without a proposal."

Ezra felt the words like a kick to his gut. If he could find the peace to trust her, he would grab her away from Clay and ask her to marry him right here and now. But as difficult as it would be to see her claimed by another man, if he gave in now, he would always wonder if she might decide something was more important than being true to him and Louie.

Chapter Seventeen

Rose and Hazel spent a quiet Christmas Day reflecting on how good God had been to them the past few months. Hazel kept reminding herself that there were many things to be thankful for, even if her arms ached for Louie and her heart longed for Ezra.

Part of her still felt as though she was meant to be with them. It was the same part of her that had come to believe that though she had originally thought she was coming to Tucker Springs to marry Benjamin Gordon, God had devised a different plan for her—one that included a future with Louie and Ezra. But she couldn't listen to that part of her anymore. It would only lead to more sorrow.

Her disappointment pumped through her with every beat of her heart lately. Still, she had to believe that God would lead her on. That He somehow still had a plan for her. If that meant no husband or children, then she simply had to accept his will. Better that than a loveless marriage like she would undoubtedly have with Clay

Willow if she ever said yes to his constant proposals. God would take care of her, that much she knew.

Miz Caroline had invited them for a Christmas breakfast, but Hazel knew Ezra and Louie would be there, so they declined the invitation and decided to make apple fritters and little pies and have those alone in the cabin instead. Hazel knew that under other circumstances, Rose might have accepted so that she could spend time with Wyatt Avery. Hazel wasn't sure what sort of match they would make, but Wyatt was a good man, and she supported her sister if she chose to pursue the possibility of a courtship.

For a Christmas gift, Hazel had bought Rose a copy of the Bible. Her very first. She'd inscribed it,

> *Dearest Rose,*
> *May the words written within the pages of this holy book draw you closer to your heavenly father. And may you know His love all the days of your life.*
> *Your loving sister,*
> *Hazel*

For Hazel, Rose had purchased a copy of *Wuthering Heights* and a pen set engraved with her initials. After they read the Christmas story together out loud, they spent a quiet afternoon reading in front of a warm fire until five o'clock came and they each dressed for dinner at Miss Tucker's.

"It was so kind of her to invite us," Rose said. Hazel could hear the tremble in her voice at the idea of entering a wealthy home after she had stolen from the Wellses the last time she'd been in the vicinity of anything of value.

"Don't be nervous, Rose." Hazel gave her a quick hug. "I assure you, I have full faith that those days are behind you. And the Wellses were paid back in full."

"But how?"

"Pa didn't have the same hold on me, Rose. Once I got out, I saved the money I made. Between that and selling a few of the items Mrs. Wells gave me over the years, I had enough to live simply and still pay for the pin. I'm just glad you didn't get your hands on her more expensive jewelry."

Rose flushed. "I promise I'll repay you every cent."

"You know I don't require that," she reminded her sister, but she didn't argue any further. She knew how important it was to Rose to make amends for the pain she had caused, so she had been accepting small payments from the compensation her sister received working at the livery. At first Mr. Fulton had balked at the idea of hiring a woman to muck out stalls and brush down horses, but Rose had a way with people and rarely walked away without getting exactly what she wanted. And while she did not enjoy the dirty work, there was nothing else available in town, and she was determined to make a living.

At six o'clock sharp, Miles Jackson pulled up in front of the cabin, seated regally behind a pair of sleek, thoroughbred horses. Hazel smiled. "You look very elegant, Mr. Jackson."

He scowled. "That woman makes me wear this getup

every day. Like I can't serve her coffee and drive her buggy in my own clothes." But Hazel could tell by the proud set of his head that the so-called getup made him feel good. The black suit was exactly like the one Smith had always worn.

"Don't be too hard on her," Hazel said. "Smith has been her man for many, many years. She's a creature of habit, so it's natural she'd want you to emulate him in the way that you dress. Besides, when I lived in Boston, almost all of the drivers wore similar suits of clothing."

"That so?" Again, he looked pleased.

"It is."

He nodded as he opened the door and she and Rose climbed inside. The enclosed carriage was warm with heavy blankets and heated bricks. "I feel like a princess," Rose breathed as the carriage moved forward.

To Hazel's surprise and delight, the Jacksons and Mrs. Smith served the food and then took their places around the table with them. Smith sat in a wheelchair and asked the blessing.

"Now," Miss Tucker said, once dinner was finished and they had retired to the sitting room with strong coffee and Christmas mints. "Tell me, Miss O'Brien, what do you intend to do now that you are no longer in the employ of Ezra Murphy?"

Her words shot like an arrow into Hazel's heart. She had come so close to being more to Ezra than just his son's nanny. But that was all in the past now. "Well, as you know, I've been helping Miz Caroline at the café. She has offered me a permanent position as well as a room in their home."

"With all of those children? How, pray tell, do they have a room available?"

Hazel smiled. "Well, Sally's husband has returned from out West for the holiday and will stay until the baby is born. Which will be any day now. When the baby is old enough to travel, they will go West, and that will leave Sally's room vacant." Hazel was trying very hard to be grateful that she would have a way to earn a living and a roof over her head. It was better than living in the woods.

"So, Ezra's just throwing you out of his cabin." She shook her head. "I wouldn't have thought he could be so mean-spirited."

"He said I could stay until spring, but I wouldn't feel comfortable living there when I'm no longer working for him." She felt her face flush. "He's been much too generous as it is."

"Humph." Miss Tucker's shrewd gaze shifted to Rose. "You," she said just as Rose popped a mint in her mouth.

Rose's eyes rounded. "Hmm?"

Rather than the annoyance Hazel expected, the lady chuckled. "Caught you off guard, didn't I?"

Rose nodded, still chewing the mint.

"I hear you're working as a stable boy. Is this true?"

"Stable girl," Rose said, dabbing at her lips with a napkin. "But yes, I am."

Miss Tucker gave a derisive sniff. "In my day, females did not do filthy work."

"Well," Rose said. "I don't have an inheritance or a husband, so if I do not want to beg in the street, I must do any honest work I can find. Even if it means cleaning up horse manure."

The old lady gave a distinct nod. "That's what I thought. I like a woman who isn't afraid of hard work. That is why I have recommended you both for positions in Jamesburg. My good friend Mary Chesterfield has two positions open in her household. One is as nanny to her grandchildren. Her daughter and son-in-law were unfortunately killed in an accident, leaving the children to be raised by her. And clearly, a woman of her age with social responsibilities can't possibly raise six children alone. She is interested in you, Hazel, for that position. And you, Rose, I have recommended as a lady's companion."

Hazel wasn't sure whether to be grateful or annoyed by the assumption that Miss Tucker could dictate her life, including sending her away from Tucker Springs. But the truth was that she would be relieved to leave behind the pain she endured daily working so close to Ezra, seeing Louie every day without the freedom to teach him. Go with him on adventures. Listen to his stories. Not to mention, she missed her talks with Ezra. Missed the way he shook his head when she grabbed a shawl instead of her coat.

"Thank you, Miss Tucker," she said. "As much as I will miss Tucker Springs and all the wonderful friends I've made here, I believe it is for the best."

She nodded. "Very sensible." She turned to Rose. "And you, young lady? May I tell Mary Chesterfield that you accept, as well? Or do you prefer your position as a stable *girl*?"

"Well, if Hazel is going, I suppose I'll go, as well."

"Very well, then," she said. "I will inform Mary of your acceptance. She'll expect you Monday, January second."

"That will work out perfectly." After all, she had promised Ezra that she would be out of the cabin the first week of January. He certainly didn't need another reason to accuse her of not being trustworthy.

As she lay in bed next to Rose that night, Hazel stared at the ceiling. There wouldn't be many more nights on this straw tick mattress that Miz Caroline had given her. She would have to leave the beautiful furniture Ezra had ordered from Wyatt. She recalled with a sad smile the excitement of that day when they had brought it into the cabin and set it up while she was putting up apples with Miz Caroline and the town ladies. Ezra had picked her up at the Averys', and when they got to the cabin, Louie had insisted she cover her eyes and led her inside. He could hardly contain his excitement over the surprise, and she remembered the happiness on Ezra's face when he saw how delighted she was. She had known then that they were meant to be together.

Even though she had been wrong, she couldn't help but thank God for opening another door for her. For making a way. There was a chance that in Jamesburg she would find new friends and become part of another community. But this time, she would be more careful with her heart.

Chapter Eighteen

Ezra stood at the door of the livery stable on New Year's Eve, watching the snow fall outside. It was coming down in an endless whirl now. A light dusting had begun around supper time, but within an hour, fluffy, white flakes had begun to blanket the fields, the roads, the trees. The beauty was breathtaking, but as the temperature dropped and the wind lifted, it seemed less and less likely there would be much of a turnout for the dance.

But for those close enough to attend, the livery stable had been transformed into a place of wonder. His gaze followed the path toward the cabin. He didn't have to wonder if Hazel planned to attend. Wyatt was bringing Rose, and Hazel came with the bargain. According to Wyatt, if Hazel hadn't agreed to attend, Rose would have stayed home, as well.

Impatient, Ezra bounced on the balls of his feet. He had finally admitted to himself how miserable he would be not to see Hazel every day. For the last month, at least he had been able to watch her at work at the café, hear her voice, speak to her on occasion—mainly pleasantries, nothing of importance. But it had been something. Something he wouldn't have after tomorrow.

He felt a presence next to him and turned to see Jennie standing next to him, staring out at the snow. "You think this is going to turn into a blizzard?" she asked.

He shrugged. "I suppose it could. The wind isn't too strong, but it is blowing."

"Do you think we should cancel and send everyone home?"

"I suppose it wouldn't hurt to end sooner than midnight. Townsfolk can stay since they will be able to get home safely."

"So, you're eyeing that road over there pretty closely." Her voice had just an edge of humor and a little bit of a singsong lilt. "You waitin' for someone?"

"Nope." He cast her a sidelong glance. "Are you?"

"Yes, as a matter of fact. I'm waiting for Hazel—just like you are. I want to tell her goodbye." She gave him a pointed look. "You do know she's leaving tomorrow."

"Yes. I do. I wish her well in her new position."

She paused, as though trying to decide whether to respond, then forged ahead. "I've never known you to be this stubborn, Ezra." She shook her head. "It's almost cruel. No, I take that back. It isn't *almost* cruel. It's just plain mean."

"I gave her a good reference. What more do you expect? You know, I could have mentioned about her pa, but I didn't."

She narrowed her gaze. "Well, aren't you sweet?"

"No, Jennie. I'm a man whose son was almost harmed because the woman I entrusted him to didn't tell me the truth."

"You know as well as I that she would give her life for that child, Ezra. Those times when she saw her father were only glimpses. She was afraid and she thought her fear was making her see what she didn't want to see—the man she came all this way to run away from. I think you know that. Your pride just won't let you admit it. Well, you're an idiot, Ezra. Hazel is the one tailor-made for you. She's the woman you've been waiting for your whole life, but just because Marie ran off, you are afraid Hazel will do the same thing."

"How about if you just keep your opinion to yourself?" he snapped. Miz Caroline had said very nearly the same thing. It seemed as though all the people he loved thought he was a fool. Maybe he was.

"How about if I don't, Ezra Murphy? Because I hate to watch a man I love like a brother make such a colossal mistake." Jennie turned. "I have to get to the refreshment stand before Chester Rubles takes all of the cookies we spent two days baking. I swear, that's another man who needs a wife." She took in a breath and spoke on the exhale. "I'd take a really good look inside yourself, Ezra. You only have a few hours before she's gone. And brother, if you let her go, I'm not sure she'll ever take you back." Without another word, she moved off to tend the refreshment table. Her anger stung him, and he looked around for something to distract him from the uncomfortable emotions he didn't want to feel.

He located Louie playing a game of tag with Henry

Avery and Fannie Willow. The one thing he was grati-
fied to note was that Hazel hadn't been escorted to the
dance by the widower. He was sure she had been invited
to accompany Clay and his children. He knew he had
no right to feel glad about her apparent refusal, but he
did. He glanced out one more time, and his heart lifted
as he recognized the Averys' wagon. Wyatt had bor-
rowed it tonight.

He moved away from the door and walked to the
other side of the room. Of course, Jennie had been right
in her implication. He had been waiting for Wyatt to
arrive with Hazel. And now he wanted to see her when
she walked in the door.

"Hello, Mr. Murphy." A decidedly female voice interrupted his reverie.

Ezra gave an inward groan even as he politely smiled
at Miss Stewart. She had been especially attentive since
he had gone to her and asked for Louie's readmittance
to school. He knew she had been sweet on him for quite
some time. He just hoped it wouldn't be much longer
before she realized that he wasn't interested. Not in her.

The door opened, and Hazel walked inside. She un-
wrapped her scarf. And her gaze took in the room. He
held his breath and waited.

Hazel brushed the snow from her coat as she stepped
into the livery stable. Rose had been working for two
days to clean out all the hay, move the horses and wagons to the corral out back, and open up the barn for
tonight's New Year's dance. Wyatt had lent a hand.
Candles burned all around the room, giving the trans-

formed stable a romantic feel. That, combined with the soft waltz that played when they arrived, caused an ache of emotion in Hazel's throat.

This would be the first and last time she attended a dance. Not just in Tucker Springs but, she felt sure, in her whole life. The Wellses had held one gala per year in their spacious home. It happened every March to celebrate the coming of spring. Of course, she was never invited to attend. But each year, after putting the children to bed, she had made herself very small against the upstairs railing and watched the exquisite women in beautiful gowns as they danced with elegant men in handsome suits. Oh, the dreams she had concocted for herself during those times.

More recently, dreams of a life with Ezra had quickly eclipsed any notion of life as a grand lady.

For the past week, she had become quite eloquent in her negotiations with the Lord. "Please, Lord, I will never take Ezra and Louie for granted if only you will cause Ezra to trust me again. To see that I would give my life for Louie before I would allow him to come to harm." When the Lord responded with silence, she once again surrendered and prayed, "Nevertheless, not my will, but Yours be done."

She could not imagine that anyone could be better for the Murphy men than she was, but if God knew she wasn't the best wife and mother for them, she just had to let them go. She glanced around the room for Ezra and caught her breath when their gazes met. He stood across the dance floor, and if she didn't know better, she would have thought that he was waiting for her.

When a woman's hand touched his arm, he looked down into Lucy Stewart's face. Hazel drew in a soft breath. She didn't want to tell the Lord how to do His business, but for mercy's sake, there was simply no way the schoolteacher was a better mother for Louie than Hazel was. That woman had believed that Louie wasn't even bright enough to learn his letters and hadn't bothered to notice that he could already read.

Jennie waved her over to the refreshment stand. "Oh, Hazel. I'm so glad you decided to come after all."

"Rose gave me no choice." She took a glass of lemonade. "She refused to come with Wyatt if I was going to stay home." She glanced around as she took a sip of the sweet and tart drink. "Did your ma decide not to attend?"

"Sally's in labor. It will likely be a long while before the little boy or girl appears, but Ma didn't want to take a chance. She says no two births are alike and Sally might have this one quick."

Hazel was disappointed that she wouldn't have a chance to tell Miz Caroline goodbye in person. But of course, a new grandbaby was more important. "Please give your mother my regards. Tell her I'll miss her and that I appreciate everything she's done for me."

"She knows. She's sorry to miss you tonight." Jennie smiled. "She told me to tell you she'll be seeing you. It's only ten miles."

"I know. But it seems like a hundred. Things just won't be the same without you close by."

Hazel reached out and embraced her friend. The first friend she had ever had. Her eyes misted at the thought that she would be leaving this town. Tomorrow, Miles would be picking them up in Miss Tucker's carriage to drive them to Jamesburg.

"So how many children will you be caring for?" Jennie asked, as though she had been privy to Hazel's thoughts.

"Six."

Jennie's eyes widened, and she gave a long whistle. "Oh, Hazel. Are you absolutely sure that's what you want? You always have a home at Ma and Pa's. Ma thinks of you as another of her children. She's sincere about wanting you to work at the café and live in Sally's old room."

"I know. And I can't tell you how much that means to me. I've felt more at home in the last three months than I have my entire life."

Jennie clicked her tongue and stared with a frown behind Hazel. Hazel turned to see Ezra and Lucy Stewart begin to waltz. Jennie frowned. "Mercy, Hazel. You know full well she forced him to ask her, making him choose between that or being rude. Go out there and take him away from her. He will be miserable if that woman gets her claws into him. And poor Louie can't abide her."

Though her heart ached and her indignation flared, she knew Ezra had to make his own choice. She shook her head. "You know I can't."

"I suppose."

"Have you seen Louie around? I want to tell him goodbye. Surely Ezra won't object to that."

"Oh, who cares if he does?" Jennie nodded and gave

a little wave to someone across the room. "I saw him with Henry and Fannie Willow not too long ago."

Hazel moved away from the table and in the direction Jennie had indicated. She spied Fannie Willow walking onto the dance floor with Clay. She smiled as father and daughter danced. Clay had invited her to the dance. He'd invited her to dinner. He'd asked if he could take her for a drive or a walk. The fact was that Clay was one of the nicest men any woman could find. And any woman would be blessed indeed to become his wife. But Hazel's heart was taken, and so she had finally requested of Clay that he please honor her with his friendship and nothing more.

Though clearly disappointed, he had been a perfect gentleman. "I understand, Hazel." He'd smiled, then his eyes turned toward Rose. "You think your sister might be interested?" She hadn't had the heart to tell him that Rose only had eyes for Wyatt.

She found Henry alone standing against the wall. "Hi, Henry," she said. "Have you seen Louie?"

His eyes were wide, and he shook his head. But it was the sort of gesture Hazel knew all too well. She narrowed her gaze and scrutinized his expression silently. Just as quickly as he'd shaken his head, his expression clouded, and he dropped his shoulders in resignation. "Yes, Miss Hazel."

She chuckled. "Can you tell me where he is?"

"I'm not sure."

"Is that the truth?"

"Well, I told him something, and he got mad and ran off."

Normally, Hazel believed children who learned to work out their differences when they were young became adults who were able to resolve conflicts, so she tried not to interfere. But something about Henry's behavior worried her. "Tell me where Louie is, this minute. I'm sorry to sound harsh, but I need to speak with him. If you've had a disagreement, that's fine. You won't be in trouble. But I need to know."

His eyes clouded as though trying to decide if he should give in or persist. Finally, he glanced toward the door. Hazel thought of the snow outside, and her heart nearly stopped. "Did Louie leave the dance?"

Henry nodded, slowly, reluctantly. "He was mad because I told him that Fannie told me her pa was going to marry you. And you were going to be her ma and the queens were going to be her chickens."

Hazel gasped. She looked around, desperately trying to find Ezra. He was no longer on the dance floor. As a matter of fact, only a few people were still dancing. Her ears caught the sound of the intensifying wind whipping up outside. She knew that sound from within and without. Inside a warm, cozy home, it was nothing more than something to lie in bed and listen to. But outside, she had seen people freeze to death during weather that sounded just like that.

Fear gripped her, and prayer poured from her. The child she loved as fiercely as any mother could was in danger. She gripped Henry by the arm. "Listen, I don't see Mr. Murphy anywhere and I don't have time to go looking for him. I want you to go and find him. Is that clear?"

Alarm covered the boy's face. When he just stared, she gave him a shake to startle him back to the present. "Sweetheart, did you hear what I said?"

"Yes, ma'am."

"What are you going to do?"

"I'm going to find Mr. Murphy."

"Right." Hazel leveled her gaze at his. "This is important. Once you find him, tell him that Louie left the dance and that I followed him. Tell him about Louie getting upset. And tell him that I think Louie is going to my cabin."

Henry ran off to do as he was told. Hazel gave another sweeping gaze around the room but still, there was no sign of Ezra anywhere. *Oh, God. Please.* It was much more difficult to pray "Thy will be done" when it was your child. Or a child you loved as though he were your flesh and blood. So, she didn't pray that. She prayed for strength, for speed. She prayed for wings.

The snow danced and darted around her and blew straight into her face, stinging her cheeks. She was barely across the street on the road that led to her cabin when she realized she hadn't grabbed her coat, scarf or gloves. She paused only a moment to consider turning back. There was a good chance Louie had run outside on the spur of the moment and in his despair had not taken his coat, either. If that were the case, he could be in danger much sooner than if he were properly bundled up. That meant she had not a moment to spare. "Louie!" she called. She couldn't be too far behind him. Fortunately, there weren't more than two or three inches of snow. Fortunate for her anyway, since she could trudge through it without too much difficulty. But Louie's small legs could sink into a drift and he would not be able to get back out. "Lord, please help me get to him. Even though You have not chosen to give him to me as my own, allow me to return him safely to his father."

"Lou-IE," she called out again and again. Even when her lips no longer had feeling and her teeth chattered so badly she was sure the word was unintelligible. Still, she called out. Where on earth was Ezra? She had expected him to grab a horse and follow immediately. And if he had any inkling at all that his son was in the smallest amount of danger, she knew with certainty he would have dropped whatever he was doing and come right away. If Henry had reached him even five minutes after she'd sent the boy to look for Ezra, he should have caught up with her by now. She craved his warmth. Though her gown was long-sleeved, the neckline dipped a bit lower than her throat rather than reaching her chin as most winter gowns did. Oh, her vanity. She should have worn something more serviceable. But she'd seen the way Ezra looked at her at Jennie's wedding, and she couldn't help but wear the blue satin again. Now she regretted that decision.

A gust of wind blew out the lantern, and her path faded in front of her. Oh, Louie. How would he have ever seen the path? Only the snow provided a contrast to the black sky, which was void of stars or the moon.

Relief weakened her as she made her way into a clearing and saw the light she had left in the window just up ahead. She picked up speed, even though her legs were numb from the wet and cold. She trudged through the snow, determined to find Louie. Then it hit her. What if he hadn't come here? What if he'd gone somewhere else in this blinding snow? Without a coat, in the dark? It was all she could do not to sink to her knees right there in the freezing snow to beg God to save him.

She ran up the steps to the cabin door. She gasped as she saw that the door was wide-open.

Someone had kicked in her beautiful new door that Wyatt had made.

"No!" Her heart stopped at the sound of a child's cry. She whipped around, willing him to call out again. Suddenly, she saw a flicker of a light from the chicken coop, and relief washed over her. Louie had to be there. "Louie!" she called out. She ran to the coop and stopped short as dread hit her stomach. Louie couldn't have kicked in that door—so who had? And why had the boy cried out?

In answer to her questions, a hulking shadow appeared in the doorway to the queens' palace.

"Well, look what we have here."

Hazel froze at the sound of that voice she knew all too well. "Pa." Fear gripped her as she realized he held a knife.

"Don't you hurt her!" Louie yelled from inside the coop. Hazel tried to look around her pa to see the boy. She had to know if he was warm. If he had been harmed. She had to see him. No matter what this vile excuse for a man did to her, she had to know Louie was safe.

"Where is it, daughter?"

"Pa, why? Why do you want it so badly? Is it because

Ma's image is inside? Is that it?" If the reason had any sentimental claim, she would gladly hand it over. But one look at the evil grin on his face and she knew that wasn't the case.

"The locket is solid gold. You've been hiding it from me all these years."

"You could have saved yourself the trip here, Pa. I'm sure you could have stolen a dozen lockets from other people in the time you've wasted here."

"No one gets the best of Liam O'Brien, girlie. Where is it? I've looked everywhere in that house."

Then he looked down, and his eyes flickered as he reached out.

"Don't you touch her."

Shock registered in his eyes as something came barreling through the air and landed hard against the side of his head. An egg slid down his cheek, shell, yolk, white. He reached up and grabbed the mess, flinging it to the ground with a look of fury on his face. Then he turned toward Louie.

That roused the mother bear in Hazel's heart. "Oh no, you don't go near him."

Another egg hit its mark, and despite the dire situation, Hazel couldn't help but think perhaps they really should have let him pitch the baseball at the festival.

The sound of a horse's whinny stopped her pa before he could get anywhere near Louie. "I'll be back," he threatened.

"You'll not leave. Throw down that knife."

Micah had crept up behind them, covered by the snowfall and darkness, as Ezra moved toward them.

Pa glanced at his knife, and for one terrifying minute, Hazel thought he might prefer to go out fighting. Instead, he tossed the knife into the snow.

Micah grabbed him and wrapped a rope around his thick wrists. Ezra handed the reins of his horse to Micah. "Use this one to take him back to town."

"Louie?" Hazel ducked her head into the chicken coop to find the boy holding tightly to Maisie, his favorite chicken.

He rubbed his cheek against her feathers. His teeth chattered in the cold, but to Hazel's relief, he wore a coat, scarf and gloves. He set the chicken down and ran to her. She caught him easily and held him close.

"I saved you!" he said, squeezing her tightly, his warm little body pressed tightly to her.

"You certainly did." She didn't care who was there; she didn't care that the snow had soaked her gown, her hair, her skin. All she cared about was that this boy was safe.

Chapter Nineteen

Ezra stared at the two people he cared about the most in the world, safe and here with him. *Thank You, God, for your continual mercies.*

He shrugged out of his coat and wrapped it around Hazel, leaving his hands on her shoulders. "Let's get you two inside the cabin so you can warm up." Shivering violently, Hazel nodded. He wrapped his arm around her and pulled her close to him while she continued to cling to Louie.

Micah helped Liam onto the horse, keeping the reins. He climbed into his own saddle. "How will you get back to your house?" Micah asked.

"Wyatt has to bring Hazel's sister home eventually. So I'll ride back with him."

Micah nodded. "All right, we'll be going, then."

Ezra noticed Hazel didn't watch them ride away. He got the sense that in that moment, she had finally put away her past.

"I'm sorry about your pa," he said as they reached the porch.

She shrugged. "I came to terms with who he is years ago. God is the only one who can change him. And Pa will have to make the decision to let Him. I forgive him and I pray for him. But that is all I can do." Her teeth chattered a little as she spoke. "I'm so glad you came when you did."

Ezra walked her into the cabin, noting the door frame was shattered at the lock. He could give it a makeshift repair in a matter of minutes and then have Wyatt make it like new again later.

Hazel slipped out of his coat and hung it on the peg by the door. Without being told, Louie rushed over to grab a quilt and brought it back to Hazel. Ezra draped it around her shoulders and tucked her into the rocking chair.

"Stay with Miss Hazel, son, while I heat some water to soak her feet."

"Want I should take off her shoes, Pa?"

Hazel laughed. "I'm frozen, but I'm still capable of taking off my own shoes." She smiled at Louie. "You could sit here with me and get me warm, though."

He clambered up onto her lap, and Ezra saw Hazel's smile grow wider.

When he carried the water to her, he bent down and touched her shoe. "May I?"

The cabin door burst open, and Wyatt and Rose rushed in. Ezra felt a rush of disappointment he didn't really understand.

"Hazel!" Rose cried and crossed the room to where Ezra still knelt at Hazel's feet. "Did Pa hurt you?"

"Nope!" Louie said proudly, cradled in Hazel's lap as she sat in the rocking chair in front of the fire. "I saved her."

"Ezra," Wyatt said, "if everything is okay here, we need to let Rose take care of Hazel while we go make sure everyone gets home safely from the dance. Micah would normally handle it, but with him dealing with... you know, he asked if we would. The snow is letting up a little, but it is still coming down pretty hard."

Ezra stood. "We need to fix that door first." He wanted to hurry back and be of assistance to the town. But he wasn't going to leave Hazel here with a broken door.

Rose waved away the comment. "I can take care of that. A blanket stuffed in the hole will keep out the cold and I'll use a belt to make sure the door stays closed. That'll keep it until one of you can fix it."

Wyatt smiled at Rose. "I can get to it tomorrow."

"It'll hold until Monday," she said. "Your ma wouldn't like you working on the Lord's Day."

Ezra's gaze met Hazel's. "Is all of this okay with you?"

She nodded. "Do you want Louie to stay with Rose and me tonight? You could come get him in the morning on the way to church."

And that would give them a chance to say a proper goodbye tomorrow.

"Louie, do you want to sleep here tonight?"

"What about Archie?"

"Don't worry. I'll make sure Archie's not too lonely."

"Then, I reckon I'll stay here and keep an eye on Miss Hazel."

Ezra swallowed down a lump in his throat at the tender look on Hazel's face as she looked at Louie. There was no mistaking her love for the child.

Louie went into his arms and Ezra held him close. The realization that he might have lost Louie tonight—to the elements or to violence—made him thank God for his protection and mercy. He held him until Louie squirmed. "Be good for Hazel. I will see you in the morning."

When he got to the door, Hazel's voice stopped him. "Ezra."

He turned back and saw that she was staring at him. "Please be careful out there."

Warmth rushed through him. "I will. You get some rest."

After the door closed behind him and Wyatt, they hurried to the Averys' wagon. On their way back to town, Wyatt said, "For someone who can't even have her as your nanny because you don't trust her to be around Louie, you sure were quick to let him stay the night."

Ezra opened his mouth to answer, then closed it again as the truth of Wyatt's words hit him. He stared into the darkness, hardly feeling the light snow hitting his face. Wyatt was right. His head had been telling him he couldn't trust her, and he had been filled with doubt and fear. Fear that she would hurt and disappoint him and Louie, like Marie had. But his heart knew—and if he was honest, had known all along—that he did trust her. Completely.

* * *

Hazel woke to the smell of breakfast cooking and opened her eyes. She could hear voices in the kitchen, and as she left the dregs of sleep behind, she realized it was Rose and Louie. *Happy New Year.* She had one more day to spend in Tucker Springs, and she intended to soak in every second.

She got up and dressed quickly, then walked out of the bedroom. "Good morning, you two."

They turned around and both rushed over to her for a hug. "Good morning," Rose said and kissed her on the cheek. "You look so much better than you did last night."

Hazel chuckled. "I feel better."

They had just finished breakfast when a knock sounded at the door. Hazel's heart leaped in her chest. What would Ezra be like today? Would he be in a rush to gather Louie and say goodbye? Or would he and Louie be willing to spend the day with her?

She hurried over to open the door. Wyatt Avery stood on the doorstep, looking more than a little uncomfortable. "Ezra sent me."

Her heart sank. He had sent Wyatt to pick up Louie. She had never imagined that Ezra wouldn't say goodbye to her in person. She stepped back and let him enter.

"You came to get Louie?"

"Actually, Ezra asked me if I would drive Rose and Louie out to Ma's for breakfast before service. He wants to talk to you alone."

Rose frowned. "Your ma won't mind?"

Wyatt shook his head. "Sally had her baby and Ma's

all set to celebrate with a New Year's breakfast to show off her new grandson. She insisted."

Rose beamed and grabbed her coat. Louie shrugged into his.

After they were gone, Hazel sat nervously in the rocker, just waiting to hear from Ezra, her mind frantically churning over the possibilities of what he would want to discuss. It had to be something serious for him not to want Louie present. If he were just coming to say goodbye, he would have included Louie.

So, either Ezra just wanted to explain to her again why she couldn't be in Louie's life and maybe tell her again how sorry he was. Or…and her heart pounded at this possibility…he was considering allowing her to continue as Louie's nanny but didn't want to get the boy's hopes up until they had confirmed the agreement.

By the time the second knock sounded on the door, she jumped in her chair. This time when she opened the door, Ezra stood on the doorstep. He looked stern and solemn, and suddenly she was sure of which one of her possibilities was about to take place. "Would you like to come in?" she asked hesitantly.

He nodded. "Yes, please."

She stepped back and stood without speaking while he took his coat off and hung it on the peg.

When he turned back, his gaze locked on her face, and there was something unfathomable in the depths of his brown eyes. "I'm glad to see you don't seem to have suffered any ill effects from last night's events."

The formality was worse than the not knowing.

"Thank you," she said, then braced herself for whatever came next.

It was…not what she expected.

"I owe you an apology."

Her eyes widened. "You do? For what?"

"For inferring that you couldn't be trusted with Louie."

She shook her head. "No, you were right. I shouldn't have kept my fear that my pa might have been in town from you."

"Maybe I was right about that, maybe not. But I know that in spite of that, I can trust you with Louie. So I was hoping that you wouldn't leave after all."

Her heart pounded. He was offering to let her stay on as Louie's nanny. Even though she longed for more, she would accept this and learn to live with it. She considered her words carefully. She needed to prove to him that she could accept an employee-and-employer relationship without expecting more.

"Mr. Murphy, I would be happy to be Louie's nanny again." He opened his mouth to speak, but she gently held up her hand. "And I promise that I will never do anything to knowingly endanger him. I would give my life for his without hesitation."

"And I would give mine for yours."

Her eyes widened, and she stared at him.

He pulled something from his pocket. "I wasn't asking you to be Louie's nanny."

She stared down at the object in his hand, unable to believe her eyes. Her mother's green glass trinket box that had been broken on the storeroom floor. "Ezra, how did you find one like mine? And what did you mean when you said you don't want me to be Louie's nanny?"

"I gathered the pieces that day and dropped them into a drawer instead of throwing them away. I don't know why. But last night, I remembered that I had some of that new glue in stock that you can barely see, and I glued the pieces back together."

Tears filled her eyes that he would do such a thoughtful thing.

"I would like for the box to represent me and you, Hazel. Now that I've let go of my foolish pride and fears, I'm hoping to put us back together. I'm not asking you to be Louie's nanny." He flipped open the top of the box and pulled out a gold ring with a heart shaped ruby in the center. "I love you with all my heart, Hazel O'Brien, and I am asking you to be my wife."

She drew in her breath. "I would be honored." She held out her hand and watched him slip the ring on her finger. "I love you, too, Ezra Murphy."

Outside they could hear the horses stamping in the cold. Ezra smiled. "I reckon we ought to get going. I told Wyatt we'd be along for breakfast soon. He was worried about what people might say if he left us alone." But he made no move toward the door. Instead, he pulled her into his arms and bent his face close to hers.

"You had better kiss me quickly then," she murmured against his lips. "So that we can go."

Without a moment of hesitation, he pressed his lips to hers, and no new year had ever looked more promising.

* * * * *

LOVE INSPIRED

Stories to uplift and inspire

Fall in love with Love Inspired—
inspirational and uplifting stories of faith
and hope. Find strength and comfort in
the bonds of friendship and community.
Revel in the warmth of possibility and the
promise of new beginnings.

Sign up for the Love Inspired newsletter
at **LoveInspired.com** to be the first
to find out about upcoming titles,
special promotions and exclusive content.

CONNECT WITH US AT:

f Facebook.com/LoveInspiredBooks

🐦 Twitter.com/LoveInspiredBks

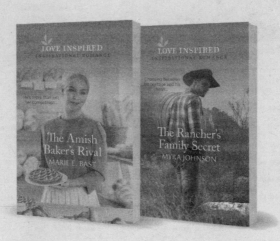